SANCTUM

MADELEINE ROUX

HARPER

An Imprint of HarperCollins*Publishers*

For my family,
who never fail to amaze with their belief,
support, and love. If there are better people
on earth, I haven't met them.

Sanctum

www.epicreads.com

Library of Congress Cataloging-in-Publication Data
Roux, Madeleine.
Sanctum / Madeleine Roux. — First edition.
      pages   cm
Sequel to: Asylum.
Summary: "Plagued by nightmares from their summer in the Brook-
line asylum, Dan, Abby, and Jordan return to New Hampshire College for
a prosective students' weekend, only to find themselves caught in a dark and
dangerous mystery"— Provided by publisher.
   ISBN 978-0-06-222100-1
[1. Supernatural—Fiction.   2. Universities and colleges—Fiction.
3. Haunted places—Fiction.   4. Horror stories.   5. Mystery and detective
stories.]   I. Title.
PZ7.R772San 2014   2014008723
[Fic]—dc23   CIP
                                               AC

Typography by Faceout Studio

   16 17 18 19 CG/RRDH 10 9 8 7 6 5

❖

First paperback edition, 2015

"Reality denied comes back to haunt."

—PHILIP K. DICK

*I*t was a fantasy of lights and sounds and smells, crooked candy-striped tents, and laughter that burst like cannon fire out of the winding paths. Curiosities lurked around every corner. A man belched flames from a podium. The scent of fried cakes and popcorn hung sweet and heavy on the air, tantalizing until it became sickening. And in the very last tent was a man with a long beard—a man who didn't promise riches or oddities or even a glimpse into the future. No. The man in the last tent promised the one thing the little boy wanted most of all.

Control.

You guys are not even going to believe this, Dan typed, shaking his head at the computer screen. *A "memory manipulation expert"? Is that even a real thing? Anyway, just watch the video, and let me know what you think!*

His cursor hovered over that last line—it sounded so desperate. But whatever, Dan was starting to get desperate here. His last three messages had gone unanswered, and he wasn't even sure if Abby and Jordan were still reading them.

He hit send.

Dan leaned away from his laptop, rolling his neck and listening to the soft pops of his spine adjusting. Then he closed the thing—maybe a little too sharply—and stood up, shoving the computer into his book bag between loose papers and folders. The bell rang just as he finished packing, and he filed out of the library into the hall.

The students in the wide corridor surged forward in one long column. Dan spotted a few kids from his third-period calculus class, and they waved at him as he approached their bank of lockers. Missy, a short brunette with freckles splattered across her nose, had decorated the door of her locker with just about every *Doctor Who* sticker and postcard she could get her hands on. A tall, gangly boy named Tariq was grabbing books from the locker next to hers, and beside him stood the shortest guy in twelfth grade, Beckett.

"Hey, Dan," Missy greeted him. "We missed you at lunch. Where'd you run off to?"

"Oh, I was in the library," Dan said. "I just had to finish something for AP Lit."

"Man, you guys have to do so much work for that class," Beckett said. "I'm glad I stuck with regular English."

"So, Dan, we were just talking about *Macbeth* when you walked up. Were you planning on going?"

"Yeah, I heard the set is amazing," Tariq said, shutting his locker with a clang.

"I didn't even know we were doing *Macbeth*," Dan said. "Is it like a drama club thing?"

"Yes, and Annie Si is in it. That's reason enough to go right there." Beckett shot the boys a mischievous smile, one Dan only barely returned, and then the group started down the hallway. Dan couldn't remember what classes the rest of them had next, but even if he hadn't been doing any work in the library, he really was headed to the second floor for AP Lit. It wasn't his favorite class, but Abby had read most of the books on the syllabus and had promised to give him a rundown at some point, which made it better.

"We should check it out," Tariq said. He was wearing a sweater three times too big for him and skinny pants. It made him look a little like a bobblehead. "And, Dan, you should join us. I might be able to get us free tickets. I know the lead techie."

"I don't know, I've never really liked *Macbeth*. It hits too close to home for OCD people like me," Dan deadpanned, rubbing furiously at an invisible stain on his sleeve.

Both Missy and Tariq stared back at him blankly.

"You know?" He chuckled weakly. "'Out, damned spot'?"

"Oh, is that from the play?" Tariq asked.

"Yeah, it's . . . It's like one of the most famous lines." He frowned. Abby and Jordan would've gotten it. Didn't everyone have to read *Macbeth* for school? "Anyway, I'll see you guys later."

Dan peeled off from the group and headed upstairs. He pulled out his phone and sent off a quick text to both Jordan and Abby: "Nobody here gets my sense of humor. Help!" Twenty minutes later, when he was sitting bored in class, Jordan still hadn't texted back and Abby had sent a lukewarm "LOL."

What was wrong? Where had his friends *gone*? It wasn't like they were that busy. . . . Just last week, Jordan had been telling him on Facebook chat how insanely tedious his classes were. Nothing was challenging, he'd said, after the classes at the New Hampshire College Prep program. Dan sympathized, but honestly, the classes were the last thing he remembered from their summer in New Hampshire. What he couldn't stop thinking about was what had happened in their dorm, Brookline—formerly an insane asylum run by a twisted warden, Daniel Crawford.

When he wasn't thinking about *that* small detail, though, he was thinking about Jordan and Abby. When they'd first returned from the college campus, he'd gotten texts and emails from them constantly, but now they hardly talked. Missy, Tariq, and Beckett were okay, he supposed, but Jordan and Abby were different. Jordan knew how to push his buttons, but it was always good-natured and made the three of them laugh. And if

Jordan pushed a little too hard, Abby was there to call him out and restore the balance. Really, she was the linchpin that held their group together—a group that in Dan's mind seemed worth keeping up.

So why were his friends ignoring him?

Dan glanced at the clock, groaning. Two more hours until the end of the day. Two more hours until he could dash home and get online to see if his friends wanted to chat.

He sighed and scooted down into his seat, reluctantly putting his phone away.

Strange to think that a place as dangerous as Brookline had brought them together, and normal life was pulling them apart.

✗✗✗✗✗

A half-eaten peanut butter sandwich sat on the plate next to his laptop. At his feet, his AP History textbook collected leaves. The crisp fall air normally helped him focus, but instead of doing homework, like he really ought to, he was busy going through the file he had made about Brookline. After the prep program ended, Dan had made sure to organize the notes he'd made, the research he'd done, and the photographs he'd collected, and turn it into one neat file.

He found himself returning to browse through it more than he should. Even with all these original documents, so much of the warden's history was still missing. And after learning that he might actually be related to the warden through his birth parents—that this horrible man might be his great-uncle and even his namesake—Dan felt like this was a hole in his personal history, a mystery that he very much needed to solve.

At the moment, though, the file was just a distracting way to pass the time while he waited for Jordan and Abby to log on. What was that phrase his dad always liked to use? *Hurry up and wait. . . .*

"Could I be any more pathetic?" Dan muttered, pushing both hands into his dark, messy hair.

"I think you're just fine, sweetheart."

Right. Better to keep the gloomy asides silent in the future. Dan looked up to see his mom, Sandy, standing on the porch, smiling at him. She was holding a steaming cup of cocoa, one he hoped was for him.

"Hard at work?" she asked, nodding to the forgotten textbook on the floor at his feet.

"I'm almost done," he replied with a shrug, taking the cocoa from her with cupped hands, his sweater sleeves pulled over his fingers. "I think I'm allowed a break every once in a while."

"True," Sandy said, offering him an apologetic half smile. "It's just . . . well, a few months ago, you seemed so excited about applying early decision to Penn, but here we are in October and that deadline's coming up fast."

"I've got plenty of time," Dan said unconvincingly.

"Maybe for the essay, but don't you think the admissions people will find it odd that you stopped doing all your extra-curriculars your senior year? Couldn't you get an internship? Even if it was just one day on the weekends, I think it would make a big difference. And maybe you should visit some other campuses, too—you know, early decision isn't the best choice for everyone."

"I don't need more extracurriculars as long as I keep my four point oh. And besides, NHCP will look great on my apps."

Sandy's pale brow furrowed, a chilly wind ruffling her shoulder-length hair as she looked away from him, staring out at the trees surrounding the porch. She hugged herself and shook her head. This was how she always reacted when NHCP came up; unlike Jordan and Abby, who had been able to spin and massage the truth for their parents when it came to Brookline, Dan's parents more or less knew the whole story. They had been there when the police questioned Dan; they had listened as he recounted being attacked, pinned to the ground. . . . Just mentioning that place in their presence was like whispering a curse.

"But sure," Dan said, blowing on the hot chocolate, "I could look for an internship or something. No sweat."

Sandy's face relaxed and her arms dropped to her sides. "Would you? That would really be amazing, kiddo."

Dan nodded, going so far as to open a new browser window on his laptop and Google something. He typed in "zookeeper internship" and tilted the laptop slightly away from her.

"Thanks for the cocoa," he added.

"Of course." She ruffled his hair, and Dan breathed a sigh of relief. "You haven't gone out much lately. Doesn't Missy have a birthday coming up soon? I remember you going to her party around Halloween last year."

"Probably," he said with a shrug.

"Or your other . . . your other friends?" She stumbled over the word *friends*. "Abby, was it? And the boy?"

She always did that, asking about Abby as if she didn't

remember exactly what her name was. It was like she couldn't believe or accept that he had actually gotten a sort-of girlfriend. To be fair, Dan could hardly believe it sometimes himself.

"Yeah," he said with a noncommittal grunt. "They're busy, though, you know . . . school and work and stuff."

Dynamite job, Dan. Your Oscar's in the mail.

"Work? So *they* have jobs?"

"Subtle, Mom," he muttered. "I can take the hint. . . ."

"I'm sure you can, sweetheart. Oh, before I forget—the mail came. There was something in there for you. . . ."

That was unusual. He never got snail mail. Sandy flicked through the various envelopes that had been tucked in her jacket pocket before dropping one in his lap. The letter looked like it had gotten run through a washing machine and then dragged through the dirt. Dan checked the return address and a cold pain shot through his stomach.

Sandy hovered.

"It's probably junk mail," Dan said lightly, tossing the envelope onto his books. She took the hint, giving him a thin-lipped smile before turning away. He hardly heard the door close as Sandy disappeared back into the house. Dan scrambled for the letter.

Lydia & Newton Sheridan

Sheridan? As in Felix Sheridan? As in his former roommate, the one who had tried to kill him over the summer, either because he went crazy or because he was, what, possessed? When he closed his eyes Dan could still see Felix's maniacal grin. Possessed or not, Felix had absolutely believed he was the Sculptor reincarnated.

Dan's hands shook as he tore open the envelope. Maybe it was just an apology, he thought—it was entirely possible that Felix's parents wanted to reach out to him and say they were sorry for all the trouble their son had caused him.

Dan drew in a deep breath and double-checked to make sure he was alone. Through the half-open window he could hear Sandy washing the dishes in the kitchen.

Dear Daniel,

You're probably surprised to hear from me, and I'd hoped to avoid sending this letter, but it's become clear that this is the only option.

I really have no right to ask this of you, but please give me a call as soon as you receive this letter. If you don't get in touch . . . Well, I can't say I would blame you.

603-555-2212

Please call.

Regards,

Lydia Sheridan

CHAPTER

2

*D*an couldn't decide whether to chuck the letter in the garbage or dial the number right away. Inside, he could still hear the quiet clinking of his mother washing and drying the dishes. He read the letter over again, tapping the paper against his knuckles as he weighed his options.

On the one hand, he would be perfectly happy to forget Felix altogether. On the other . . .

On the other hand, it would be a lie to say that he wasn't curious about his old roomie's condition. They had left everything so unresolved. The cold sensation in his stomach refused to go away.

Felix probably needs your help. You needed help, too. Is it really fair to say that anyone is a lost cause?

He looked to the window on his right. His mother was humming now, and the music of it drifted softly out to where he was sitting. A few leaves floated down from the maple tree that lorded over the porch. No matter how many times Paul cut back the branches on it, it kept reaching for the house. But that didn't stop his dad from trying.

Dan picked up his mobile and dialed Lydia Sheridan's number before he could think of an excuse not to.

It rang and rang, and for a moment he was certain she wouldn't pick up. He almost hoped she wouldn't.

"Hello?"

"Hi, Lydia? I mean, Mrs. Sheridan?" His own voice sounded high and strange to his ears.

"That's me. . . . Who is this? I don't recognize the number."

She had Felix's same soft-spoken manner, but hers was a more relaxed and more feminine version of the voice he could still recall.

"This is Dan Crawford. You sent me a letter asking to get in touch. So . . . Well, I'm getting in touch."

The line went quiet for what felt like a lifetime. Finally, he could hear Felix's mother drawing in ragged breaths on the other end.

"Thank you," she said, sounding like she was on the edge of tears. "We're just . . . We don't know what to do anymore. It seemed like he was getting better. The doctors treating him really thought he was improving. But now it's like he's hit a wall. All he does is ask for you, day in and day out—Daniel Crawford, Daniel Crawford."

This news was more than a little unnerving.

"I'm sorry to hear that, but I'm not sure what you want me to do about it," Dan said. Maybe that was cold, but what was he supposed to do? He wasn't a doctor. "It'll probably pass. I bet it will just take time."

"What about for you?" Lydia demanded.

Dan jerked his head back, startled by the sudden chill in her voice.

"Has it passed?" She sighed. "I'm sorry. I'm . . . I'm not sleeping. I'm just so worried about him. I really hate asking this of you . . ."

"But?" Dan prompted. He didn't need to. He saw the question coming from a mile away.

"If you could just go to Morthwaite. See him. See . . . I don't know. I'm begging at this point, do you understand? Begging. I just want him to get better. I just want this to be over." Dan could hear the tears cracking through in her voice again. "It's not over for him, Dan. Is it over for you?"

He had to laugh. Did it feel over? No, not by a long shot. The dreams persisted, as terrifying as ever, often featuring the warden himself. It *wasn't* over, and as twisted as he knew it was, Dan felt a little relieved to hear that he wasn't the only one for whom that was true.

"This might not work," Dan said slowly. "It could make him worse. You realize that, right?" *I don't want that on my head. I can't have that on my head.*

He felt guilty enough for having dragged Abby and Jordan into the mess at Brookline. At least with Felix, he'd been able to tell himself that he was blameless—that that two-faced Professor Reyes had all but admitted to luring Felix down to the basement, where his mind—well, where his mind had *stayed*, is what it sounded like.

"But you'll go?" Mrs. Sheridan sounded so happy. So hopeful. "Oh, thank you, please, I just . . . Thank you."

"So where exactly am I going?" Dan asked, his stomach still one giant knot of dull fear. "And how am I getting there?"

CHAPTER

3

*T*he following Saturday, Dan found himself sitting in the passenger seat of Lydia Sheridan's charcoal Prius. Tall and willowy, she hunched over the steering wheel as she clung to it. Tight brown ringlets kept escaping from a tortoiseshell butterfly clip that struggled to keep a grip on her hair. Thin-rimmed spectacles crept down the steep slope of her nose.

"Are you sure your parents are all right with this?" Mrs. Sheridan had asked when Dan walked up to her car that afternoon.

"Yeah, of course," he'd replied, waiting for her to unlock the passenger side door. "It's just, they're remodeling the house. Trucks everywhere. We can't even park in the driveway right now. But they were happy to hear I was headed to see Felix."

After these awkward pleasantries—exchanged in a McDonald's parking lot—Dan had gotten in the car, and the ride had been silent ever since.

Not that he wasn't dying to know more about what he was in for, exactly. He just couldn't muster up the nerve to ask.

Instead he stared at his phone, reading responses from Abby and Jordan to a message he'd sent that morning, informing them both that he was going to visit Felix. This proved they were still reading his messages, at least. But right now, Dan was wishing he had gotten their responses sooner, *before* he was trapped in someone else's car.

Lipcott, Jordan

to me, avaldez

So I read your message and thought, "Are you sure about this?" And that was before my mom brought in the mail. Somebody mailed me a photo, Dan. Abby got one, too. It feels like some kind of sick joke. Circuses and sideshows and crap. I'll attach the picture for you, but there was no return address. What the hell is going on?

—J

PS Wait until you see the back, blegh.

[Download Attachment 2/2]

And Abby's response proved even more surprising. . . .

Valdez, Abby

to me, jlipcott

I've been trying to move on, Dan, but I got a picture in the mail, too. I really, really don't want to rehash the past, but . . . I don't know. Did you get a photo? It seems weird that only Jordan and I did. This is freaking me out, Dan. It feels like someone is targeting us. Be careful, okay? Let us know how it goes with Felix so I don't worry so much. Why can't we just be allowed to move on?

Abby

[Download Attachment 2/2]

It was all well and good to want to *move on*, but that was such an abstract, nothing phrase in his head. How was he supposed to forget that he had been strapped down to a gurney and almost killed? Forget that after he broke free, *he* was almost the one doing the killing? How did a person move on from something like that? Abby's use of the word *just* was especially cruel. *Just* decide to move on. *Just* decide to forget. *Just* stop having nightmares. As if it were as simple as unpacking a bag of groceries and putting the milk and juice away in the fridge.

Dan tapped on the two attachment links and waited for the network to kick in and download the images. His foot shook anxiously as he watched the black-and-white pictures fill his screen—first Jordan's, then Abby's.

He squinted, turning them this way and that. They looked like they could have been taken on the same day at the same place—they were even torn as if maybe they had been ripped from the same photo. When he examined the backs of the photos more closely, he understood why Jordan was so creeped out.

A single word in black ink was scrawled on the back of each picture. Jordan's read, "You're," and Abby's read, "finished."

You're finished.

Dan glanced up and away, then focused on Felix's mother. She didn't notice his darting eyes. *Why did they get photos and not me? If it's some kind of warning, why would I be left out?*

That's a good thing, Dan, he reminded himself wryly. *Nobody should want to get a note saying "You're finished."*

Though it was orange and red now instead of green, the densely wooded terrain outside the car triggered a memory. He could practically smell the cheap air freshener from the cab that had first brought him to New Hampshire College.

"How much farther?" Dan asked, glancing up from his phone.

"Half an hour," Mrs. Sheridan said. "Maybe forty minutes."

Dan's knee bounced; they had been driving for an hour already. The only way to Morthwaite Clinic, apparently, was through miles and miles of forest far from any main traffic arteries.

A text message arrived from his mother.

Hope you are having fun with Missy and Tariq. Please be responsible but call if you need a ride after the party tonight! Love you.

At last there came a break in the trees and Dan pressed himself closer to the window, watching as they drove up a steep climb that brought them to a wide-open field, fenced and gated. Dan had hoped to find a cheerful, modern clinic, but Morthwaite looked like it could be Brookline's twin. It was cleaner, at least, although nobody had bothered to clear the vines overtaking the stone facade. Gray and tall, the building perched like a weary sentinel on the hill, and even at this distance Dan could make out grates protecting the windows.

Mrs. Sheridan stopped the Prius at the gate and a security guard asked to see both of their IDs. The pimply, heavyset guard scrutinized Dan's license with hooded eyes, looking skeptically from the card to Dan's face before finally calling up to the main building to confirm their appointment.

"Looks like you check out. Here's your guest badge," the guard said, practically tossing Dan's ID and a plastic name card back through the window. "Have a nice day."

Dan tucked his license away and clipped the visitor badge to his coat. The car slowly navigated the gravel driveway, then idled under the stone overhang that enclosed the entrance to the clinic. Dan wiped his slick palms on his jeans and looked across the center console to Mrs. Sheridan.

"So this is it," Dan murmured.

"If you need a minute . . ."

"No," he said. "Let's get this over with."

Gravel crunched under Dan's shoes as he got out and stared ahead into the clinic. He shuddered, struck by the same sense of foreboding he'd felt when he first set foot in Brookline. He couldn't believe this was an actual, functioning mental hospital, where people still went for treatment and even, in some cases, long-term stays. Maybe this summer he had been one more fainting spell away from just such a fate. He put his hand in his jeans pocket and closed it around the familiar shape of his pill bottle. It felt like an anchor, like a ward. He was seeing a counselor and keeping up with his meds; there was no reason he couldn't live a normal life.

Why couldn't Felix do the same?

Right. Normal. Because having nightmares every night and obsessing over your dead great-uncle is completely normal. And bonus! Your best friends are receiving threatening messages.

As he walked up the driveway to the front entrance, Dan glanced at the windows on the first floor. A face peered out at him, stark and white, and for a second he could swear it was Warden Crawford's, smug smile and all. But another step closer, Dan realized it was only a docile old man.

A nurse in tidy blue scrub pants and a chunky-knit sweater greeted them just inside the door. There was another series of gates here, though smaller, and the nurse asked Dan to empty his pockets and step through a metal detector. He handed over his wallet, his keys, and his water bottle, then gave her his medicine quickly, hoping she wouldn't ask him about it. The nurse just took his things and put them in a plastic bag, then labeled it.

"You can have these back when you're all done," she said.

Another wave of dread overcame him, this one harsher than the last. Without his things, Dan felt that much closer to being a patient instead of a visitor. But the nurse smiled and directed him through the security gate, chatting amiably as she led him down the brightly lit halls.

"I'll wait here in the lobby," Mrs. Sheridan told him. "You go on ahead."

Dan paused. "Are you sure? He probably wants to see you."

She shrugged her tiny shoulders and looked anywhere but at him. "No. He's seen enough of me. He only wants to see you, I think."

"You're the one Felix keeps asking for?" The nurse furrowed her brow, giving Dan a closer look. Her name tag said "Grace."

"I am, yeah. We know each other from summer school."

"He was doing so much better," she said with a sigh. They rounded a corner, leaving behind the lobby and Mrs. Sheridan. "Nobody really comes to see him except his parents and the occasional teacher. I'm sure he'll be glad to see a friend. His room is just down this way. You're Daniel, right? He talks about you all the time."

"Dan," he corrected instinctively, "but . . . yeah. He does? That's . . . really something. What does he say about me?"

The nurse was slightly shorter than him, and had to look up

to meet his eyes. She leaned against the doorframe and chuckled. "All good things. That you were always so kind to him, and one of the only real friends he's ever had."

Dan's face burned. Felix rarely entered his mind these days, and when he did, it wasn't for pleasant reasons. His pace slowed, his hands sweating again as he hid them in his pockets. Maybe he should've visited sooner, *cared* more.

Nurse Grace coughed politely, nodding toward the door. "Ready to go in?"

"Sure . . ."

"There are a few rules, obviously," she said, taking out her passkey. "Don't touch the patient, don't accept anything from him to take out of here. We'll be observing, of course, in case he becomes overstimulated or upset. I need verbal confirmation that you understand these rules."

"I understand," Dan said.

He swallowed uneasily. The last time he had seen Felix face-to-face, it had been in an operating theater, and there'd been a scalpel flashing between them. The door beeped softly as the nurse used the passkey over the electronic lock. A soft hiss, a click, and the heavy white door swung open. They stepped into a small antechamber with a few plastic chairs and a glass window that looked into the adjoining patient room. There was Felix, sitting behind the observation panel, dressed in crisp white flannels with blue pinstripes. His hands were folded in his lap, resting on a checkered blanket. He was looking out the actual window, the one with bars over it, his eyes far away.

This was not the same tidy, upright Felix Dan remembered— it seemed as though he had shrunk, now just a frail husk of the muscle jock he had become over the summer. All the weight Felix had put on from his strict diet and exercise regimen seemed to weigh him down now, his whole body drooping toward the floor.

The nurse let Dan through another electronically locked door into the room with Felix. Dan heard the door whisper shut behind him and lock into place. It seemed as though all the air rushed out of the room, leaving them in a cool, hermetically sealed box.

Felix didn't even turn at his entrance, though Dan saw the beginnings of a smile tug at the corner of his thin lips.

"Hello, Daniel Crawford," Felix said calmly. "I've been waiting for you."

CHAPTER

4

$\mathcal{A}$n empty chair waited not far from where Felix sat gazing out the window.

It wasn't a padded cell, exactly, but Dan would hardly call it a living space. An antiseptic scent permeated the room—it smelled like every high school bathroom Dan had ever been in. The only object with any personality whatsoever was the blanket draped over Felix's lap; everything else was either white or pale blue.

"Hi," Dan said, meandering awkwardly to the chair. He sat down, fidgeting. "Your, um . . . your mom sent me a letter. She said you wanted to see me. Or maybe *want* is a strong word. You were asking for me, is what she said."

Felix swiveled to observe him. No more glasses, just his mother's thin, steep nose. Were Felix's eyes always so huge and staring? Dan saw his own face reflected back at him, glinting in Felix's stare.

Felix twitched as if to shrug. "No more spectacles. The frames, you see, could be snapped and used for self-harm. I now use contacts instead."

Dan nodded, clasping his hands together and forcing them down on his leg.

"Personally, I think sawing through the carotid artery with a piece of jagged plastic would be a crude and inefficient way to die, but I'm told it has happened before and so . . ." Felix tapped just under his right eye. "Safety first."

"I'm sure they know what they're doing."

"You don't look well, Daniel," Felix observed matter-of-factly. "Sleep proving elusive?"

"Nightmares," Dan explained. He didn't see any point in being coy. Felix wasn't coping with the aftermath of Brookline and neither was Dan, no matter how much he might try to pretend otherwise. "But I bet you know that already."

Felix nodded, looking out the window again. "I do, I do. . . . The nightmares are what hurt the most. I dream of all the sculptures I had yet to make, and even though when I have control over my mind, I know that wasn't really me, those failures still haunt me. But I'm sure you understand. You're special, too, special like me. You see things you shouldn't be able to see. You know things you shouldn't be able to know. Things like other people's memories. . . ." He paused, smoothing the blanket across his legs. "The doctors here do what they can. The violent urges are gone. But the dreams, the burning in my head, that will never go away. A bright burning star . . . It burns when my eyes are open and when they're shut. It burns right now when I look at your face."

"I'm sorry? You lost me for a second there. You know what? Never mind. Honestly, man, I don't know what to tell you. I thought once we left that place the nightmare would be over for good."

A short burst of laughter almost caused Dan to fall out of his chair. He hadn't expected Felix to laugh, let alone so suddenly.

Then Felix fell silent, pursing his lips.

"That was very naive."

"I guess so," Dan admitted. "Still, there are worse things than being naive."

Felix leaned forward, gesturing for Dan to do the same. When he did, a waft of strong soap smell hit him hard. Felix grinned, his eyes wrinkling at the corners. He laughed again, almost gleefully, as if a secret waited to burst out from behind that toothy grin. "Are there?"

"What do you mean?" Dan whispered. He glanced over Felix's shoulder at the observation glass. Felix burbled out another high-pitched laugh, then squinted, squeezing his eyes shut tight. "Maybe I shouldn't have come here," Dan added.

"It's . . . It's all right now. I . . . The star burns but I . . . Yes, I can hold on for just long enough." Felix leaned in even closer—any closer and his chin would have brushed Dan's shoulder. Dan was so riveted, he almost didn't feel the object that fell on his leg.

"Don't let them see it," Felix hissed. "Cover it with your hand. There. There, that's good. Don't let them take it from you. If they take it, you'll never find your way, and then it's trouble for me. So much trouble for me. More burning."

"What is it?" Dan pressed his hands over . . . a card? A letter?

"Follow them, Daniel. You'll see. You'll see!" Felix rocked back into his chair, covering his face with both hands. A half-choked cry escaped. "Forgive me, Dan. What we did to you . . . Awful. Terrible. I don't know if it can be undone."

"*What?* Are you okay? Are you in pain?" Dan looked around frantically, and just as he expected, he heard the lock mechanism on the door click. The nurse was coming. "I think we need help here!"

"Follow them," Felix sobbed through his fingers. "Follow, Daniel!" Every word sounded as if it were being tortured from his throat. "It's okay to be afraid!" he cried. "I'm afraid all the time."

Nurse Grace rushed in behind Dan, pushing on his shoulder. "You'll need to leave now," she said, then kneeled down in front of Felix. "Please," she said as an orderly appeared to escort Dan out. "It's time for you to go."

Dan stood, numb, and backed away, watching as Grace tried to sooth the frantic Felix, who clawed at her shoulders, pushing himself up until he could see Dan again.

"Follow, Daniel! Follow! It's time for me to wake up now. Wake up, Felix! Wake up!"

The sound of Felix's screaming echoed in his head, following him out into the corridor. A male nurse guided him back out to the main hall and Dan slumped along behind him, carefully palming the note Felix had slipped him. He flicked it into the kangaroo pocket of his hoodie just as they reached the lobby. Mrs. Sheridan stood up from a low, worn couch. Dan didn't say a word, but the corner of her lips began to tremble.

"Do you think it helped?" she asked softly.

"I don't know, maybe," Dan said. His cheeks burned with the lie. "No, I don't think it did. I'm sorry."

Mrs. Sheridan nodded, placing a shaking hand on his shoulder. "Thank you for trying." Without another word, she turned and led him to the security gate. Dan picked up his bag of personal items, lost in a haze.

Nurse Grace appeared just as they reached the doors to the outside. She pulled Mrs. Sheridan aside, speaking to her in hushed tones. That was Dan's chance to sneak a look at the card Felix had given him.

He turned to face the wall, his nerves buzzing with excitement and fear as he reached into his pocket and drew out the note.

No, not a note—a photo on heavy card stock. Black-and-white faces stared at him, vacant—two little boys in front of a striped circus tent. He was sure of it now: Abby's and Jordan's photos were connected. The photo in his hands was the missing link.

"What the hell is this?" Dan mumbled.

He flipped the card over to find rows of numbers scribbled hastily on the back. Felix's voice echoed in his head.

Follow them, Daniel. You'll see. You'll see!

"Follow what?" he said aloud. "And to where?"

Under the numbers he found a single word: *not*. He imagined this photo in a line between Jordan's and Abby's, and he realized the message was only now complete. Felix must have sent them those pictures, then. Or maybe he had some help.

The hairs at the back of Dan's neck stood up as he pieced together the sentence.

You're not finished.

CHAPTER

5

an peered at his friends as, in two pixelated windows, they blinked into their webcams, momentarily mute. Abby pushed a piece of black hair behind her ear, flashing a thin wrist blotched with ink and paint stains.

"Poor Felix," she murmured. There was a half-second delay between when her mouth moved and when Dan heard her. In a normal conversation, the effect might be comical. "I was sure he'd be at least a little better by now."

"No way," Jordan cut in, tossing his head of shaggy curls. He took off his thick hipster glasses and wiped them on his shirt-front. "I wasn't hoping for anything with that kid. He tried to kill us, Abby. And now these pictures? Frankly, I almost liked it better when they just said 'You're finished.'"

"It sounds to me like he's still haunted by what he did. You heard what Dan said—Felix wanted forgiveness. Even if he's still . . . Even if he's not better, it does sound like part of him is sorry." She yawned, leaning closer to her camera, just close enough to show the dark smudges under her eyes. "Be cynical if you want, Jordan, but it's not like you're getting much sleep either."

"Nope, but my calc grades are ridiculous. Who knew insomnia could be so great for your work ethic?" He forced a laugh.

"Listen, Dan, I'm taking a look at these numbers for you, but I'm not promising much. It sounds to me like Felix has gone way, way off the deep end. Probably best just to forget we ever met the guy and move on. We can burn these pictures and never think about him again."

"You didn't see him," Dan insisted. "He wasn't just urgent . . . He was . . . possessed, almost."

What we did to you . . . Awful. Terrible. I don't know if it can be undone. . . .

An icy stone settled in Dan's stomach. Felix didn't know if *what* could be undone?

"Not a word I like to think about in conjunction with that creep," Jordan muttered. The camera caught a head full of hair while he looked down toward his lap. Over the microphone, Dan heard the scratch of a pen on paper.

"Jeez, I have got to get some sleep. These stupid numbers keep turning into blobs," Jordan said with a sigh. "I swear the pattern looks familiar, though. It's like it's on the tip of my tongue. . . . Freaking frustrating."

"You can do it, Jordan," Abby said, perking up in her video window. "If anyone can figure them out, you can."

"I don't know," he replied. He really did sound exhausted.

"Let's start from the top," Dan suggested. "You said it's probably a code of some kind, right? This is Felix we're talking about. He was a wackjob, sure, but he was smart. A genius. We have to assume he gave me the code knowing it was something we could figure out."

"I'm not even sure it's a code anymore," Jordan said. "They're groupings, but there are so few of them. The way they're spaced looks intentional, but . . ."

Dan had been so sure Jordan would know what to do with the numbers. The kid could solve a master sudoku puzzle in his sleep, or ace the kind of calc test that made Dan sick with stress. If Jordan couldn't crack this puzzle, they'd be left with nothing.

"But what?" Abby prompted. She squinted into her webcam. Dan had emailed them both a copy of the numbers on the back of Felix's photo, along with the image on the front.

"But I don't know. Sometimes these things are crazy complex. Not like A equals one, B equals two," he explained. "Maybe it can't be solved on its own. We might need the cipher—"

"Did you guys hear that?" Abby suddenly whispered, glancing over her shoulder and into the dark bedroom behind her.

"Hear what?" Jordan asked absently.

"That *voice*." Her eyes grew wide and she shrank back in her chair. "You really didn't hear it?" she whispered.

Dan leaned closer to the computer screen, brows knitted with concern. "Hear what? Abby, I mean, are you *okay*? I didn't hear anything." He hadn't. "Did you, Jordan?"

"No . . ."

Abby's head flew to the side. "There it is again!"

Dan was beginning to worry. He didn't hear anything but the impatient tapping of Jordan's pen on his desk. "I really don't hear it, Abs."

She blinked, hard, trembling a little in the window on Dan's screen. "It sounded like . . . Never mind."

"Like what?" Dan prompted.

"No, it's idiotic," she said, sighing. "Forget it."

"Abby. What did it sound like?"

She looked away from the camera. "My aunt. Lucy."

All three of them went quiet for a moment. Four months ago, when they first met, Dan might have been tempted to crack a joke to fill the silence. But hearing voices wasn't a joke to them anymore, not after the summer they'd shared, and Abby wasn't the kind of girl who got scared easily.

"Has this happened before?" Dan asked.

"Maybe once or twice," Abby said, looking down at her lap. "Maybe more than that. Ever since we left . . . I don't know. I just hear her sometimes. Whispering."

"Abby," he started to say, his stomach tying itself in knots, "that's not—"

"I've got it!"

Both he and Abby jumped a little at Jordan's sudden shout.

"I've got it," he cried again. "I mean, I don't *got* it got it, but I think I know what we need to do."

Dan wasn't ready to leave behind the possibility that Abby might be hallucinating mysterious voices. This was probably the point when a real boyfriend would give her a hug, or at least sit with her until she calmed down. Stupid distance. Stupid webcam.

"Go on," Dan said, tearing his focus away from Abby. "What do we need to do?"

"He said to follow, right?" Jordan said, speaking quickly, excitedly. *Tip-tap-tip-tap.* Jordan typed so noisily Dan almost couldn't hear his voice. "I didn't see it at first because of what's missing. Look at the photos again, all three of them—mine, then yours, Dan, then Abby's."

Dan slipped the picture off his desk and steadied it in front of the monitor, comparing it to the photos his friends had received. They made a complete panorama, one wide carnival tent and a bizarre group of people, posed in a vacant tableau. What did a weird old carnival have to do with this code?

"See?" Jordan cried. "Right there, behind the tent and the Ferris wheel. Do you see it?"

"See what?" Abby said flatly. "A blurry smudge and, I don't know, a roof maybe? I can't make it out. . . ."

Dan had already pored over the photos a dozen or so times since returning to his house, but now he tried to study the panorama with fresh eyes. Abby was right—it looked like a roof, a tall, slanted roof. "A steeple?"

"Nope," Jordan replied. "Here. Look at this picture I'm sending."

The messenger window below the videos flashed, and Dan scrolled to check out the image Jordan had found. It was almost impossible to describe the hard jab of excitement and dread that hit him like a punch to the throat. It felt like he might choke on his next breath.

Sloped, white with dark trim, falling to pieces . . .

"Brookline," he whispered, his eyes mere centimeters from the screen. "That's the campus. That carnival—it's on the green in front of Wilfurd Commons."

"I thought it looked familiar, so I checked the college's website and voilà! It's hard to see at this resolution, but it's definitely Brookline," Jordan explained.

"Nice catch," Abby said.

"Thank you, thank you very much. I'm here all week."

"Okay," Dan said, leaning back in his chair. He stuck his thumbnail in his mouth and worried it, his eyes shifting from the color photo on his screen to the black-and-white one on his desk. "Okay, so that's Brookline. That's the campus. What are the numbers then?"

"They're coordinates," Jordan said, his voice punctuated by the staccato of his speedy typing. "They don't make any sense without the cardinal indications, but I looked up Camford's coordinates and they're close. Really close. If you substitute in the right letters, you'll see what I mean."

"Slow down, Jordan, we can't all be misunderstood geniuses," Dan teased.

"No, I see what he means!" Now Abby sounded just as caught up, just as thrilled as Jordan. Dan couldn't match their enthusiasm, not yet.

"Like this," Jordan said, and a new message appeared.

43°12'24"N 71°32'17"W

"Holy crap. Forget misunderstood, you're just a genius."

"Oh, that's not all. With coordinates this precise, we can get pinpoint accuracy. Give me five minutes with Google Maps and I can have a list of addresses for you."

So the first part of the mystery was solved, at least. Coordinates. *You're not finished.* It couldn't be any more obvious that Felix was handing them a map.

"Dan? What's the matter?" Abby asked. She peered into the screen at him, her brow creased with worry. "You got quiet there."

"I'm just thinking."

"As usual," Abby said with a laugh. "Come on, fill us in."

"It's not a happy thought," he warned.

"A happy thought? Dan, we've all been so sleep deprived and stressed lately, I've forgotten what a happy thought looks like. Between these photos and senior year, I'm this close to checking myself in to the loony bin." She coughed, scrunching up her eyes before squeaking out, "Sorry. Poor choice of words."

"But not the worst segue, actually."

"Oh boy, here we go," Jordan said.

"It's just . . . Felix said 'follow,' and it was . . . I don't know. A cry for help, I think. I was sure getting away from Brookline would help him, help all of us, but that hasn't been the case, has it? We're still messed up and I keep wondering if maybe the only way forward is to go back. 'You're not finished'—that's what the photos say, right? Well, maybe we're not."

"I was worried you were going to say that," Abby replied, pursing her lips. Her skin, ashy from an obvious lack of sleep, didn't at all match the bright homemade paintings decorating the room behind her.

"But not surprised," Jordan added. Abby gave him a warning look. "What? It's too late at night to worry about feelings and crap. Meanwhile, I'm all finished with these coordinates. Survey says ten-twenty Ellis is the first address. Thirteen-eleven Virgil is address number two. Then we've got nine-twenty-two Blake and finally thirty-nineteen Concord. They're all, surprise, surprise, in spitting distance of the college."

"So what's it going to be?" Dan asked, trying his best to keep the undercurrent of excitement out of his voice. "Do we forget today ever happened and hope this all goes away? Or do we see what's behind door number two?"

"And by door number two, you mean the place where we almost died," Abby said. "I don't know, Dan. What are you thinking, we'll just waltz back onto campus with a set of directions and say, 'Excuse me, sir, do you know why our psychotic sort-of friend might have sent us here?'" Abby took a deep breath. "I mean, no offense. I just really don't follow."

For once, Jordan didn't have anything snarky to add. He was clearly awaiting Dan's answer, too. But Dan had thought this through already. Really, he had Sandy to thank for the inspiration—she was the one to suggest he look at other colleges.

"How would you guys feel about a prospective students' weekend?"

✗ ✗ ✗ ✗ ✗

In the dream, Dan could actually feel the heat of the flames as they spouted out in front of his face. He began to sweat, ducking the gout of fire just as it left the performer's mouth. Then he spun to glare at the man—didn't he see him there? But the man was laughing, wiping the fuel off his lips and slapping his thigh. The whole carnival began to tip slightly, the ground shifting under Dan's feet. *This was probably what being drunk felt like*, he thought, wandering aimlessly through the striped tents.

No, not aimlessly . . . Something was guiding his path. He didn't know what he was heading toward, only that he had to get there. Answers. Answers to questions he was only now brave enough to ask. What if he could make his family do anything he wanted? What if mind control wasn't magic, but science?

He was getting closer, just barely staying upright as he left the last of the tents behind and approached a ragged stage. In his sweaty hand, Dan clutched a slip of firm paper. "Admit One." The old coot waited for him onstage, patient, watchful. He really didn't look like much, but appearances could be deceiving. . . .

A shrill bell pierced the vision, and just like that the dream vanished.

Dan sat up fast in bed, instantly dizzy. The dinging outlived the dream, and he scrambled, trying to find his phone on his bedside table. In the process, he knocked over the bottle of Benadryl, which he'd left open after taking a pill to fall asleep.

Bleary-eyed, he found the phone next to the overturned bottle. He rolled onto his back, bringing the screen close to his face.

Missy had texted him.

Wish u had made it 2 the party. We all missed u!

Dan groaned and dropped the phone back on the bedside table. He probably should have at least texted her to say happy birthday, but it had slipped his mind. Too tired to reply, he pulled the blankets up over his head and tried to fall back asleep.

A single thought kept him awake, and for once, it wasn't a bad one: soon he wouldn't have to worry about Missy and Tariq. He would get to see Abby and Jordan, his real friends.

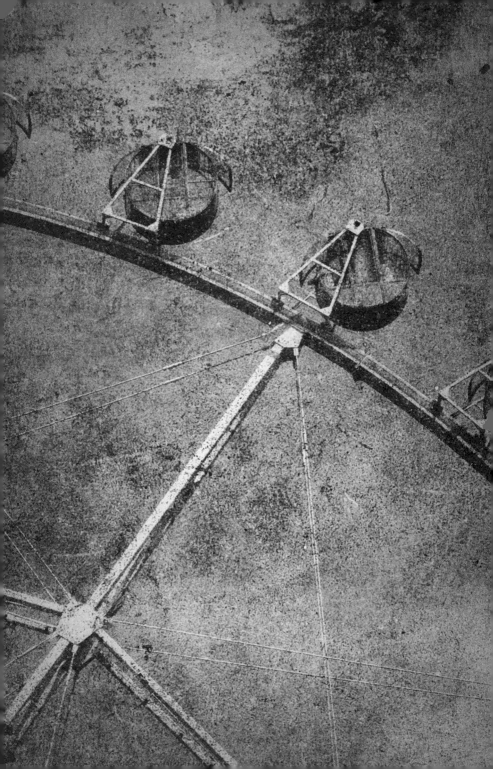

CHAPTER 6

*C*hill drizzle flattened his hair, and Dan parted it and combed it with his fingers again. He fidgeted on the sidewalk, cold and anxious, drumming on his legs from inside his pants pockets. Cars drifted by, filling the air with the soft *shhush–shhush* of tires slicking across wet pavement.

Finally, a new bus pulled up, brakes squealing, and he could see Abby's bright face peering out at him from above.

He waved, adjusting the heavy laptop bag slung over his shoulder. Already he had checked three times to make sure he had packed all of his meds, but now he checked the laptop bag again, almost as a nervous tic.

Just like when they first got to NHCP, Jordan and Abby had taken the same bus. The smell of diesel wafted over Dan, mingling with the wormy petrichor scent lingering on the pavement. He hunkered down into his jacket and stamped his feet to get warm. It was slightly colder here than at home, already wintry in late October. Tiny filaments of rain clung to the cold trees, benches, and cracks in the sidewalk. Down the block from the bus stop, the town businesses had put jack-o'-lanterns and twinkling purple lights out to decorate for Halloween.

Mist rolled down from the hilltop campus, blanketing the town in a milky glow.

"Hey," Dan greeted. "You guys finally made it."

Abby was the first one off the bus, and he hurried forward to help her with her bags. She wore a bright yellow peacoat with a sprig of peacock feathers pinned to the lapel and a floppy knit cap. Sometime since the last time he had seen her, Abby had dyed a chunk of her hair electric blue. They hugged, and Dan gave her a light kiss on the cheek.

"It's good to see you again," she said, blushing. "Here, let's get Jordan's stuff."

She turned to assist Jordan, who wore his usual dark, stylish clothes—a leather jacket and skinny jeans, with woolly socks just visible above the tops of his scuffed ankle boots.

Dan had forgotten how tragically unhip he felt in their presence. He also noticed slips of scrap paper poking out of Jordan's jacket pockets.

"I don't suppose those are hangman games?" Dan asked.

"These?" Jordan pulled out one of the slips. "Just messing around."

From what Dan could see, "just messing around" meant hundreds of rows of mathematical calculations. He had to wonder what it was like inside Jordan's genius head. They picked up their bags and waited for the street to clear, then they crossed to the paved path winding up toward the college itself.

"How was the trip?" Dan asked, walking as close to Abby as he could without tripping her. "It's been raining like this since the second I stepped off the plane."

"Jordan wouldn't shut up about his host," Abby replied. "He looked him up on Facebook. Very rich. Very athletic. And very handsome with a capital H-O-T."

Dan laughed nervously.

"And probably very straight with a capital Disappointment," Jordan added.

"I doubt we'll see much of them anyway," Dan pointed out. "We're here on a mission." He tried to say this lightly, like it was all a funny joke, but neither Jordan nor Abby laughed. "Besides, they probably don't have time for lame high school students like us."

"Yeah." Jordan tossed his curly hair and gave Abby a sideways look. "Let's hope they don't pay too much attention to the Scooby gang sneaking off."

"I don't remember this hill being so steep," Abby said, puffing. "Man, this place must get *freezing* in the winter."

With every step they took up the hill toward the college, Dan felt his breath becoming shorter and his mood darker. It was one thing to talk about coming back here; it was another thing entirely to be here, to be *back*. Felix, possessed or inspired by the Sculptor, had tried to kill them. Dan had seen an actual dead body. But as anxious as the place made him, it was as if someone had opened him up and hidden a magnet in his chest—he felt pulled back to this place and its as-yet-undiscovered secrets.

A buzz in his pocket jarred Dan out of his thoughts. He pulled out his phone to find a new text message from Sandy.

Hey! Make it to Jordan's safely? Just checking in. Have fun on your visit!

Dan chewed the inside of his cheek, his finger dodging over the screen to type back a vague if reassuring message.

"Jordan's?" Jordan himself eyed the phone over Dan's

shoulder as Dan typed a quick reply. "What exactly did you tell your folks about this weekend?"

"Not the whole truth, if you want to be technical about it." It hadn't felt good to lie to his mom, but it hadn't exactly been hard, either. "I mentioned you were checking out a tour at Georgetown this weekend and said I was going to tag along. And then I *might* have changed my flight with the emergency credit card."

"At least I'm not the one obscuring my whereabouts this time," Jordan said with a wry smile. "I'm sure we'll have a blast at *Georgetown*. But seriously, Dan, let me know if you need help paying back that credit card."

"You should've just told them the truth," Abby said.

"Then I wouldn't be here talking to you two. My parents don't want me to have anything to do with this place." *And maybe they're right.*

They reached the top of the hill and Dan stopped abruptly, stunned as if someone had punched him in the gut and knocked out what little breath he had left.

"What the . . ." The words died on his lips.

They're the same, he thought, staring dumbly at a sea of tents set up in the grassy central area of the campus. *They're just like in my dream.* Or really, just like in the warden's dream. And more alarming still: just like in their mysterious photos.

He tugged the picture out of his coat pocket and held it up for all of them to see. Jordan and Abby did the same, standing in a row and completing the panorama.

"What's stronger than déjà vu?" Jordan whispered.

"Whatever this is," Abby answered.

The carnival tents were only just visible through the gaps between brick buildings; from where they stood, they could see the broad orange, purple, and black stripes. Dan half expected to smell the scent of burned fuel—to see the fire breather from his dream, and the man on the stage. . . . But all he could smell was the mud clinging to their shoes and the unidentifiable cooking-meat stench that always seemed to float over from the Commons.

Dan tucked the photo back into his jacket pocket.

"I wasn't expecting a carnival," Abby said. "Do you think it's for the prospective students?"

"There was nothing about it in the pamphlet they sent out," Jordan said, leading them forward and deeper into campus. Tall trees sprang up on either side of the path, their fall leaves shiny with wetness. "Kind of a big thing to leave out, don't you think?"

Dan wouldn't know; he hadn't bothered to read the pamphlet. It said it was for prospective students, not people pretending to be prospective students.

"At least it's twenty percent less creepy than the pictures," Jordan muttered. "Can anyone explain to me why every vintage photo looks like they used the Macabre filter on Instagram?"

"Doesn't look like they put up any rides, either," Abby said, squinting toward the tents.

"You're right." Jordan shrugged. "No Ferris wheel . . . Kind of dumb to have a carnival with no rides. Still, seems like we should check it out anyway. Who knows, Dan, it might have a big, important clue."

"If we have time," Dan said, choosing to ignore Jordan's sarcasm. "And only after we've checked out every address. We might not even be able to get to all of them, or we might have to split up." It was then he realized neither of his friends was responding, and both were staring at the ground.

"Not trying to be a killjoy," Dan assured them. "But that *is* why we're here."

"We're *here* to figure out why we're all having nightmares and hearing voices. We're *here* so we can get some closure and move on with our lives." Jordan zipped up his jacket against the wind as they walked. "That may or may not involve Felix's scavenger hunt, Dan. You have to be open to the idea that maybe that kid is just off his nut and those houses don't have anything creepier in them than Republican voters."

"You think Felix just picked a bunch of random addresses for his own amusement? No way," Dan insisted, reasonably, he thought. "I think whatever . . . *possessed* Felix . . . gave him these coordinates. They're linked. I can *feel* it."

"Yeah? Are your Super Warden powers activating?"

"Jordan, that's not funny." Abby halfheartedly elbowed him.

"You're right. Shit. I'm sorry, just . . . being back at this place . . . I knew it would be weird, just not *this* weird. The carnie vibe isn't helping any."

Dan couldn't fault him. All three of them grew quiet as they walked the path snaking through academic buildings and fraternity houses. The admissions building where they were supposed to meet their hosts was on the far side of the campus and had its own separate driveway for cars of parents dropping off their kids. It looked like Dan, Jordan, and Abby must be the only three students who'd come by bus.

The walk took them past a small, gated cemetery. Dan had never given it much thought over the summer, since it was little more than a manicured patch of grass, the gravestones haphazardly arranged in no real line or pattern. Some of the grave markers were so old they weren't much more than crumbling stubs. But now, a bright flash of red on one of the newer markers caught his eye. At first he thought it was just an ordinary flower arrangement, but when he looked closely, he saw that it was a wreath of red roses shaped, more or less, like a skull.

A thin carpet of mist wound through the headstones.

"That's an odd choice," he muttered, thinking aloud more than anything else.

Jordan followed his gaze. "Yeah. Real tasteful. Jeez. Why didn't they just put a big blinking arrow that said: 'Hey, look! A dead guy!'?"

Abby paused to look at the wreath, and Dan bumped lightly into her back. "Oh, sorry," she said distractedly, "I was just thinking it almost looks like an *ofrenda*."

"Huh?"

Jordan and Dan had said it together.

"For the Day of the Dead?" Abby asked. She drew closer to the cemetery gate and leaned forward, studying the flower wreath. "An *ofrenda*."

"Just saying it over and over again doesn't explain what it is," Jordan said.

"Right." She rolled her eyes a little and pointed to the flowers on the headstone. "Basically, it's like the flowers you take to the graves of loved ones, the offerings. Usually you bring marigolds, but skulls are a big part of the Day of the Dead, too, so maybe somebody combined them? I've never seen a design like that."

"Maybe he left it," Jordan said, nodding his head down the path to where a stout college-aged boy was curled up against the cemetery gate. His head rested on an empty rum bottle.

Someone had covered his face in marker.

"Man. Looks like someone had either the best or the worst night of his life," Dan said.

"Ugh. Hazing. I don't get that crap," Jordan cut in. His suitcase left narrow, wet tracks on the path as they continued on toward Wilfurd Commons, leaving behind the snoring frat boy. "Why would I pay a bunch of roided-out jocks to be my friends just so they can get me completely wasted, write all over my face, and leave me in a *graveyard*? What's the point?"

They stepped into the tall shadow of Wilfurd Commons just in time—a light rain had started to fall, and the mist Dan remembered from the summer was rising in full force. Other prospective students were mustering outside on the grass, herded this way and that by NHC students in bright orange T-shirts. "I don't know," Dan said. "I sort of get the appeal of a frat. Everyone wants to feel like part of something."

"Sure, but what's the point if you have to pay your way in?" Jordan snorted.

"We should hurry up," Abby said. "It looks like most people already dropped off their stuff inside."

"Yup, we need to blend in," Dan said, following her and Jordan into the big blob of high school students pushing their way into Wilfurd Commons. A knot grew in Dan's stomach as he realized just how many student chaperones were there to keep an eye on them.

He tightened his grip on his bag, eyeing the chattering high schoolers with suspicion, even annoyance. Over the summer, making new friends had been one of his top priorities; now, he wanted to do everything in his power to avoid it.

CHAPTER

7

"Don't worry about your friend there."

"Hm?" Dan hadn't noticed he was staring, but apparently he was—at Abby. She was walking close to her host, and the two girls were laughing as if they had known each other much longer than ten minutes. Abby just had that way with people. Dan strained to hear what they were giggling about. "Oh, I wasn't worried."

"Really?" His host, Micah, lifted a thick, dark eyebrow and clapped Dan on the shoulder. "'Cause you look plenty nervous from where I'm standing."

"We're, um, sort of dating, that's all," Dan said. He and the other prospective students—"coolly" called "prospies"—were being marched back across the academic side and down the short road that led to the dormitories. Paired off with their hosts, most of the students were busy getting to know their campus buddies for the next few days, no one more so than Abby.

"Hey," Dan called, waving to her. A few steps ahead, she smiled and tossed back a quick twiddle of her fingers.

"Who's that?" he heard her host say.

Abby's response was too soft to overhear.

"I think your girl is busy," Micah said gently. "Don't sweat it, man, you can catch up with her later. Do you two go to the same school?"

"Not really," Dan said. "I mean, no, no, we don't. We actually met over the summer at the program they have here."

"Really? Well, come on now, that's great. So y'all just couldn't get enough NHC? Had to come back?" He chuckled, and even his laugh seemed to have a Southern accent. Dan would almost guess his host was exaggerating the effect in an attempt to be funny or something, except that Micah didn't seem like the type to be ironic, as far as Dan could tell.

"We met Jordan there, too," Dan explained, pointing, half trying to rope Jordan into the conversation. Jordan didn't appear to be warming up to his own host, Cal, with anything resembling enthusiasm, despite Cal's previously hyped good looks. It couldn't help that Cal seemed to be doing all the talking. "The three of us sort of became inseparable," Dan said, unable to keep a note of pride out of his voice.

"Think you're keen to apply? I don't mean to be nosy, but when you intern for the admissions office it kind of comes with the territory," Micah said. They were passing back by the frat houses now. Dan wondered which one was missing a pledge.

Dan redirected his attention to Micah, still unsure whether his host was making fun of him or not. Who said "keen" in earnest, anyway? Well, Dan supposed maybe Micah did, with his neat, modern glasses and a goatee that he reached up to rub every time he spoke. "Maybe. I'm mostly into history and psychology—do you know Jung? Yeah, him—but I have a few different interests. I still have to see if NHC is a good fit."

"You should talk to Professor Reyes in the Psych Department.

She's running a senior seminar in the old asylum on campus, but I have her right before for Psych 200. I can ask her tomorrow if she'd let you sit in on a session," Micah offered.

Dan tried to think of something to say, but his mind blanked.

"The asylum's called Brookline, but you probably read about it already this summer," his host continued amiably.

"Yeah," Dan said. "I've heard of it."

"Damn it." Micah snapped his fingers at the host walking next to him, a short boy with scraggly red hair. "We got stragglers already. Grab that prospie before the frat boys eat her up."

The redheaded boy responded without question, peeling off from the group and trotting over to a girl who was caught up in conversation with a little huddle of fraternity brothers clustered near the sidewalk.

"Don't want you folks wandering off," Micah explained lightly. "'Specially not to any frat parties. Those things get out of hand fast. We've been complaining to the new dean about their parties, even made a petition. I think this year a few houses will get their charters yanked."

"Who's 'we'?" Dan asked, his eyes roaming across the front lawns of all the frat houses. Some of them had yards that were littered with trash.

"Reasonable folks," Micah answered directly. "You'd know what I meant if you went here."

"I bet," Dan replied. He pointed his thumb over his shoulder toward the way they'd come. "We saw a guy passed out near some gravestones. He didn't look too good."

"Sig Tau douche bags can't hold their liquor. Sorry, pardon my French. Just don't like those guys. They're always throwing ragers and one kid or another is getting alcohol poisoning. It's a damn disgrace. Like I said, we'll make sure they get gone this year." Micah motioned to the same redheaded boy who had collected the wandering prospie. Out of breath, the boy jogged up to them as they continued their way across campus. "Dan here says there's a Sig Tau pledge passed out near the cemetery. Get someone to check on him, yeah?"

"Sure," the boy said, nodding eagerly. "As soon as we—"

"No, Jimmy. Now. We got prospies all over the place—trying to set an example here. Don't want them thinking we're just a bunch of drunken morons."

Jimmy nodded so hard Dan could hear his neck crack.

"Wow," Dan said, watching Jimmy trail off behind the group. "Are you like head host or something?"

"Who? Me?" Micah laughed, throwing back his head. "Nah, nah . . . We just like to keep things orderly is all."

It struck Dan as more than orderly, but he wanted to disappear, not call attention to himself, so he nodded politely and kept his eyes forward.

"Hey!" Abby dropped back to walk next to him, bringing her host with her. "This is Lara. Lara, this is Dan. She was just telling me about this art installation she's working on for her semester project."

"Oh, cool." Dan reached across Abby to shake the girl's hand. She was short, only just clearing Abby's shoulder, and her dark, glossy black hair swung back and forth, cut into a severe wedge around her face. "Nice to meet you, Lara."

"Seriously, I can't wait to see her installation," Abby raced on. "It's a mixed-media room with statue pieces and music and live models. She's going to take me to check it out tomorrow!"

"*Actually*, it's an auto-destructive critique of the masks we wear as people of color to erase our heritage and become white," Lara said in a flat monotone. She was either a master of deadpan humor or deadly serious. Maybe all college students just spoke a different language.

"That . . . sounds complex," Dan said.

"*Complex*. Don't get her started," Micah bit out from clenched teeth. "She'll talk your ear off about Dada futurism mumbo jumbo, who even knows what all."

"Despite what your folksy Southern upbringing told you, ignorance is not becoming. Much to the contrary, in fact," Lara said darkly. "*Much.*"

"Jeez. Tense much?" Jordan popped up between Abby and Dan, leaning his elbows onto their shoulders. "Relationship gone wrong?"

"I'd really rather not talk about it," Micah said tightly. "Anyway, like I was saying . . . If you want in on any particular classes, Dan, you just let me know. I'll make it happen."

"That's really nice of you, thanks," Dan said, brushing off Jordan's elbow.

"Hope you guys aren't too hungry," Micah added. "We've got a bit of an orientation planned before we eat. It'll go down in Erickson, but I s'pose you know where that is since you stayed there over the summer."

"Actually, we stayed in Brookline," Dan said.

They crossed one last street that separated the row of fraternity and sorority houses from the main circle of dorms.

Micah looked at him funny, and Dan realized he'd acted like

he hardly knew anything about Brookline a minute ago. He was going to have to do better keeping his stories straight.

"You'll have to tell me all about that. I've heard crazy stories about that place," Micah said finally.

And then, as if on command, there it was.

Dan thought he would be prepared for this moment—it was just a building, after all, and he had no reason to go in it now. Felix's addresses were all off campus. But it didn't matter. Dan stared up at its chipping white façade and the sagging columns struggling to support the roof and he shivered. And yet there was that magnet in his chest. It pulled him not just to the college but to Brookline itself, and a serpentine voice in the back of his head whispered, "Welcome home, Daniel."

CHAPTER

8

*I*nside the newly renovated, warm Erickson Dormitory, Dan finally felt the chilly influence of Brookline break. The volunteers led them up to the third floor, where a bank of over-stuffed couches had been set up along the walls in a U shape. A few students disappeared down the hall, taking piles of luggage to a room to be sorted and divvied out later by host and dorm building.

Dan grabbed a seat between Abby and Jordan, who clambered out of their coats and scarves, red-faced and sweating from the jump in temperature. It was almost too warm in the spacious common room, overcrowded with bodies and furniture.

"My host seems nice," Dan whispered to them.

"Mine's okay," Jordan replied with a shrug. "Not very bright, and a little WASPy, but okay."

"Lara is awesome." As if to prove it, Abby gave her host a little wave. All the student volunteers stood near the archway leading out into the hall. There was an elevator on the right side of the room and windows all along the wall behind where the prospies sat. Dan felt the cold from outside seeping in when one of the hosts finally opened a door. Jordan's host began pulling orange folders from a few cardboard boxes and passing them out to the various rows.

"You don't think she's a little . . . frigid?" Jordan asked. "I'm getting some serious *robot, type A* vibes off of that one."

"She's serious about art, Jordan," Abby muttered. "There's nothing wrong with that."

"Find your folder, please," Jordan's host instructed. "They're all labeled."

"At least you two got paired with hosts who have stuff in common with you. Don't ask how I got paired up with Cal because I have no frakking clue," Jordan whispered. "He's an *economics* major."

"Economics involves math," Dan suggested. "Right?"

"Maybe for most people. I get the impression Cal is just trying to learn how to handle a trust fund."

"How could you know that already?" Abby whispered. "I say give the guy a break."

"I will not. He's wearing boat shoes. Ugh. Boat shoes and he is nowhere near a stupid boat. Justify that, Captain Tolerance."

"What are you even—you know what, never mind."

Abby handed him one of the orange folders, and then Dan quickly located his before passing the remaining stack along. He cracked open his folder to find a long schedule of events he did not plan on attending. Abby had been right—the "Campus Carnival" for prospies took the top spot in a huge font.

"If you have an emergency," Cal was saying at the front of the room, "you'll find the list of campus numbers in your folder. Any phone on campus can connect you easily to the main switchboard if you just dial 555 . . ."

He droned on about safety precautions and campus policies, but Dan had stopped paying attention. A small, sharp elbow was prodding him repeatedly in the ribs.

"Ouch. What?"

"That kid," Abby murmured, nodding discreetly to a boy just down the row from them. He glared back at Dan through a curtain of stringy black hair. "He's been staring at you ever since we walked in here."

"So? He's probably just socially awkward." Dan would know. He couldn't rightly say he was completely out of his shy nerd phase himself. "Or is there something on my face?"

"Dan, it's not funny. He's . . . *off*. I don't think he's blinked for the last five minutes."

"She's right," Jordan hissed, chiming in so suddenly Dan jumped a little in his seat. "His eyes are all glassy."

"He's a host, too," Abby pointed out. "He's wearing one of the volunteer shirts."

"I'm calling it now," said Jordan. "Dude's wasted."

Carefully, Dan turned his head to look at the kid again—he didn't even seem to be *breathing* he was so still. And Dan had to admit, that look did make him feel unsettled. There was no mistaking it—unless the kid was bird-watching out the window behind Dan, he was staring unblinkingly, intently, directly at him.

"Maybe Jordan's right, he's stoned or something. Anyway, we're not here to worry about that crap, or Jordan's problem with Cal's stupid shoes—"

"*Hey,*" Jordan said.

"So let's keep some focus," Dan finished. He didn't want to look at the staring kid anymore. Between him and the cold air radiating against the back of his neck, Dan was starting to get a distinctly creepy vibe about their weekend residence.

And this is supposed to be one of the good dorms.

"I hope you all plan on coming to the carnival," Cal said,

flashing them a trust-fund-worthy smile. "We're bringing it back this year and you lucky folks are just in time to see it. Usually Student Affairs just organizes some half-assed trick-or-treating thing for the weekend."

"The volunteers here and the college faculty really went all out," Micah assured the room. "Food, entertainment, the whole nine yards. The Dance Department volunteered a few kids to do acrobatics, and the fencing club is doing a demonstration. We hope all of you find the time to make it down with your hosts—we haven't had anything like this on campus in, well, definitely not since I've gone here, so who knows."

"Any questions?" Cal didn't seem much interested in Micah's clarifications. Jordan, apparently bored already, had taken out a slip of paper with a sudoku puzzle on it and was solving it against his leg.

"Good. Now, if you could all find your hosts again we can help you choose which classes you'd like to sit in on and make sure you find your luggage and room." Cal beckoned for them to come and reunite with their hosts. Dan stood up and stretched, watching as Abby shuffled forward to reconnect with Lara.

Over the fireplace to his left hung a giant black-and-white photograph of a man, ironically, standing in the exact spot where the picture now lived. The subject bore a vague resemblance to Cal, he thought, same privileged smile and casually coiffed hair.

"Daniel Crawford?"

Dan started, feeling a clammy breath rush right against the side of his neck. Turning, Dan found the staring black-haired volunteer standing so close to his shoulder they were practically touching. His breath smelled of an old tuna sandwich.

"Can . . . Can I help you?" Dan stammered, finding that even when he took a step back, the boy followed. His eyes, Dan noted, didn't just look glassy but *hollow*.

"Daniel Crawford." It wasn't a question now, but a statement.

"Uh, yes, that's me. What's up?"

"Daniel Crawford . . . Daniel Crawford . . ." The host repeated his name over and over again, each time louder, a note of hysteria and then panic pitching his voice higher and higher. "Daniel Crawford. DANIEL CRAWFORD."

Dan reeled back, knocking into the couch behind him and slamming down into it so hard his jaw rattled.

"Jeez, what the—"

The rest of the room heard the commotion and suddenly they had an audience. Dan scrambled back deeper into the couch, convinced the weird kid was going to start crawling all over him.

"Daniel Crawford . . . Daniel Crawford . . . You're not finished. Daniel Crawford, you're not finished, not yet . . ."

"Stop it! STOP SAYING THAT!" Dan hoped his own screaming would drown out the boy's voice. For a second, it did. Then the boy went quiet, smiled a strange, sad smile at Dan, and said softly, "You're not finished, Daniel Crawford. Time is running out, Daniel, and you're not finished. Get out, get out of here now, go, go . . ." He clutched his head, grimacing.

Above the noise he heard Cal's voice across the room, his snapping fingers. . . . "Hey!" Cal was shouting. "Hey! Doug! Snap out of it! *Wake up!*"

Then as if in slow motion, Dan watched the boy scramble onto the next couch over, shoulder open the window, punch out the screen, and throw himself toward the cold open space.

CHAPTER

9

*D*an froze. He knew somewhere in the back of his mind that he needed to help, but none of his limbs responded when he tried to move.

Someone screamed, maybe Abby, and then Dan came to. The black-haired boy hadn't quite managed to fit himself through the window with his first try, and one arm and half a sneaker were still visible hooked around the ledge. With a grunt, Dan shot forward, leaping onto the couches and grabbing what could still be seen of the host. Dan heaved backward with all his weight. The two of them crashed to the floor, and in the time it took Dan to draw his next breath, Cal and Lara were there to help wrestle the boy to the ground.

A hand closed around Dan's right biceps and squeezed. He started away violently.

"It's me! It's just me!" Abby was there at his side, peering down into his face with concern. "What happened? Why was he screaming at you?"

"Back up!" Cal thundered, standing and pushing curious onlookers out of the way. "Give him some air! Give us some room. . . . Jesus, Doug."

Micah arrived and helped Lara pull the boy to his feet. The boy didn't fight them, going limp as a rag doll in their hands.

They dragged him toward the door, Cal herding prospies out of the way as they went. The other hosts tried as best they could to keep order, but as soon as the door shut, the room exploded with noise.

"What the hell?" Jordan trotted up to them, pale and staring. "Did he just try to hurl himself out a window?"

"I—I think so." Shaking, Dan blinked and passed a hand over his face, feeling a cold sweat along his forehead and nose. "He just kept saying my name. I don't get it. I've never seen him before, I don't know how he knew who I was. . . ."

"Are you all right?" Abby knelt, touching his knee gently. "Guys, this is bad. We've been here all of ten minutes and—"

"It's not like Dan *did* anything," Jordan interrupted. "But you're right. This was probably a mistake, coming back here. Dan, what do you think? Should we just pack it in now? I can call my folks. It would take some explaining but they'd probably let you stay if Abby came, too."

"No." Even now, even when he kind of wanted to go, Dan knew it wasn't an option. He didn't really believe it himself, but he said, "Maybe it was a prank?"

"A prank?" Abby stood up suddenly, throwing her hands in the air. "Dan, get real."

"What? I don't know what to tell you, Abby. Let's just . . . Let's just all stay calm. We only just got here. Our hosts helped take him away, right? I'll ask Micah what happened later and we can get some answers." Dan stared up into her eyes, silently pleading. He couldn't do this alone, even if he wanted to. And he didn't want to. He wanted them here.

"People are staring," Dan told them, inhaling deeply. "We

have to decide now—stay or go."

Abby chewed her lower lip furiously, twining a piece of dark hair around one finger. She glanced at Jordan, who was still worrying the puzzle paper in his hand.

"I at least want to see Lucy," Abby said. "I want to do that much. I'm not sure when I'll be back here from New York again."

"And I actually do want to see what those addresses are about," Jordan added. "Not exactly dying to get back to Richmond and the parental lockdown, so we stay, I guess."

Dan breathed a sigh of relief and got to his feet—shakily, but he got there. The remaining hosts gathered up the prospies, preparing to take them down to the Commons for lunch. Dan wondered when he would see Micah again.

"Let's stick with the others," Dan said. He kept wanting to stare at the still-open window, but forced himself not to. "We can discuss how we're going to start over lunch."

"We'll have to find some way to sneak off," Abby whispered as they fell in with the other prospies. "Lucy doesn't live far from campus, but I have a feeling our hosts are supposed to keep tabs on us constantly."

"Maybe if we can get to her place she can tell us about some of the addresses from Felix," Jordan suggested. That was a big ask, Dan thought, considering how fragile Lucy had been the last time they'd seen her. They shuffled out of the lounge and into the hall, following the trail of kids and hosts to the stairwell at the far end of the corridor.

"I think that's up to Abby," he said, giving her a quick glance. "She can judge better if Lucy is in any condition to talk about that kind of thing."

"Thanks, Dan, I . . . I think that's a good call. Give me some time to consider it."

When they stepped outside, Dan pulled up his coat around his neck, shivering.

"I'm just saying, she's been here for like ever, right?" Jordan said. He tried to smooth out the sudoku puzzle in his palms, then gave up and shoved it in his jeans pocket. "She might have heard rumors, or, I don't know. She just seems like the best authority on Brookline we have right now."

"And she also just lost her husband and had her whole traumatic childhood shoved in her face, so she probably won't want to talk about Brookline at all," Abby shot back hotly. "Jeez, Jordan, I want to figure this out as much as you two do, but not at the expense of my aunt's peace of mind."

Even if he was eager to question Lucy, Dan sided with Abby on that one; after all, the woman had been checked into Brookline as a child against her will, suffered a lobotomy under Warden Crawford, and then escaped that place only to lose her husband, Sal, at the hands of Felix. Or the Sculptor. Both, Dan decided.

"All right, all right," Jordan muttered, putting up his hands. "Forget I even mentioned it."

"Jordan and I could check the first addresses while you go visit her," Dan suggested, with what he hoped was a calm, diplomatic tone. "Or maybe we can ask around to see what's going on with Brookline's excavation."

"Excuse me."

Their conversation trailed off as Abby's host, Lara, ran up to them, slightly out of breath, her blunt haircut wild and stringy around her face. Dan felt immediately suspicious, and then tried to curb that impulse—she was probably just checking to see if he was okay, given that a kid had screamed and screamed and then tried to jump right in front of him.

"You said your name was Daniel, yes?" she asked, pushing the hair out of her face.

"No, Dan. It's Dan."

The other hosts and prospies continued on without them, trekking across the muddy open field in front of the dorm on their way to the Commons. Some of them looked back at Dan curiously, but most of them seemed to want to get as far away from him as they could, and that was fine by him. "I was told to make sure you were okay. Do you need to call your parents? Will you be staying?"

Dan shrugged coolly. "I'm okay, I guess. That student . . . Is he . . . Is *he* okay?"

"Doug?" Lara frowned, shaking her head slightly. "He's a first year. I don't see him around much, kind of a loner. Students get stressed this time of year, with midterms and everything. His parents will be here soon to see that he is taken care of."

"I'd never met him before," Dan said. He didn't *mean* to sound defensive, but how could he not feel a little on trial? "I don't even know how he knew my name."

Abby coughed theatrically, and Dan decided not to say much more to Lara unless she really pressed.

But Lara surprised him. "That's simple enough," she said. "Not exactly rocket surgery, mm?" She pointed to the orange orientation folder tucked under his arm. A white sticker practically glowed on the front. "DANIEL CRAWFORD." "Your name is right there for anyone to see."

"So it is," Dan said with a nervous laugh. That was fine if it was explanation enough for Lara, but it didn't nearly satisfy Dan. Doug had been staring at him well before they had their folders. And how did he know to say "You're not finished," just like it said on the backs of their photos?

"I hope he feels better soon."

"He's not the first student to lose it a little over exams," Lara added, starting toward the Commons and the rest of the group. "I remember my first year like it was yesterday—many lost hours of sleep, moments of panic, even delirium from the lack of rest. I even lost clumps of hair over my first final. My parents were dead set on me being a pre-med, and the pressure was significant. Then I changed my major from bio to studio art. I'm sure you can imagine how that conversation went. But that's enough of that—I'm supposed to be convincing you that NHC is awesome all the time!" She clenched her teeth in something that resembled a smile, brushing the stray hair out of her face. "Anyway, lunch. We'd love it if you joined us."

"We?" Abby asked.

"Micah and me. Cal may come, too, but I think he's still assisting Doug and contacting his parents. He can be quite a talker, so I'm sure he'll be reassuring them for the next hour or so." The light drizzle from before began to pick up in a steady rain, and all four of them quickened their pace. Damp, cold to the bone, Dan was only too happy to make it to the white overhang outside the Commons.

He huddled under it, hugging himself. Brookline was to their immediate right. He looked up at the empty windows, rows and rows of them staring out like dozens of vacant eyes. Maintenance had only halfheartedly trimmed the weeds sprouting up along the edge of the entrance, leaving Brookline to look like it had been abandoned in decay all over again. So much for the excavation effort.

The moody clouds overhead shifted, until a stray beam of light illuminated Brookline's top floor—the floor on which Dan had fended off a man with a crowbar, sure that he was going to die. The way the light hit the windows, it almost looked like a pale face with ragged holes for eyes was watching him from inside.

Just a trick of the light, Dan, you know better.

"Hey," Abby said, touching him on the back. "Let's go inside. Don't think about that place. It's harmless now."

She couldn't even look him in the eyes as she said it. Dan knew she didn't for a minute believe that. Neither did he.

CHAPTER

10

$\mathcal{D}$an pushed a triangular piece of deep-fried macaroni and cheese around on his plate. Across from him, Lara demolished a heaping bowl of salad. In between bites, she elaborated on her art installation for Abby.

"It's dedicated to my parents," she explained, "and centered around my Korean-American heritage, but like I said, it's a critique too. My parents were obsessed with being just like the other white suburban families. They needed the next big SUV, the next fancy television—"

"There's nothing wrong with having a nice TV," Cal said. He stretched, yawned, and then straddled the bench of the long table where they sat. With a casual flick of his fingers he pointed at one of the prospies walking by with a lunch tray.

"Seven," he said. He pointed again, not even subtly, to the next person going by. "Sixish. Never mind, didn't see the nose. Five. *That* one's a three on a good day."

Abby brooded over her untouched pork chop while eyeing the slice of pie she had saved for dessert. "Is he *rating* girls?" she asked, aghast.

"Not girls," Micah said as he cut apart his own pork chop.

"Maybe there's hope for you yet." But Dan's whispered jest didn't amuse Jordan at all.

"Don't make me gag," he whispered back.

Cal, it appeared, had a sharp ear. He swiveled to face Jordan and chuckled. "Relax. It's a joke. Besides, don't whine, you're a solid eight."

Dan reached up to tug Jordan down to the bench, holding him tight by the elbow. "Don't. He's trying to get a rise out of you."

"Yeah?" Jordan scoffed. "Well, it's working. An eight? Ha!"

"If they're going to be this boring, I don't want them coming to the party tonight," Cal said, inspecting his nails. Down the bench, a short volunteer Dan didn't recognize perked up, waving at Cal.

"Is there a house party tonight?" The boy practically gurgled with excitement. He was the polar opposite of Cal, thickset and stumpy, with frizzy blond hair and Coke-bottle glasses.

"Yes, Henderson, and you are not even the slightest bit invited." Cal sneered. Dan had never seen anyone with teeth so white, and Cal's evenly golden-brown tan only made them more blinding. He looked the way Dan pictured the archetypal Californian.

"*Must* you, Cal?" Lara snapped, taking her bowl and retreating to the salad bar.

"I thought college kids were supposed to be hip," Jordan told Dan in a bitter undertone. "Are we supposed to look up to these weirdos?"

Micah had turned to swat at Cal, persuading him at least to stop rating the passing students.

"Look on the bright side," Abby said, leaning in close to Dan so they could both hear. "They're just our hosts. Soon they'll forget about us and we can sneak away."

"I thought you liked Lara," Dan pointed out.

"I do, but not if it means hanging around with Cal, too. Do you think they'll miss us if we don't go to the party?"

"No way," Jordan whispered. The three of them sat in a row, Lara's temporarily abandoned tray sitting across from them on the long, white table. "This isn't a middle school field trip. This is supposed to give us a taste of college, right? I'm sure we can go off on our own if we really want to."

"Jordan's right," Dan decided, "but we have to be careful not to draw too much attention. I think we should at least go to the party, then see if there's a chance for us to leave without being spotted."

"And just what are we whispering about?"

Ridiculously, all three of them snapped to attention at once, likely giving off the complete opposite of the innocence they were going for. Dan forced a smile as Micah leaned his elbows on the table, fingers busy combing through his dark brown goatee.

"Don't let me interrupt you," Micah added good-naturedly. "Y'all just look as thick as thieves."

Not entirely untrue.

"We were discussing the party Cal mentioned," Abby blurted. "It sounds like a blast."

"Ugh." Micah pulled off his glasses and ran both hands over his face. "I'm sorry about all this. It's not very, uh, academic. We weren't going to say anything. . . . It's not really a, well, prospie-friendly event. There might be adult beverages being served, if you take my meaning."

"We do," Jordan said flatly. Dan remembered how Jordan had been sneaking booze in his room all summer, and had to suppress the urge to laugh.

Lara returned, and she and Micah shared a weird look as she sat down. Maybe Jordan had been right. . . . It really did seem like there was some kind of unhappy history there. So why even sit at the same table?

"Well, just saying, if you don't want to come to the party, there's other stuff planned, too," Micah said. "And then tomorrow there's the carnival. You folks are gonna be busy bees this weekend."

"What is it with this carnival?" Dan didn't really think before he said it, and his question came out sounding a little harsh. He tried a lighter tone. "I mean, it looked unusual—especially for a college. Is it for Halloween, or just for the prospies?"

"Well, all of the above, I suppose," Micah said, cleaning his glasses on his button-down shirt. "It's an old college tradition that hasn't happened since . . . since . . . shoot, I don't actually know. I think sometime in the twenties, maybe? Could have been longer. An old wagon used to come through the town and set up. Fortune-tellers, freak shows, that sort of thing. Here, look." Micah ducked under the table and dug around in his bag. He resurfaced with two photographs that he smoothed out on the table in front of them. One was of a man on a horse—a horse whose tail was being tugged by a clown. The other photo depicted a man who could have been the circus ringleader, happily sitting on the lap of a woman who was twice his size.

"We spent a day digging up old stuff in the library when we were putting this whole thing together. Camford tried to throw

them out, but the college allowed it, so they started setting up on the campus every year. I guess Student Affairs thought it might be fun to bring back the tradition."

"The twenties?" Dan asked. "The nineteen twenties?" He shot a look to Abby and Jordan, making sure they were catching this.

"Yeah," Micah replied, squinting. "The nineteen twenties. Why? You big on old carnivals or something?"

"Just . . . interested in local history is all." Dan felt Abby's sharp elbow work its way into his ribs. That was a familiar feeling by now. "We'll definitely have to check it out for ourselves."

"God, no thank you. I'll call them back later." It was Cal. Across from Jordan, he took out his mobile and watched it vibrate and chime in his palm. With his free hand he flopped the reddish-brown fringe of hair out of his eyes and then tucked the phone away. "It's the counselor's office. Probably about Doug. Poor little dude."

"How is he doing?" Abby asked politely.

After swallowing a mouthful of spinach, Cal dabbed his mouth with a napkin, folded it into a precise square, tucked it onto his lap, and said, "He's a good kid. Just under too much pressure, I think. Grades'll make anyone crack. But he'll be all right once he sees his parents. And the college takes this kind of thing very seriously. They'll make sure he's safe until they can cart him out of here and back home." Cal spoke with his hands, and a huge class ring flashed on his middle finger as he did.

"Did he . . ." Abby cleared her throat, then spoke up more clearly. "Did you find out anything about why he might have homed in on Dan like that?"

"No clue," Cal said casually, turning back to his salad. "Was kinda spooky though, right? Daniel Crawford! Daniel Craaaawford . . ." He stuck his arms straight out like a wandering zombie. Snorting, he shook his head, laughing at his own joke. Then he paused, frowning and glancing up from his food. "Say . . . Crawford? Dan Crawford? Like Daniel Crawford the old Brookline warden?"

Dan felt a cold stone sink to the bottom of his gut. "No relation," he choked out.

"That's good, that's good. Guy was a piece of work." Cal chuckled, forking down another helping of spinach.

"Who is this?" Lara asked absently.

"Yes, pray tell," Jordan said shrilly, "who *is* that?"

"Some genius who ran the old Brookline asylum back in its glory days. He had some pretty radical ideas but he was working with some of the most insane criminals in the country, so you have to give the guy credit for trying." This time when Cal laughed, Dan wanted to smack him. "Learned all about him in seminar this semester. Professor Reyes made us write like ten papers on the dude. Major overkill, but better than busywork, I guess."

"You don't and shouldn't have to give the guy *credit*." Unbelievable. Professor Reyes was teaching students that the warden was some kind of misunderstood genius. Dan's face felt hot, sweat breaking out at his temples. Next to him, he saw Abby go rigid with fear.

"Excuse me?" Cal finally put down his fork.

Dan felt a tremor start in his leg. "Did you know he based his experiments off of eugenics and exceptionalism? You can't give him a pass just because he was working with the criminally insane. That doesn't excuse anything."

"I think you have to acknowledge the gray area here . . . ," Cal started, but he wasn't allowed to finish.

"What do you know about it?" Dan interrupted, smacking his hand on the table.

"Uh, probably more than you, man. And no offense, but I'm not going to sit here arguing with a *prospie*."

"Who'd like some air?" Micah said suddenly, standing and knocking his tray halfway off the table. He caught it just before it fell. "I should show Dan where he'll be staying for the weekend. You two should do the same."

"Yeah," Cal said with a shrug. "Yeah, whatever. See ya."

Dan got to his feet, but not before turning to his friends. While Cal concentrated on his food, Jordan mouthed "economics major" and then "boat shoes."

"I'll text you guys soon," Dan said quickly.

"I don't like us getting separated," Abby whispered, a little frantic.

"We'll meet back up right after this," he replied. "I promise."

Outside, the same light rain fell, and Micah pulled out an umbrella that looked big enough to be a backup tent for the carnival. Dan kept his eyes averted from Brookline as they left the Commons, unable to shake the fear that discussing the warden had been enough to wake his presence, like some kind of urban legend. Who was he kidding? If the nightmares were any indication, the warden had never really gone away.

"Ignore Cal," Micah said, walking briskly next to him. "He was just showing off. Probably trying to impress your friend."

"My . . . ?" Dan frowned. "You mean Jordan? God, I hope not. Jordan deserves way better."

"Oh." Micah laughed, maybe with sudden clarity. "I'm sure your friend can fend for himself then."

"If Cal's such a jerkbag, why are you friends with him?"

Micah just shrugged. "Good question."

They traveled along the paved path that snaked across the quad. Brookline now loomed behind them, and Micah cut through the wet grass diagonally, taking them back to Erickson. Micah held up his plastic ID card to the sensor outside the door and it swung open, allowing them inside.

"There's a temporary one in your folder," Micah explained. "It only works on some of the buildings, but just let me know if you want to see the gym or anything like that."

Dan followed Micah to the elevators in the dorm lobby. Micah turned to face him, looking like he had something important to say.

"Listen, Dan, Cal's not always a bad guy," he explained. "He was one of the first people I ever met on campus. We were fast friends back in freshman year and even roomies for second year, but people change. I mean . . ." He shrugged, crossing his arms and leaning against the carpeted wall in the elevator as it pulled them up to the third floor. "What if one of your buddies changed? Would you just drop them?"

Dan didn't have an answer for that. It wasn't like Jordan or Abby could ever become as nauseatingly vapid as Cal, who'd parroted what Professor Reyes told him without questioning it. Dan grimaced. Professor Reyes. He'd known he was going to have to confront her sooner or later.

"And not to pry," Micah continued, stopping Dan from answering what he now assumed was a rhetorical question, "but how do you know so much about Brookline just from staying there? Most prospies get here and they don't know thing one about this school, but you seem like some sort of expert."

The elevator doors opened, allowing Dan a moment to think up a clever enough response. After having a strange kid scream in his face and nearly jump out of a window, Dan wasn't exactly *keen* to cozy up to anyone on campus.

"I'm not most kids," Dan said. He followed Micah out through the common room—not the same one from before, luckily—and into a corridor. They turned right and then stopped outside a door marked 312. "I mean, besides staying in Brookline this summer, I've also just been looking forward to college since I can remember. I've been taking the whole search seriously."

"Like me, then?" Micah smiled crookedly at him and unlocked the door. It swung open to reveal a shoe box of a room, cramped but extremely tidy. An air mattress was already set up next to the window. Micah wandered in that direction. "I couldn't wait to get the hell out of high school. Small town. Small minds. Scattered family. Good people, sure, but I was ready for a change."

"I know the feeling," Dan said absently.

A soft knock came at the door behind him. Micah went to answer, and Dan heard his luggage being dropped off by another host student. He took the moment to gaze around the room, spotting two acoustic guitars in the corner, a desk with the biggest computer he had ever seen, and walls choked with posters for sci-fi movies. On the dresser, a row of martial arts trophies was lined up underneath a huge map of Louisiana. Dan leaned in close to the map, looking at the red Sharpie circle around one city.

"Cata . . . Cata . . ." He couldn't get his mouth around the word.

"Catahoula?"

"*Gesundheit*," Dan said with a smirk. "Is that home?"

Micah set down Dan's bag next to the air mattress and stretched, then nodded. "For a little while, it was, then Shreveport, then Baton Rouge."

Dan circled the room, picking up other little details as he went—the dean's list taped above Micah's computer, commendations from the Biological Sciences and Philosophy Departments, a few photos of what he assumed was family back home, and a whole line of miniature *Star Wars* figurines underneath his monitor. A row of frames hung near his academic accolades, black-and-white photos showing an old plantation house with a tall oak on the right and what looked like a stream behind it. A formal family portrait filled the next frame, in which a woman in a frilly dress sat in the middle of a herd of befrocked children, all of them staring out at the camera with that old-timey, dead-eyed stare.

"Family?" Dan asked, leaning in closer to the photos. He bumped one of the *Star Wars* figurines and hurried to right it.

"Mom's side of the family. That's the old Arnaud Plantation house. Just my grandmother lives there now but she never liked me much. The place is falling down—haunted too. The way my grandma tells it, that's a badge of honor." Micah chuckled and joined Dan near the desk. "You mentioned wanting to major in psych—you analyzing me now?"

"Sorry, I guess I'm being pushy," Dan replied, a little sheepish. "Social stuff isn't my strong suit."

"Don't worry, Dan, I was kidding. 'Sides, you seem social enough. I don't think I talked to anyone I didn't have to the first week I was here." Micah sat down at his desk, watching as Dan circled back to the window and the air mattress. "I'd spent some time in juvie for stealing, and I straightened myself out after that. My uncle went to NHC, and it was his big idea to get me to work hard and apply. No tearful good-byes with family; nobody really gave a damn that I was going except my uncle. Cal was one of the first people to pull me out of my shell. Guess that's why we're still buddies, even if he can be an asshole."

Juvie? That gave Dan pause, not because he was judging, but because he felt some newfound respect at the way Micah had been able to turn his life around after something like that.

Dan moved to look out the window. Through the mist rising between buildings, he could make out another window across the way, where the rough shape of a human being watched back. Squinting, Dan leaned in closer to the glass and then felt a cold finger trace up his spine; *Doug, poor Doug*, was staring back at him.

"What the hell . . . ," he murmured. "Is that—what building is that?"

Micah joined him at the window, bounding there in two big steps. "Oh, Goddamn it. That's the health center. You'd think they woulda had that kid out of here by now."

Dan couldn't look away, not when he could tell, even from this distance, that Doug was shouting "DANIEL CRAWFORD" at the window. Someone appeared over Doug's shoulder then and dragged him away. The last thing Dan saw of him were pale fingers knotted into claws, pawing at the foggy glass.

"You okay?"

Dan nodded. He leaned onto the dresser pushed under the window, then straightened his elbows and stood up tall. A little disoriented, he wavered, grabbing the dresser again and knocking over a candle. He steadied it, turning it over in his hand. It was red wax and half-melted, but what was left of it looked like the base of a crimson skull.

When he refocused his eyes he could see his own frightened reflection in the glass.

"Fine. Yeah . . . Fine."

"Have you thought about what classes you want to sit in on? A few professors are having special sessions over the weekend so you guys can check out what kind of discussion and workload you can expect."

Only half listening, Dan felt his head go up and down, up and down. Nod . . . Nod . . . The fear inside him transforming, slowly, but transforming nonetheless.

"Yeah," he said, setting his jaw. "Didn't you say that this Professor Reyes was teaching a seminar? That's the one I want to see."

CHAPTER

11

"Running late," the text message from Jordan read, "be @ dinner in 5."

Dan sat alone at one of the long, glistening cafeteria tables, Felix's photo tucked surreptitiously in the shadow of his tray. Out of the corner of his eye, he watched Abby, who was just now hovering at the cereal dispenser, tapping her forefinger on her lower lip while she decided between Cinnamon Toast Crunch and Corn Pops. It was cute the way she felt comfortable eating breakfast for dinner, even tonight, when other high schoolers might be more concerned with impressing the college students.

Dan heard a soft voice behind him, and he might have thought it was Abby's if he wasn't still looking right at her. But the voice, he realized, couldn't be hers anyway. It was too low, too breathy, too monotone.

"Daniel, Daniel, come out and play. . . ." It was like a song, a child's rhyme. "Come out and play, won't you come out to play, Daniel, Daniel. . . ."

He twisted, fast, following the sound of the voice, an angry shout dying in the back of his throat. Tucked in the corner, hidden from view by the shadow of the dessert station, was a little boy, seemingly abandoned. Frantic, Dan glanced in every direction. Nobody else saw him—thin, maybe nine or ten years old, dressed in a striped sweater and torn, too-short pants. It looked like the top of his head was lumpy, almost misshapen, and *bleeding*.

The little boy was clasping something hard in his hands, holding it tight to his chest. His eyes bugged, hollow and empty like Doug's, like—

"Dan?" Abby sat down across from him, frowning. "You look like you've seen a ghost." She laughed, but Dan could hardly breathe enough to respond.

"Do you . . . Is there a boy in the corner?" he whispered. "Is there a boy behind me in the corner? A little one—striped sweater. Funny pants."

"Um, no, I don't think so." And then indulgently, "Let me check." Abby hoisted herself up, looking over his shoulder for a long, tense moment. She lowered herself back to the bench and politely cleared her throat. "There's nothing there, Dan. Well, maybe like a wrapper or two, but not a little boy. Are you *seeing* things now?"

Yes.

"No." Dan swatted haphazardly at the sweat popping out on his forehead. "I mean, I'm just starving. Are you starving? I'm *starving*."

He glanced at the photo under his tray. Jesus, the little kid had looked just like the one in the picture.

"It's not like I'm going to judge," she said, taking up a spoon. "Remember? I'm hearing voices? None of us are exactly in tip-top mental shape at the moment. If you are seeing things, you have to tell us."

"You win. I *am*, all right? There was a boy standing right

behind me, and I heard him singing some kind of nursery rhyme, only it had my name in it." But it wasn't his name, not really. Nobody called him Daniel. "God . . ." He shook his head, scrambling the ten different thoughts all warring for dominance (*I shouldn't have told her; of course I had to tell her*, etc.). "This place is some kind of collegiate Bermuda Triangle."

"Hey," she said. Abby's warm hand reached across the table and closed around his. The tiny squeeze she gave his wrist almost made him forget where they were. For a second they were just two normal teenagers. Boyfriend and girlfriend, having dinner. "Even if it is, we'll find a way out."

"Thanks, Abby, I . . . That makes it better. You make it better."

"Hey, kiddos, buckle up—I've brought homework!" Jordan arrived in a burst of busy energy, sitting down hard next to Dan before shifting a two-foot-tall stack of newspapers, almanacs, and books onto the table. "Oof. Man, those were heavy."

"What's all this?" Abby asked, taking back her hand so she could eat her cereal.

"Couldn't get that damn picture out of my head," Jordan explained quickly, divvying up the stack of stuff evenly into three piles. The rain had splattered and streaked his glasses. "And I also needed an excuse to ditch Cal. So I thought, okay, why not see if we can dig up more on the carnival? I hit up the library and smooth-talked the kid working the front desk to let me take a peek in the archives. I figured someone must have written about the carnival back in the twenties, right?"

Crunching an apple, Jordan pushed his copy of the addresses across the table. Already, a print of a local map waited underneath, with each of the coordinates circled in red ink.

"There's tons of stuff in there about what was going on in Camford last time the carnival was here, plus stuff about the carnival itself."

"Wow," Dan said. "Nice work."

"Eh, it was nothing." He shrugged. "It's easier to stay busy. If I just sit around it's like my mind starts to, I don't know, implode or something. Busy is better."

The top folder on Jordan's pile teemed with photographs and news clippings—so many, in fact, that the bottom seam of the folder had started to tear. Dan carefully plucked the file off the stack and opened it, watching a cascade of old pictures spread out onto the table. He glanced through one after another. . . . Bearded ladies, muscle men, a tightrope walker, a carousel. Ghostly remnants of a happier time in Camford, before it had been marred by the warden's legacy.

"There's, um, been another development, too," Abby said. She nodded toward Dan, a gentle prompting that made him feel both sheepish and protected. They were his friends. He had to trust them.

"She's right. It's . . . It's weird to admit, but I'm starting to *see* things. Well, just the one thing so far, so maybe it's nothing. Maybe it'll stop at that."

"Whoa." Jordan slowly lowered his half-eaten apple to the table. "What kind of things? Er, thing?"

"A little boy," Dan replied. Automatically, he pictured the kid again and shivered. "But he looked . . . old, like he was from another time. The weird thing is, he looked like the kid in the picture Felix gave me. I don't think it's a coincidence."

"Yikes. That is some M. Night Shamalamadingdong shit." Jordan took another bite of the apple, but slowly this time. With a full mouth he added, "Do you think it's stress, maybe? Or the lack of sleep? Are you sure it was . . . Are you *sure* you weren't hallucinating?"

"Well, I guess not," Dan murmured. "He was singing my name at me, and it reminded me of that Doug kid, the way he just said my name over and over again. So maybe I was thinking of that and conjured up the kid from the photo?"

"I keep hearing Lucy," Abby confessed, chewing her lip. Her hair was still damp from the rain. "It's getting worse. It's like being here is . . . accelerating something. I'm hearing her all the time now." She took Dan's wrist again. "I'm not sure coming back was such a good idea. Maybe we should've left all of this alone."

"We could still leave," Jordan said, losing interest in his apple. "If you guys really don't think we should be here . . ."

"No," Dan said. His eyes rested on the photo, focusing on the pale, strange little boy in the image. "We have to start tracking down those addresses. Tonight."

"Okay then," Jordan said. He took a newspaper off the top of his stack and opened it, getting down to work. "Tonight. Before we lose it altogether."

CHAPTER

12

$\mathcal{D}$an couldn't hear his own thoughts over the *THUMP-WUB-THUMP* of the bass. If this was what hanging out with friends was like in college, he'd take a book, a chai latte, and a quiet corner in the library, thank you very much.

"It's like the stereo is inside my head!" he shouted at Jordan as they stood in the cramped, sweaty foyer.

"Yeah!" Jordan screamed back. "Isn't it fantastic?"

Well, there was no accounting for taste. The police would probably show up any second to break up the party. What sort of neighbors wouldn't complain about noise this loud?

Dan turned a full circle, trying to spot Abby among the sea of heads bobbing along to the music. It didn't help that he couldn't remember what she was wearing. He hadn't changed from earlier, but he'd turned up in the quad at nine to find that literally every other person going in their group—Abby, Jordan, Micah, Lara, and Cal—had done something large or small to freshen up or completely change their appearance.

Lara had worn a pair of high-waisted denim cutoffs over purple tights. The dye job on the shorts made them look like a rainbow, something that he pointed out trying to make conversation, only to have her rebut coldly that it was "*ombre*, not rainbow." She managed not to freeze to death outside by wearing a huge, bulky coat over everything. It reminded Dan vaguely of a flasher.

Heads half-glued together, Abby and Lara had engaged in rapid-fire chitchat as they all hurried across campus. Both girls had dark hair, and Abby had braided hers into about ten different designs and pinned it up in a sort of starburst. She'd looked amazing, and Dan had wished he was seeing her all dressed up under circumstances where they could actually enjoy themselves. Instead, they would be spending the night skulking around in the dark. But then, he might not even be doing that much with her if the first time they ever met had been under better circumstances.

Jordan had worn a fresh pair of black skinny jeans and a baggy dark shirt with a Transformer bleached onto the front.

"I thought we were just going to sneak off," Dan had whispered to him as they neared the party. "Why did you guys dress up?"

"It's a trick, Dan," Jordan had said, as if it were the most obvious thing in the world. "You know? A disguise? If we showed up looking scrubby, they'd probably get suspicious."

"Scrubby?" Dan had looked down, scrutinizing his sweater and khakis. "Is that what I look like?"

"No, you look just fine. You've always been able to pull off that effortless you thing."

"What *me* thing?"

"Just take the compliment, Dan," Jordan had said with a breathless little chuckle. They could see the laugh actually hang in the air as puffy white mist. "You're doing you and it's working just fine."

Now, inside the off-campus house, with people everywhere, lights flashing, and music blasting, Dan understood why Lara had worn practically nothing under her coat: it was sweltering here.

He tugged on his strangling collar and kept searching for Abby. Where had she gone? Didn't she know they were supposed to sneak off? Maybe some smooth older guy had grabbed her for a dance.

Perish the thought.

"Lost?" Micah shouted, wading over to him through the sea of thrashing bodies. "Here! I brought you something, but it's our little secret."

A red plastic cup emerged, smelling distinctly like rubbing alcohol and smoke. Dan stuck his nose down into it and felt his throat close up. "What is it?" he yelled.

"Bourbon and Coke! Didn't know what you wanted, figured this was all-purpose."

"Thanks," Dan said, sipping carefully, then forcing the liquid down over his protesting taste buds. The tailpipe of a beat-up old truck probably tasted better. He scanned the party, trying to think of something to say. "I don't see many other prospies here."

None, in fact.

"We're a selective bunch," Micah said, slurping down his own drink like it was water. With the red cup between thumb and forefinger, he pointed toward the milling dance crowd. "Looks like your buds are having a good time."

He wasn't kidding. Abby and Lara twirled around each other, laughing hysterically at what, Dan could only guess. Jordan, meanwhile, seemed to be trying to yell at Cal and dance with him simultaneously. Cal's hand landed on Jordan's hip, and Dan didn't know whether to drink more or rush into the crowd and yank his friend away protectively.

"Don't sweat it," Micah said, as if reading his mind. "Like I said, Cal isn't always a bad guy."

"He didn't make the best first impression," Dan muttered, but Micah managed to hear him and shrugged.

"Honestly, he's had a rough couple years. Lost his dad. It was a big blow. They were close. That kind of thing can knock you loose for a while, you know? I'm just hoping he'll land on his feet again. I miss having him as a friend," he said.

Dan's throat still burned from the single sip of alcohol. "I didn't know his dad died. . . . That sucks."

"Yeah, back when we were roomies." Micah shook his head, watching Jordan and Cal drift away from the dancers to chat near the stairwell in the corner. "He was a big-shot alum. They buried him in the campus cemetery."

Before Dan could respond, a fumbling, drunken boy in a football jersey slammed right into Abby and Lara, both of whom turned on him, pushing back. The three shouted back and forth before the girls managed to spin him around and toss him outside the circle of dancers.

"She's tough," Micah observed with a laugh. "Your girl, I mean."

"Yeah." He felt the wind leak out of his sails as she turned back to Lara and kept on dancing. Why didn't she want to hang out with him? "My girl."

"Something the matter there? I mean . . . Shoot, don't share if you don't wanna."

Dan took a quick slug from his cup, feeling the whiskey burn down his throat. God, his parents would murder him if they could see him now. *Sorry, Mom and Dad.* He turned his back on the dancers, worried that if Abby so much as glanced at him she would know he was talking about her. "We just never really defined what we are. Sometimes it seems like things are great, but sometimes it feels like we're not even really a couple. And I'm afraid if I ask what we are, it will, like, pop the bubble, and we won't be anything."

"Just ask, man," Micah said. "She's not a puzzle box. The next time you two get a down moment just lay it out there. Trust me, you'll feel better knowing exactly where you stand."

"Maybe I will, but—"

"Telling secrets?"

Dan spun quickly, almost slopping half his drink down his shirt when he found Abby right there behind him, cheeks red and forehead shining with sweat. His pocket buzzed. Startled, Dan almost dropped the cell phone as he retrieved it, venting a long internal groan.

Just checking in, sweetie. How's campus? Behaving yourself?

Mom. How did parents have just the perfect timing? He would answer later, he decided, when he wasn't facing down both Abby and Micah.

"Dan was just telling me what a special girl you are," Micah said, smooth as silk. "Weren't you, buddy?"

"Um, yes. Yes exactly," Dan stammered. He tried to give Micah a grateful smile, but his host didn't notice.

"Now, see?" Her face broke into a wide smile, and she leaned heavily on his arm, touching her cheek to his shoulder. "That's just . . . That's really sweet, Dan." She grimaced, pointing at the boy in the football jersey who had crashed into her and Lara. "That jerk, on the other hand, is not what I would call sweet. Can you believe he actually called me princess? Princess! He doesn't even know me. Like that's some kind of compliment . . ." He had never heard her talk this quickly or with so many hand gestures. Abby whirled on him, pressing her pointy forefinger into his breastbone. "Tell me you would not call me that."

"Um," Dan stalled, thankful he hadn't had more to drink. "Khaleesi?"

"Better." She smirked, putting both hands on her hips. "Yeah, I'll take that."

"How many drinks have you had?" he asked gently. Micah left them behind, slipping through the dancers, aiming for Football Jersey.

"Two . . . ish? Twoish or threeish?" It wasn't funny exactly, especially not when they were supposed to be sneaking off any minute, but she kept poking her tongue out to the side in the silliest way. . . .

"Guys!" Both he and Abby turned to find Jordan, balancing three red plastic cups in his hands. "Here! Drink up!"

Dan sniffed the cup curiously. "Rum? Vodka?"

"No, idiot, it's just soda. Drink more or we'll stand out. The others will be tipsy soon and we can disappear. Finish the one you've got, Dan, then have this one."

Jordan was right. Everyone had a red cup in their hand. Some had two. Dan spotted Cal in the corner tossing his back like a man dying of thirst.

"Good call, Jordan," Abby said, peering out from behind the lip of her cup. "Very sneaky."

"Hey, you're not allowed in here. . . ." It looked like there was a bottleneck forming at the door, with two girls in matching sorority sweatshirts attempting to elbow their way into the party. The girls were forced to turn around when both Micah and Cal blocked the entryway.

"Turn around," Cal snapped, pointing over the girls' heads to the cold, dark night outside. "I said turn around. Now, slomo, or I'll call the cops."

That had to be an empty threat. If the cops really did show up, they'd find underage drinking and music so loud it was rattling windows down the block.

"God, I had no idea this party was VIP only," Jordan muttered.

"We should go now," Abby said. "While they're distracted."

Dan followed her to the edge of the room, skirting the dancers, careful to avoid Lara, who was chatting up someone not far from the doorway leading out of the living room. Dan's shoes stuck to the floor as they left the house through the kitchen and the open back door, where two girls were practically glued together against the jamb.

"And I believe we call that 'sucking face,'" Jordan said with a snort.

"Don't be gross, Jordan," Abby chided.

"What? It's true!"

"You're *staring*."

"I'm just trying to be encouraging," he said glumly, then he

sniffled and wiped at invisible tears under his eyes. "It's just . . .
It's just so beautiful. Ha. I should snap a pic and send it to Mom
and Dad. Surprise!"

"You absolutely will not," Abby said, cackling.

"Guys? Can we concentrate, please?" Dan led them to a stand
of trees a little ways behind the house. They huddled together in
the dark under the leaves. He pulled out his mobile and opened
the GPS application. The coordinates they had been able to
pinpoint online were already saved as bookmarks and popped
up as little red triangles on the display. Next to the triangles,
tiny letters indicated their distance from the various destina-
tions.

"This one looks closest," Dan said, pointing to one just down
the road from the party. "Hopefully we can check it out and get
back to the party before anyone notices we're gone."

"I got Lara's cell number," Abby assured them both. "If we're
out too long, I'll just text her to say one of us got sick and we
went back to campus."

"That's all well and good, but the real question here is, what if
someone lives at this address? We can't just barge in and go, *Hi!
We think your house might have something to do with a dead guy and his maniacal schemes, mind if we take a look in your kitchen?*" Jordan plastered on a
giant, phony smile. "What's the plan?"

"If it's occupied, we'll have to come back in the daytime,"
Abby suggested. "Or skip it."

Dan looked up and away from the phone, considering Jordan's
question. He stared blankly into the shadows for a moment, his
eyes unfocusing until they landed on a spot of silvery, almost
glowing light. He squinted, watching the shape resolve into the

image of a little boy. It was the same wide-eyed child from dinner, his head still bruised and bleeding, but this time he was reaching forward, holding something.

What is it? What do you want to show me?

"Daniel, come out and play, come out and play. . . ."

He couldn't see what was hidden inside the tiny clenched fist, and then the boy was gone and Jordan had him by the shoulder, shaking.

"Hey! Dan! Snap out of it. Dan? Earth to Dan!"

"Did you see it again?" Abby asked, accurately interpreting his sudden pallor, the slight tremor in his hands. His hand tightened around the phone.

"I'm fine," he murmured. "It's gone. We should . . . We should get going."

But moving away from the presumed safety of the tree and the now-comforting glow of the house party lights proved harder than Dan expected. Every step he took into the darkness came with the threat of seeing that silver glow again, and then the boy, and maybe the next time he wouldn't vanish.

Abby leaned in to glance at the GPS map, and together they cut across the back lawn to the street behind it. Half a block east, and they came to the crossroads. A single streetlamp illuminated the sign.

"Ellis," Abby read. "And that house is ten-fourteen. We must be close."

"I don't know if I'm excited or about to puke on myself," Jordan whispered as they crossed the street. The rain had stopped hours ago, leaving the pavement slick and shining. They left behind the wan glow of the streetlamp and plunged back into darkness. It was late enough that most houses sat quiet, all their lights turned off.

Dan walked more quickly without meaning to, half jogging as they traveled down the street. At precisely the midway point of the block, he stopped, watching as Abby's phone lit up the mailbox at the edge of the lawn.

"This is it," she said. "No cars in the driveway. No lights. What do you guys think?"

"What did you *think* we would do? Ring the doorbell?" Jordan muttered. "Come on, let's find a back window and hope they don't have an attack dog."

"It looks abandoned," Dan added.

"And creepy. Yuck."

Jordan had a point. The Victorian house had seen better days. Paint peeled in long shavings, stuck to the clapboards by the damp. Three stories high, the house pushed to the limits of the property, too much building for too little land. It had been dark green once, or maybe blue.

Dan refused to look up at the windows, convinced he would see the pale, bleeding boy staring back at him.

The second they set foot on the side porch, the boards creaked. The trio shuffled along slowly, each of them trying to minimize the noise as they neared the back of the house. Jordan stuck his head out and peered around the corner.

"Looks clear," he said, "and I don't hear anything or anyone. I should be able to get us inside." And with that, he pulled a small tool out of his pocket—not a lockpick, but a kind of flat, wide trowel.

"Why am I not surprised?" Dan murmured, smirking.

"Good for windows," Jordan whispered. "I had to use this baby a few times at home."

He slipped the edge of the tool into the sill, sliding it into the rotting gap. With a few pumps of his elbow, the window rattled and then Dan heard a faint popping noise.

"No alarms. I still don't hear anything. . . ." Jordan lifted the window a few inches, waited, and then pushed it the rest of the way up. "After you."

"You're too kind," Abby said with a sarcastic chuckle. At least she seemed to be stone-cold sober again. Dan knelt and made a cradle of both hands so she could climb up safely. He boosted her in and then followed. When Jordan landed next to him, they lowered the window and softly closed it. Dan took out his cell phone to light the way.

"Don't flip the light switches," he told them. "We don't want to alert the neighbors."

He swept the phone screen around the room, revealing a kitchen that could have been a museum for a bygone era. Dan shivered, remembering the same musty, untouched chill from Brookline's lower levels, as if the air hadn't been breathed in decades. It looked as if nothing here had been touched in years, but strangely, it seemed *clean*, or at least organized.

"Someone is taking care of this place," he observed, going to the sink on his left. He tried the hot water handle, and the pipes groaned and chugged before releasing a thin spout of orange goop. It ran clear after a second and he turned it off. "Water is still on, so someone is paying bills on this place."

Jordan's and Abby's cell phone lights bounced around the kitchen. Dishes were stacked next to the sink; a teacup on the counter still had a film of ancient tea in the bottom.

"Look at this!" It was Abby, whispering excitedly from the next room, a spacious dining room with a chandelier and a stopped grandfather clock. "Newspapers, hundreds of them, and tons of mail. What is all this stuff?"

Dan followed the sound of her voice, joining them in the dining room.

"Mailbags," Jordan said, knocking one with the toe of his boot. "They don't look like they've been opened or even touched in years. Look at that dust."

Abby had already begun to pick through the stray letters stacked on the dining room table. Gingerly, she peeled open one of the unsealed envelopes. "This one is from 1968. This one, too. And this one. These are from the year after." She sorted through the envelopes more quickly, slightly breathless. "They look like local addresses, but there are dozens of different recipients here."

"Who would bother collecting this junk?" Jordan asked, going to stand behind Abby and read over her shoulder.

"Mailbags in here, too," Dan said, moving beyond them and into the foyer. He stooped and picked up a handful of letters, blowing a thin layer of dust from them. "Same years. Sixty-eight and sixty-nine." Shuffling through the letters, he began to notice a pattern, if a small one. He pocketed the letters with street addresses he recognized. "They're all addressed to women. Local ones, from the looks of it. And, oh man, check this out. . . ."

Dan had come to a stack of photographs, paper-clipped to a manila envelope that had no name or address at all. The photos

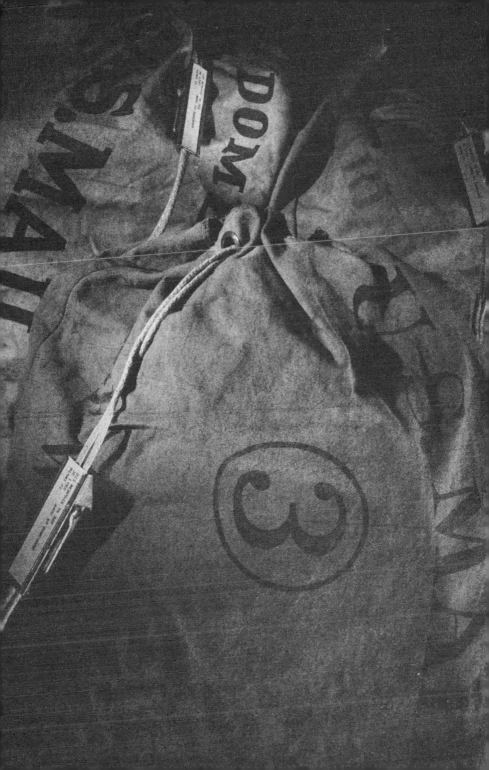

were all of girls (young women, really—they looked to be college-aged), and while none of the photos was exactly compromising, there was something intimate, even voyeuristic, about them that made Dan's blood run cold.

"They look so sad," Abby said. "What do you think—"

She fell silent, stunned by a sudden scraping noise from outside. Not just outside, but the porch and the way they had come.

Dan ducked down instinctively; the others followed him an instant later. He crawled toward them across the foyer, and they huddled together against a china cabinet near the dining room window. Even though it was dark inside and out, he could tell the difference, the flicker, when a shadow passed across the window directly above them.

"Someone is here," Jordan breathed, then clapped a hand over his mouth.

The shadow flickered again, then stayed. Dan held his breath, squeezing his eyes shut. He didn't dare look up.

Through the window, he heard someone draw in a long, rattling breath, and then a girl's voice sang out, high and clear.

"Daniel . . . Daniel . . . Come out and play, Daniel. . . ."

CHAPTER

13

*I*t felt like an eternity, the time between when the voice stopped and the scraping sound came again, this time receding. None of them moved, frozen in silence. Minutes crawled by, but even so, Dan held his breath until his lungs burned.

"T-Tell me you guys heard that, too," Dan whispered. He lifted his head just a little.

"Yup," Jordan squeaked, white-faced. "Most definitely."

"Dan . . ." Abby shook next to him, gripping his knee. "You said you saw a little boy. That was a girl's voice. Is there more than one ghost?"

"Jesus Christ." Jordan leaned heavily against the cupboard. "You're making it worse. Shut up, shut up!"

"We have to get out of here," Abby said. "Now is not the time to get caught breaking and entering."

"Let me look. . . ." Dan shifted onto his knees, carefully peering up and around until just the top of his head rose above the windowsill. With no streetlamps near the house, he found it hard to determine whether or not the coast was clear. But nobody waited outside the window or in the immediate, admittedly limited area Dan could see.

"I think we're good." He turned and led them back into the

kitchen and to the window they had come in. "Do I need to do anything special to the window or will it just slide right open?"

Jordan leaned across him and pushed up under the bottom of the window. It groaned as if the edges had become too wide for its frame. He shoved harder and it finally shuddered open.

"I'd say 'after you,' but screw that, I'm out of here." Jordan hoisted himself onto the kitchen counter and then out into the night. Abby followed. She turned to Dan before ducking through the open space and paused.

"What is it?"

"You know that weird feeling you get when you feel like you're being watched?"

"Yeah, I've got it too," he said. "We need to hurry."

No sooner had the words left his mouth than he heard a single, solitary footstep on the floor above him. The one heavy footfall sent a rippling groan through the house.

"*Go*," he said urgently, waving her out the window. Dan scampered up after her and wedged himself through the window, ignoring the sharp splinter that scraped across his arm. Back out in the cold, Dan pushed the window shut and followed his friends down the porch.

Nobody needed to say anything; Jordan took off, sprinting. Dan matched his pace, glancing back over his shoulder once as they left the house behind. Paper scratched against his belly, and he touched his stomach where some of the mailbag letters were tucked into his waistband. His arm throbbed where the splinter had caught him. He clasped his hand over the ache, and his palm came away slick with blood.

When they reached the crossroads about a block from the

house, Dan slowed down to a walk and pulled out the letters.

"Not a total loss," he said, catching his breath. "At least I got some of these."

"I took some, too," Abby added. "Do you think anyone will notice them missing?"

Dan shrugged, frowning down at the letters in his hand.

"Not to be a total downer," Jordan began, "but what the hell happened back there? Am I the only one who thinks Felix tried to lead us into a trap?"

"These must be important," Abby said, not quite answering his question. "We can read through what we took and see if there's any mention of Brookline. If not . . . Well, we could always try going back another night."

Dan remembered the sound of that footstep shaking the house and shivered.

"Let's hope we don't have to," he murmured. "Anyway, that was only the first address. Maybe whatever Felix wanted us to find is at one of the coordinates and he just wasn't sure which one."

"Man, all these maybes are starting to freak me out," Jordan said. He spun and strode defiantly out of the pool of lamplight they had stopped in, and Dan followed, clutching his hurt arm.

"Hey!"

"Watch it!"

Dan felt Abby's hand on the arm of his sweater, tugging him back as they watched Jordan stumble under the streetlamp. Jordan was holding his chest, panting.

"God! You scared me half to death!" he cried.

"Sorry! Sorry." It was Micah, sliding into the light with his hands raised in surrender. Dan puffed out a sigh of relief. "I didn't mean to scare y'all, but you weren't anywhere at the party. I've been looking and looking. . . ."

His eyes landed on the hand Dan had clasped tightly over his biceps.

"You okay?"

"Fine, we were—" What *were* they doing? Why hadn't he bothered to concoct a convincing story in case this very scenario unfolded? He swallowed hard and forced himself to look Micah in the eye. "Just out exploring the neighborhood. The party got sort of crowded, so we went out for some air." Dan smiled, allowing his shoulders to drop. *Relax. Relax and sell it and he will never know the difference.* "I think we must've taken a wrong turn, though. Couldn't find our way back."

He looked to Jordan and Abby for confirmation. They nodded in suspicious unison.

"Yes!" Abby finally blurted. "Yeah, we got lost. The party was . . . way too hot, right? So many people in that tiny little house!"

"Yeah, I found it a little stifling myself," Micah said, reaching up to adjust his glasses. "You want me to show you guys back? I think that might be best. Not sure I'm supposed to allow y'all to wander around town in the middle of the night."

"Allow?"

Jordan was going to give them away if he kept up the attitude.

"Oh." Micah laughed nervously. "Not like—I mean, we're just supposed to look after you kids is all."

"Thanks for finding us," Dan said quickly. He strode out ahead in the direction he hoped would lead them back to campus. Micah didn't object, so he assumed he had chosen correctly. "It's crazy how confusing these streets get in the dark. I bet in the daytime you can spot the campus chapel from just about anywhere."

"That's a fair guess."

"But I'm sure you can find your way blindfolded now. Does it feel weird to have somewhere else feel like home? I mean when you first got here you were probably as hopeless as we are at finding your way around, but now it's second nature." Dan could hear his voice speeding up as he talked but did nothing to stop it.

"It surely is."

Dan felt compelled to keep talking, not just because he wanted to prove their innocence, but because he could not handle silence right then. Silence gave the shadows and the darkness power. Silence meant he might be ambushed and taunted with his own name. The constant stream of inane chatter felt like a ward against that possibility, and even made him relax a little.

It wasn't until they were in view of the house party and Abby tugged on his sleeve that Dan realized just how long he'd been monologuing.

"Hey, motormouth," Jordan said when Dan slowed down to walk beside them. "You're being the definition of suspicious."

"I am?" Dan asked. "Crap, I suppose I am."

"Nobody talks that fast unless they're hiding something," Abby added. "Unless you're really trying to make friends? Which would be ironic, since you're the one who said we didn't have time to make friends."

"Right. Yeah. I just thought . . ." They were outside the back porch now. Micah didn't seem keen to let them out of his sight again. Abby breezed by him wearing a big, fake smile. The kitchen was much less crowded at this point.

"Wow," Jordan muttered. "Who needs a drink?" He went to the punch bowl on the counter and scooped out a cup for himself. Cal joined Micah in the doorway, and as they talked, Cal kept looking over his shoulder at them.

"You just thought what?" Abby prompted. They stood in a close huddle in the corner by the empty chip and dip bowls.

On the counter behind the bowls was a row of candles burning away. Dan stared intently at the candle on the far right, a dark red glob that was almost completely burned down, so that all that remained was the hint of a sculpted jaw and chin.

"I just thought anything would be better than silence." He laughed pitifully at his own explanation. "If it gets quiet, I might see that little boy again. Or hear voices. I'm sure that sounds completely stupid."

"It's not stupid, Dan," Jordan said softly. "I get what you mean."

Abby opened her mouth to respond, and judging by her furrowed brow, it wasn't going to be in the affirmative. She didn't get a chance to say her piece, though—Micah had broken off from Cal and was now hovering over Jordan's shoulder.

"Hey, guys, could I steal Dan for a moment?"

"He's all yours," Jordan said, grinning through clenched teeth.

"Thanks." He didn't give Dan an opportunity to say goodbye, just took him by the arm and dragged him away. A herd of drunken students thundered in from the living room, and

Abby and Jordan disappeared into the crowd.

Micah brought him to the opposite end of the kitchen, where a shadowy alcove sheltered a butler's staircase that hardly looked wide enough for one. This didn't bode well—what if Micah was going to report them for running off? Maybe his host wasn't nearly as friendly and forgiving as he seemed.

"What's up?" Dan asked neutrally.

"I wasn't going to mention this," Micah began, wiping at invisible sweat on his brow. "But I need you to warn your buddy Jordan about Cal. I was just talking to him, and that boy was *all lit up*."

Dan mouthed the words "all lit up" with one brow lifted.

"Drunk," Micah explained. "Point is, his behavior's been, uh, erratic lately. This stuff with his dad . . . He's just unpredictable right now and he doesn't always hold his liquor well. He can be a little on the mean side when he's sober, but *drunk*? Look, a word from me might not mean much to your friend, but he'd listen to you. It's nothing serious, I just think it's best if we all keep a collective eye on them."

"Is the drinking unusual?" Dan asked, still not fully following.

Micah nodded. "Bad drinking, bad grades, bad new crowd. It's a mite early to say 'downward spiral,' but it's getting there, know what I mean?"

It was Dan's turn to nod.

"You see it lots," Micah continued, scratching at his goatee. "More than you might think. Lots of pressure here to do well, to perform, sometimes it's enough to make a person crack. Then his dad . . . It's been a lot for him to handle. When I saw your friend dancing with him tonight I just thought it might be best to warn you."

"So if Cal is on some downward spiral, what is he doing hosting a prospie?"

Micah laughed, guffawed really, pausing a moment afterward and staring at Dan. "Well, you know how I said his dad was a big-shot alum?"

"Yeah . . ."

"His pop was the dean. The whole administration has been on eggshells around Cal since he died. Cal could probably get away with murder if he had a mind to."

"Ha." Dan forced out a nervous laugh. "Well . . . I'll, um . . . I'll tell Jordan to be careful."

"That's all I'm asking," Micah said, clapping Dan on the shoulder. "Thanks, man, I had a feeling you were a stand-up sort, and it's good to know I was right."

✗ ✗ ✗ ✗ ✗ ✗

That night, after pulling Jordan aside to fill him in about Cal, Dan returned to Micah's room and fell asleep without even glancing over the new clues they had collected. He collapsed into a heavy but fitful sleep, and even unconscious he knew the dreams would come, could feel them gathering on the fringes of his mind like a bank of growing storm clouds.

The dream swallowed him up whole.

He stood in the entryway to a shabby house, stamping the fresh mud off his boots. There was an umbrella in his hand and he shook the rain from it. He checked his pocket watch, a well-polished antique, and felt himself become overwhelmed by the tedium of this visit. There was so much to do. His time was so precious. Why did he waste it on these cretins and fools?

That was when Harry stumbled into the dining room. Rows and rows of stuffed mailbags filled the room, grayish and fat, like sows turned onto their sides. He went to one and toed it, which made Harry visibly recoil. It didn't matter. Harry, like all of them, was a tiny man and a tiny thing. But tiny things could be made to grow, and that, he knew, was his calling.

"Letters, letters, none for me," Harry was saying, worrying over the mailbags, tending to them like a doting father. "Never any letters for me."

"They're all for you, Harry. You're the minder of these things. You're the keeper. That gives you power. You bring the letters where they need to go. For a while, at least, all letters are for you." That seemed to calm the man; he stopped compulsively tucking his stringy hair behind his ear. "But you've been naughty again, haven't you, Harry? You've been snooping, reading what you shouldn't."

"Yes. Naughty. Yes, I shouldn't. . . ." Harry tucked his hair behind his ear, and again, and again.

There was nothing to do but sigh and nod. "Who is it this time?"

"The girls. The girls write to each other, but never to me. Letters, letters, never any for me."

"I told you, Harry, they are for you, if only for a time. How does that make you feel?"

"Good. It makes me feel good." Harry, gnarled and hunching, straightened up a little.

"I'm not here to cure you." He consulted his pocket watch again. Running late. Ah well. He detached the watch and cradled the warm metal heart of it in his hand. "So put yourself at ease. I'm not here to cure you, Harry. . . ." Then he smiled, and beckoned Harry closer. "I'm here to set you free."

Dan woke in a cold sweat. It was just his imagination, obviously. He had been in that old house with Abby and Jordan and now his mind was making up stories. Micah had left the window open a crack, and a steady breeze seeped in, unpleasantly damp. With jittering hands, Dan nestled down under his blanket, the tremor getting worse when he thought of Felix's sure, strange voice.

You see things you shouldn't be able to see. You know things you shouldn't be able to know. Like other people's memories.

That wasn't a *thing*, was it? Dissociative disorder was a thing—a thing that was hard enough. And who knows, maybe that's what Felix had, too, and he just had a more severe case or something. But Dan's dreams and visions felt so real, about things he couldn't possibly know. Unless they were totally in his imagination, there was something else going on here, something deeper that was wrong.

Dan wasn't sure which was worse—the idea that he was actually being haunted or *possessed* or whatever, or the idea that this was all in his head.

CHAPTER

14

"Micah didn't *have* to say anything," Dan was explaining, aiming for casual but landing somewhere closer to petulant. "I'm just glad Jordan knows to be on alert. What were they doing dancing together, anyway? It doesn't seem like Jordan even likes the guy."

"Oh, come on. When do you think he's ever gotten the chance to be himself? I can see why he'd want to let loose a little. It's not like he gets to dance with boys at prom." Abby cradled a steaming cup of coffee in her mittened hands. They had stopped at the student union just as it opened. Dan could hardly stay awake this early, but the caffeine helped.

"I hadn't thought of that," Dan admitted.

"Jordan's not an idiot, he knows not to get attached. We're only here for three days," she said lightly.

"Our hosts do seem interested in getting to know us, though, don't they?" he replied. "I can't tell if that's a good thing or not."

"Right? Under normal circumstances I'd be flattered, but these aren't exactly normal circumstances." She had ordered a skinny vanilla latte with an extra shot, and, not knowing what to get for himself, he'd asked for the same.

Vanilla-scented steam rose through the tiny hole in the top

covering his drink. He breathed it in, using the warmth like a shield against the October chill. Fog rolled across the crisp grass, unfurling around them like a cloudy carpet. Abby kept leading them off the paths that crisscrossed the campus, taking the most direct route to the street that led east toward their destination.

"Well, I for one am glad to get away from Micah for a minute," Dan replied. "I mean, I'm glad you and I get to spend some time together."

She paused, cocking her head to the side. Finally, she said, "Me too. I don't think I could have made this trip by myself."

"How was Lara's art thing?"

"Her senior installation? Oh, it's beautiful, Dan, really haunting. She's so talented, I can't help but be a little jealous."

When Abby texted that morning to ask if he wanted to go with her to see her aunt Lucy, she had mentioned going first with Lara to see her installation-in-progress. Apparently, Lara did all her best work at sunrise. Dan couldn't imagine being up even *earlier* after the night they'd had, but he seemed to be the only one—Micah had been dressed and ready to go the moment Dan woke up. He'd made sure to confirm plans with Dan for lunch, at which point he'd know whether Dan could sit in on Professor Reyes's seminar or not, and he'd reminded Dan that the carnival was still going on that night. Once he was alone, Dan had called his mom to tell her about how great things were at Georgetown.

"You and Lara seem to be hitting it off. Do you think you'll stay in touch with her after we leave?"

They were at the edge of campus, the paved paths giving way

to sidewalks. The campus chapel rose up on their left, and just beyond that stood the library.

"I hadn't thought about it," Abby said, sipping from her coffee. "Sometimes I feel like it would be best to just leave as much of this place behind as I can."

There was that horrible word again, *just*.

"I don't know how you can do that," Dan said, not totally sure if they were talking about the same thing anymore and unable to keep all the hurt out of his voice. "I can never seem to stop thinking about this summer."

Abby nodded and held her coffee up close to her face. She touched the warm surface of the cup to each of her pink cheeks. "But if you *could* leave it behind, if you could, I don't know, magically just make yourself forget or move on completely, would you?"

He didn't have an immediate answer for her.

Smiling, she touched her elbow to his jacket sleeve. "Thought so. Obsessions aren't healthy, Dan, I know you know that. When we leave this weekend, whether we find anything to explain what's been happening to us or not, you have to try to put some distance between you and all this. Have you talked to your therapist about it? Not that it's any of my business . . ."

"I have, but she doesn't say much, she just lets me talk, which is good, I guess. . . ."

Dan stopped, feeling his pocket buzz. He pulled out his cell phone to find Jordan had just texted.

Where are you guys? Need to talk ASAP

"It's Jordan," Dan said absently, texting back.

We're by the chapel on campus, going to visit Lucy.

Wait there for me plz

"He wants us to wait. Sounds urgent. Do you mind?" Dan tucked his phone away, taking a half step into the sun for more warmth.

Not even ten minutes went by before Jordan appeared in the mist, sprinting toward them. He careened to a stop, out of breath, the buttons on his coat done up incorrectly.

"What is it?" Abby pressed, touching his shoulder.

"It's . . . Cal . . ." Jordan bent at the waist, panting. When he looked up, his wild eyes fixed on Dan. "Your BFF wasn't lying. Something is not right with that kid."

"What happened?" Abby began rubbing small circles on Jordan's shoulder.

Jordan stood upright and shook his head, his breaths still coming short. "He was pretty hammered when we got back to the room last night. I figured he'd sleep in, try to take the edge off his hangover. But when I opened my damn eyes he was right there. I mean *right* there, standing over the futon staring at me."

That rang an uncomfortable bell for Dan. "Did he say anything?"

"No! He was just watching me sleep. It was the creepiest thing ever, and I have seen some seriously creepy shit lately."

"Did he snap out of it?" Abby asked, still rubbing his back.

"No. I started yelling at him, clapping. Nothing worked. I didn't know what to do. I panicked and flipped over, thinking maybe I was dreaming, you know? Imagining it. I opened my eyes again and looked over my shoulder and he was back in bed. Snoring. Just . . . snoring." Jordan pinched the bridge of his nose and leaned into Abby's hand.

"Maybe he sleepwalks," Dan suggested. "It's not unheard of."

But he was already thinking about this summer with Felix, and how almost the exact same thing had happened. He could feel sweat gathering in his palms despite the cold; maybe they were making a huge mistake by staying. Jordan could be in danger. . . . Cal could be Felix 2.0.

"It wasn't sleepwalking," Jordan replied firmly. "I mean, Micah even warned you about him. Look . . . I can't go back to that room right now. I don't want to be alone with him. Can I stay with you guys?"

"Of course," Abby said. She offered him her latte and he took a sip. "We're on our way to Lucy's. You guys can wait outside if you don't feel like coming in."

They crossed the street, putting the chapel to their backs, and followed Abby to the sidewalk. The street sloped downward, bringing them past a row of houses that were used by the college for offices and guest housing.

"Are you sure you're all right?" Abby asked as they went. Dan fell in step behind them.

"I'll be fine," Jordan assured her. "Let's just talk about something else. How's your aunt? Does she know we're coming?"

"Truthfully?" She sighed and then shrugged her slim shoulders. "I have no idea. . . . She hasn't been returning my calls or my letters. I'm not sure she even knows how to use a computer so email is out of the question. I just hope she's okay. Losing her husband, being confronted with her past . . . It's a lot for anyone to handle, and after what they did to her in the asylum . . ."

"So how do you know she's even at home?" Jordan asked, taking another drink from her coffee.

"I guess I don't. She moved into a new house at the end of the summer and mailed me the address. That was the last I heard from her. My gut tells me she wouldn't leave Camford, though. I guess we're about to find out, right?"

✗ ✗ ✗ ✗ ✗ ✗

The walk was longer than Dan expected, and by the time they arrived at Lucy's small cottage he was that uncomfortable combination of freezing and sweaty. Everything covered by his jacket was clammy, but his face and hands were red from the autumn wind.

Jordan wiped at his runny nose as they stood at the edge of the lawn.

"Not one for good housekeeping, then," he mumbled.

Nobody had mowed the lawn or done anything to prepare for the colder weather. Most people had huge piles of leaves covering gardens to keep the annuals warm during the snow months. But here the grass had grown long and snarling, vines and morning glory strands twining up the outer walls. A few shingles on the roof had come loose.

Even so, a cheery wisp of smoke rose from the chimney.

"Looks like she's home," Dan said, pointing to the smoke.

"Okay . . ." Abby shook out her mittens, vibrating with nervous energy. "Just hang back. Let me see how she reacts to you guys before I ask if we can go in."

"No pressure," Jordan replied, apparently unexcited about the idea of going into the dilapidated house at all.

The windows were shuttered. The front stoop could hardly be seen under a thick cover of uncollected newspapers. Everything about the place looked abandoned except for the chimney. Dan remembered the way Lucy had looked at him . . . Accusatory. *Afraid*. Like maybe he wasn't a monster but one was inside him and she could see it. But he owed it to Abby to be here.

"Here we go." Abby drew in a deep breath and marched up to the door, pressing her mitten to the doorbell.

Dan heard the echo of the bell inside, and they waited for almost a minute before footsteps came from the other side of the door.

"Someone's coming," Dan said.

It sounded as if whoever was on the inside had to undo about twelve locks and chains before the door swung inward.

Lucy, gaunt and frizzy-haired, but very much there, greeted them with a gasp and then a smile.

"It's you," she said, fixing her eyes on Abby. She was wearing a threadbare cardigan over a knit dress, woolen tights, and house slippers. "Have you come for a visit?"

"Uh, yes," Abby replied, rocking up onto her toes and then back down to her heels. "Yeah. I, um, wanted to check in and see if you were doing okay. We never got to talk much after this summer and—"

"Come in." Lucy took a big step back and then ushered them toward her. Her gaze shifted to Jordan and then Dan, where it lingered. "Why don't you all come in?"

Abby started right forward, but Jordan and Dan both hesitated until Abby gave them an impatient look. With a shiver, Dan was the last to cross the threshold. Behind him, Lucy closed the door and did up half the dozen or so locks.

"Make yourselves comfortable," Lucy said, zooming past them toward the kitchen down the hall. "Let me get you something to eat. . . ."

"Someone call A and E," Jordan said out of the corner of his mouth. "I think we've got a bona fide hoarder."

Abby hissed softly under her breath. "It's a disaster," she said, wading through the stacks of newspapers and junk to the living room on the left. She navigated the group to a couch, where she had to displace several baskets of fake fruit to make room for them all.

"I thought you said she just moved in here," Dan whispered.

They sat all together in a row, hands in their laps.

"She did," Abby replied. "How can you even gather up this much junk in two months?"

"Did she seem weird to you?" Jordan asked, carefully pushing aside a wax apple that tumbled against his leg. "Like . . . way peppy? Way, way too peppy to see us?"

"It does seem a bit . . . irregular. Maybe she's doing better than I thought."

Or worse, Dan didn't suggest.

Lucy returned then with a plate of Oreos and Swiss Rolls. She set it down on the coffee table in front of them, and then took a seat in a grimy, overstuffed chair opposite the couch. A few crooked picture frames hung on the walls, most of them old black-and-whites of what looked like Lucy's parents or grandparents. The images were so faded and wrinkled the people

staring out of them looked like hardly more than ghosts.

One of the pictures in particular caught Dan's eye. It was of a man standing in a field, his face turned upward, balancing—impossibly—a wheelbarrow on the flat of his chin. He couldn't know for sure without asking Lucy, but Dan had a feeling this man was her late husband, Sal Weathers, in his youth. Three months ago, Dan had been the one to find Sal's body in the woods. At the time, Lucy had seemed to blame Dan for Sal's death.

Now Lucy scooted forward in her seat and beamed across the table at Abby.

"Are you getting excited to graduate? Sending in your applications? There are so many big changes in store for you!"

This was not the frail, shy woman Dan remembered. Not that he had much experience with lobotomy patients, but the quiet, slightly unhinged woman he had met this summer fit his image of a survivor much more closely than this Lucy did. As he listened to her barrage Abby with questions, he decided to accept this as a positive turn of events, rather than a frightening one—especially for Abby. He sat back and took an Oreo, biting into what appeared to be an ordinary cookie but tasted more like ashy mush. He heard Jordan cough quietly and then saw a balled-up napkin appear on the coffee table.

"What brings you back to Camford?" Lucy asked. Dan couldn't help but notice that even while she directed her questions to Abby, her eyes remained fixed on him. His knee bounced anxiously.

"We decided to come for a campus visit. One of the overnight weekends," Abby explained.

"You picked a good time, with the carnival and everything—there's so much to see."

"Will you be going? To the carnival, I mean?" Abby asked.

"No, no . . . I remember Sal mentioning it, that his father went as a child, although . . . I don't remember all of what he said, some of it is . . . Well, I can't recall some of it. But his father went as a boy. I remember that."

Dan perked up at the mention of her memory. As keyed in and coherent as she seemed to be, maybe she *would* be able to answer some of their questions after all. Abby seemed to have had the same thought.

"So your memory," she prompted slowly, "it's better? I mean, you're coping with everything okay?"

Lucy nodded, tipping her head to the side and looking at Abby fondly. "I am. I'm coping. The college sends students over sometimes to sit with me, to bring groceries, that kind of thing. Everything has been so much better since I found the bright burning star."

Jordan coughed again, but this time it was sharp. Dan had heard it, too. He must have mentally gone over his visit to Felix seventy times by now. He could recall Felix's exact intonation. . . . *Bright burning star.*

It couldn't be a coincidence.

"The what?" Dan asked, sitting up straighter.

"The bright burning star," Lucy replied matter-of-factly. She reached back behind her chair, taking a framed photograph from the table there, one Dan hadn't noticed at first. Smiling, she handed the photograph across to Dan. It was a faded, vintage photo of a piece of oblong red stone, like a geode. It hung

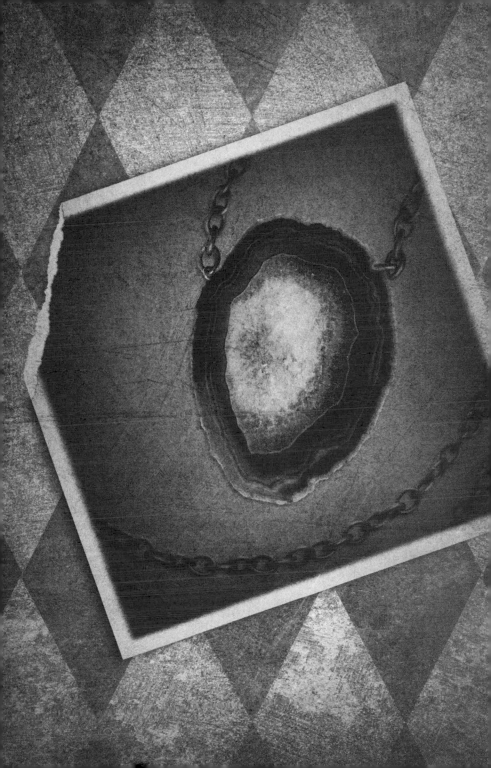

from a delicate chain. "It's beautiful," she murmured, watching him intently, "isn't it?"

"Where . . . did you get this picture?" Abby must have realized the connection, too. She stared at her aunt, breathless.

"You know, it's the funniest thing . . . I really can't remember. I feel like it's always been here with me."

"It's so pretty," Abby said, shifting to the side before sliding her cell phone out of her jeans pocket. "Could I take a picture of it?"

Lucy took the frame back from Dan and then propped it up with both hands, displaying it proudly while Abby snapped a photo with her phone. *Brilliant thinking, Abby.*

"What makes you call it that?" Dan asked, maybe a bit too eagerly. "'Bright burning star.' That's, uh, a very specific way of describing it."

"I suppose so. . . ." She looked down at the picture again. "It's not even really shaped like a star, is it?" Laughing, she turned the frame this way and that, as if she could make the stone in the photograph catch the light. "I've just . . . always called it that. I was so afraid. . . ." Putting the frame back on the table, she turned again to Dan. He squirmed under the intensity of her gaze. "I was afraid of you, Daniel Crawford. I was afraid of everything. . . . Then the bright burning star came and it was all better. All calmer."

"Oh," Dan said, looking helplessly to Abby, who stared back, just as dumbfounded. He couldn't make eye contact with Lucy; it unnerved him—the blank, unwavering stare. . . . He looked over her shoulder at the window, jolted by a face glaring back at him from outside.

It wasn't a human face, not really, but a mask. Red and black, like a skull but melting, the mouth gaping down in an exaggerated clown's pout.

"What the . . ." Dan stood up, pointing at the window.

"I see it, too," Jordan exclaimed. But then it was gone, disappearing into the hedgerow, leaving behind nothing but a few rattling branches.

"Hey!" Dan darted for the door, Jordan fast on his heels. He tore open the locks on the door and tumbled out onto the stoop in time to see someone sprinting over the lawn and the sidewalk, then disappearing across the street.

"We'll never catch up," Jordan said, "but you weren't imagining things, it was definitely there."

"A mask." He tried to catch his breath. "And a red cloak."

"What the hell is going on around here?" Jordan mused aloud.

Behind them, Dan heard the locks on Lucy's door jingling as the door opened and Abby joined them on the stoop, tugging on her mittens. She turned and gave her aunt a hug. "I'll try to stop by and see you again before we go," she said.

"Be good," Lucy said, although with the way she was watching Dan as she said it, it felt more like advice for him.

"Thanks for having us," Dan muttered nervously. "Sorry for bolting like that."

Lucy waved him off, half-hidden behind the open door. She closed it with a sigh, and Dan heard one lock after another snap into place.

"I wish we could have asked her more questions," Dan said. "About the addresses, about that picture. . . . Did she say anything when we ran out?"

"No, she froze up," Abby replied sadly. "I don't know if it was because you startled her or the mask did."

"What do we even make of all that?" Jordan asked as they reached the sidewalk and turned left. "I mean, she was *not* herself. Or maybe she was herself, but just the self she would have been before what happened to her as a kid."

"I'm worried." Eyes distant, gazing away from both of them, Abby hugged herself, rubbing her upper arms with her mittens. "How would Felix know about that necklace in the picture? It doesn't make sense."

"I think the more pressing issue is that we're now being followed by masked weirdos," Jordan pointed out.

"We have to start somewhere," Abby said. "Maybe we should check those letters we found for mentions of the burning star thing. Everything we've collected, we need to cross-reference for anything even remotely similar. It's the only real lead we have right now."

Dan nodded, debating whether to tell them about his dream. He knew, obviously, that he had been the warden again and that he was standing in 1020 Ellis. What he didn't know was whether that exchange was real or just his overactive imagination. It *felt* authentic, but even so, what had he really learned? That the warden knew someone who lived in the house, someone named Harry? That Harry saw the warden for treatment? Those two things didn't necessarily seem relevant.

If they became relevant, he decided, then he would open up. Until then he didn't want to draw attention to the fact that he was dreaming *as* Warden Crawford.

"I want to know who's following us," he said. Jordan and Abby stopped walking.

"It *is* Halloween," Abby replied. "It could've been some neighborhood kid being nosy."

"Hang on," Dan said, his eye catching on something silvery white in the grass. "I think whoever was watching us dropped something." He trotted over to the edge of the yard, crouching down to find a postcard with a photograph, similar to the one Felix had handed him at Morthwaite.

"What is it?" Abby murmured, appearing at his side.

"I think it's the carnival," Dan said, standing slowly. He showed the picture around while still studying it himself. Jordan plucked the photograph out of his hand and flipped it over.

"Nothing on the back this time," he pointed out.

"It's just a tent," Abby said. "Wait, there's a little sign. See there? On the post next to it . . ."

Dan had to squint to read the faded print. "'Old Maudire's Prison of the Mind—Hypnotist Extraordinaire.'" An empty birdcage hung next to the tent's tall, narrow opening, through which he could make out a sketchy imprint of a man's silhouette, two dark pinpricks where his eyes would be.

"Think they dropped it accidentally?" Abby asked.

"Does anything around here happen accidentally?" Dan countered. "We were given the first photos intentionally, so I have to assume this is intentional, too."

"I'm with Dan on this one. We heard footsteps in the house last night, and someone was outside calling Dan's name. . . . Someone is following us. Stalking us." As if to illustrate, Jordan cast a wary glance around them, paying particular attention to the bushes.

"Let's hope it's just one someone," Dan said darkly.

He slipped the photo of the tent into his pocket and tapped his fingers over it through the fabric.

They continued down the sidewalk together, silent until Jordan coughed and shook his head, flinging it around like a wet dog. "Oh my God, those cookies were prehistoric," he said, wrenching the coffee out of Dan's hand and tossing it back. "Ahh. Much better."

Dan's pocket buzzed. He fumbled for his phone, letting Jordan keep the coffee.

"I guess those letters will have to wait, you guys. It's Micah," he said, feeling a stone sink in his gut. "He says Professor Reyes canceled her senior seminar for the afternoon. He wants me to meet them outside his class right now."

CHAPTER

15

*E*ven flanked by Abby and Jordan, Dan felt every single one of his hackles raise at the sight of Professor Reyes.

"It's good to see you back on campus," she said, much too enthusiastically, in Dan's opinion. Micah was there next to her, looking over a paper she'd handed back during the class period. The rest of the class trickled out from the open double doors behind them. But while her students filed by, Professor Reyes only had eyes for Dan, watching him intently as he tried to keep eye contact without flinching.

To the left, the rolling lawn of the academic quad was dotted with students chatting in groups and maintenance workers raking up leaves. Through a gap in the admissions building and the world affairs center, Dan could see the bright stripes of a few carnival tents.

"After what happened over the summer," she continued softly, "I wondered . . . Well, I'm just happy to see you again. You were such a bright student, so easy to teach. I was hoping you might visit outside the program."

She wore her same dark, dramatic clothing and funky jewelry, including six or eight different necklaces and a handful of bangles decorating her wrists. Dan glanced over her necklaces, half expecting or maybe hoping to see one just like in Lucy's photo. But some of her necklaces were tucked into her sweater and Dan didn't exactly feel it was appropriate to ask to see them.

"Just couldn't stay away, I guess."

"That's not surprising in the least," she said, laughing.

Dan's brow lifted in curiosity.

"We have a promising, energetic student body," Professor Reyes clarified. "So it's not surprising you would be drawn back here. Like attracts like. I only hope that little incident yesterday didn't sour you on us."

"Incident?"

"Yes . . . That poor boy . . ."

"Doug," Micah said absently, still glancing over his paper.

"Yes! That was his name. Doug. Such a shame about him." Professor Reyes hung her head and clucked her tongue. She was wearing so much of a woody, spicy perfume that it made Dan's nose itch.

"Little incident" didn't quite seem like the right way to describe someone making a dash for an open window, but Dan held his tongue. He had this weird suspicion that Professor Reyes was specifically trying to get to him, and he didn't want to give her the satisfaction of knowing it was working.

"Next year the focus of my First-Year Initiative seminar is on college life and stress. I'm trying to set up a mental health seminar, too, but funding for those things is always tight. I'll just have to keep my fingers crossed we get a few donations at the carnival tonight," she continued. "If you choose New Hampshire College, maybe I'll see you in my FYI seminar. Right up your alley, if I'm remembering correctly—history of psychology, right?"

"Yeah," Dan said. "That's . . . that's what I want to focus on."

"No pressure, of course, no pressure," Professor Reyes said with a hearty laugh. She leaned closer and said in a conspiratorial whisper, "But really, you should apply."

Dan shifted, uncomfortable. "It's, uh, it's definitely on my list," he finally said.

"Good!" She leaned away from him. "I was hoping you would say that."

A professor Dan didn't recognize—a tall, thin man with bottle-thick glasses—strolled by. He gave Professor Reyes a wary smile and nodded toward her, but she didn't return the gesture.

"Well, it's a disappointment Doug won't get to see the carnival—he was one of our biggest helpers. You'll be attending the festivities, I hope? They were quite an effort to coordinate."

"I didn't know you were so involved with it," Dan replied tightly.

She made an open-palmed gesture, leading his eye directly to the row of tents at the edge of the academic green. Trucks from local vendors were there off-loading supplies; Dan recognized the names of the local sandwich shop, city sewage, and a Camford florist. "We all did our part to bring a little colorful town history back to life."

"Professor." Micah put up his hand, as if class were still in session. "Could you tell me what this note says? You flagged my citation but I can't read what it says."

"Let's discuss this in my office," Professor Reyes said, trying to usher him away.

"Oh, hey! Dan, one second, buddy." Micah beckoned him closer with a quick wave. "I just wanted to check in and make sure everything was okay after last night."

Dan nodded, assuming the vagueness of the question was due to Professor Reyes standing right there.

"Yeah," he said. Now wasn't the time to bring up Cal's strange behavior that morning. "We're fine, thanks."

"That's a relief," Micah said, pretending to wipe away sweat from his brow.

"Wild college antics?" Professor Reyes asked. She glanced quickly between the two boys.

"Only responsible antics," Micah replied. "You know me."

"My office, then?" Professor Reyes said. She turned to Micah, and Dan took the opportunity to slip away, dragging Abby and Jordan with him.

"Ew," Jordan said as they detoured to a picnic table on the quad, one tucked under a tall, barren tree. The sun had come out, making it just warm enough to linger outside. "Am I the only one getting a god-awful Dolores Umbridge vibe off of her? Her office isn't pink and full of cats, is it?"

"You have no idea," Dan said, sitting. "Her class over the summer was fine, I guess, but then she said this thing when I was leaving, and . . ." He watched the professor disappear into the psychology and sociology building with Micah. "Anyway, I don't trust her. I can't believe she's actually still digging around in Brookline."

"I totally believe it." Jordan snorted. "Some people just can't leave well enough alone. Take us, for example."

"That's not at all the same thing," Dan replied.

"Here," Abby said, plopping her book bag on the picnic table. "I've got our map, the files Jordan collected, and letters we took last night. We need to start looking for connections, for anything mentioning the star." She turned to Jordan with a frown. "Can you think of anything we've seen here so far that could even be connected? Posters? Books? Anything at all with stars?"

"Not on my end. Cal's room is mostly rugby jerseys and J.Crew catalogs," Jordan said with a shrug. "But I can take a closer look when I'm there next. . . . Not a happy thought."

"What are we going to do about that?" Dan asked as Abby passed around stacks of papers for them to look through. "About Cal's staring problem, I mean."

"I can't say anything," Jordan said. "If he's possessed or something, then I don't want to flip some murder switch."

"I have a few letters from last night, too," Dan said, pulling them out of his coat pocket. The top two were nothing special, bills mostly, but he hesitated over the third envelope. His eyes landed on the yellowed stamp and postmark in the corner.

"Look at this date," he said, squinting at the old ink. "This is from the last year the warden was at Brookline, I'm sure of it."

"Open it up," Abby said eagerly. "Or wait, is it a felony to open mail if it was stolen or never delivered in the first place?"

"Who cares," Jordan said. "The seal is already broken and I doubt anyone is looking for it. Go ahead, Dan."

They each dove into their respective piles. Dan scanned the letter. It was addressed to an Anna Surridge from a Caroline Martin.

"This letter never left town," he pointed out. "Check out the return address—I think we passed Tamlen Street on the way back to the party last night."

The contents of the letter started innocently enough—a date,

"Dear Anna," hopes that the recipient was well, so on and so forth. But the casual tone quickly dropped away.

"Whoa," Dan breathed, "listen to this: 'My dearest Anna, I promised I would never reveal this to anyone, but I can no longer live in this damning silence. I fear I have made a grave mistake, though I made it in good faith, with the hopes of bringing myself and the family a brighter future. A man approached me in September, cloaked all in red. You can imagine I was frightened and confused at first, but when he handed me an envelope and the wax seal was also scarlet, stamped with the image of a skull—'"

"Hang on," Jordan interrupted, dropping the newspaper he had been reading. "Red cloak? Red skull? That sounds like our Peeping Tom from this morning."

"There's more," Dan said, reading quickly now. "'My suspicions were correct. I should never have started writing that idiotic article! But my own research hardly touched on the truth. What I thought would be simply a scholastic society of like-minded men and women pursuing knowledge and success proved to be a morass of secrets too dark to tell here. To join, I was forced to reveal every skeleton in my closet, every deed I regretted or committed in shame. Mutually assured destruction is the key to their power. But that, dearest Anna, was only the beginning. Each week I saw more ugliness, watched my fellow Scarlets being taken into back rooms only to later emerge with hollow eyes and slack mouths. I knew it was only a matter of time before they took me, too. And when they did . . . I would say I recall the memories in horror, but I do not recall them at all. I will write more if I can, and I dearly want to. I want to tell

My dearest Anna, I promised I would never reveal this to anyone, but I can no longer live in this damning silence. I fear I have made a grave mistake, though I made it in good faith, with the hopes of bringing myself and the family a brighter future. A man approached me in September, cloaked all in red. You can imagine I was frightened and confused at first, but when he handed me an envelope and the wax seal was also scarlet, stamped with the imago of a skull you all of it, every last detail, name every name, but already I've risked too much. I've been in touch with a man named Harry, who says he knows all about the Scarlets and their secrets. He claims he wants to help me, and I hope I can put my trust in him. It would be nice to have an ally. I want to publish an article exposing these people, but Harry thinks it would only put me in greater danger. Now I pray this letter arrives safely and my betrayal, however insignificant, is never discovered. Love, Caroline.'"

Dan gazed down at the paper, watching the neat letters blur together until they were just thick black lines on the page. None of them spoke for a long while, and then Dan blinked and folded up the letter, handing it across the table to Abby so she could get a look.

"We might have stumbled on something completely unrelated," she said, scanning the page, "but I don't think we can rule out a connection."

"I don't think so either," Jordan agreed. "Feels like way more than a coincidence—the warden's last year at Brookline, Felix's map leading us to that house, and now that letter. It never left town. Somebody read it, too. The envelope was open."

"I had a dream about this," Dan said. He shrank preemptively from their curious looks. "I mean, that's not proof or anything, but I saw the warden speaking to someone named Harry, almost like . . . assigning him a task. Someone was stalking her," Dan murmured, but then a worse thought occurred. "Maybe even stealing her mail . . . She mentions wanting to write an article here. If she was in town, maybe it's in the archives you found in the library."

"You're right, that's not proof, but really, why rule anything out at this point?" Abby paused. "I wonder if that article would have been in the local paper or the school's," she said. "Either way, there should be copies of all the back issues. We can probably even run a search on her name with some keywords."

"It sounds like she stumbled on some kind of cult," Dan replied. A few orange leaves drifted down from the branches above them, joining the stacks of research on the table. Jordan brushed them away impatiently.

"You think the person you saw at Aunt Lucy's was in the same cult? These letters are old, Dan," Abby said. "What are the odds these Scarlets or whatever are still a thing?"

"The description matches," Jordan replied, scratching his chin. "Skull, red robe . . . Maybe it's not a cult. She said it was supposed to be about academics, right? What if it's like the Skull and Bones or the Sevens?"

"If it is," Dan began slowly, "I doubt anyone will want to talk to us about it. Isn't the whole point of those societies to remain top secret?"

He looked between his two friends, who hesitated. Jordan scratched the side of his stubbled cheek with a pencil eraser, and Abby fiddled with the zipper on her book bag.

"Let's not go asking any fishy questions just yet. I think the archives would be our best bet," she said finally. "We can spend the afternoon there, and then we have the carnival tonight. That will be a good opportunity to get away and check the next address. I don't think we should be breaking into any houses in broad daylight."

"I wonder if that bright burning star is something we can

cross-reference or LexisNexis or whatever," Jordan mused, pushing up from the picnic table. "I've never heard of it before."

"If it's tied to this secret cult society, I doubt we'll find any general information," Abby replied. They mustered under the big barren tree and then crossed from the green of the quad to the paths. The library wasn't far, just beyond a shallow hill, a half block from the chapel.

Dan tried to go over what he had dreamed one more time, before all the details slipped away entirely. The warden had been in that house with that man, going through the stolen mailbags. Could that man really have been part of a secret society? He certainly didn't fit the profile of what Dan pictured when he heard "Skull and Bones." On that note . . . could Warden Crawford?

Dan shuddered to think of the warden joining—or worse, *forming*—a secret society, extending his reach beyond the walls of Brookline. As Caroline had said in her letter, societies like that were about power and influence. Those were two things the warden definitely didn't need.

"Right, Dan?"

Starting, Dan glanced up to find both his friends watching him. He hadn't heard even the beginnings of what they were asking.

"Sorry, what was the question?"

"You were lost in thought, weren't you?" Abby smiled faintly as they reached the tall doors to the library. A few students were clustered outside, chatting over steaming coffee cups. "What's up?"

"I was just thinking . . ." His dreams had certainly become

vivid, but were they evidence or just his imagination? "We know the warden was using Brookline as his personal research playground, but what if it wasn't just him? What if he was mixed up with these Scarlets?"

"He did have a hard-on for the best and the brightest," Jordan agreed.

"That's . . . a scary thought," Abby admitted.

For all the people who'd been milling about outside, the inside of the library was virtually empty. A bored desk worker wandered over, glanced at their weekend prospie badges, and waved them through the security sensors on either side of the doors.

Since Jordan had been here before, Dan and Abby followed him to a spot near the stairs leading down to the AV archives. They set up at a row of computer terminals with a small, round table close by for their papers and bags. "It would explain how he got away with so much. . . . I mean, if he had influential people watching his back, covering up his experiments at the asylum . . ."

"Oh!" Jordan slid into a computer chair, bouncing excitedly. "That's something we can check, too. Asylums must have been subject to inspections and things, right?"

"They were, yeah." This was Dan's area of expertise, and he was glad to contribute something of value to the discussion. "Usually nurses inside the facilities secretly reported on the higher-ups, tipping off outsiders to what was going on inside the hospitals. Even then, wardens would do their best to downplay whatever horrible stuff was going on, and they'd usually get away with it, too."

"Jesus, and here I thought Brookline was an isolated incident," Jordan muttered.

"I don't know if it got as bad as Brookline anywhere else," Dan said. "I'm just saying, if there were cover-ups going on elsewhere *and* the warden here had the ear of the dean or the president of the college? It's no wonder he got away with it for so long."

"That's good," Jordan said, typing furiously. "Well . . . not good, obviously, but it's another angle to check. We can easily find out who was running the college when the warden was at Brookline, then we can start digging on this alleged secret society."

He tapped the enter key and then they heard a soft *bew* as the monitor turned off.

"What the . . ." Jordan smacked his palm against the computer monitor. "It turned off!"

"These are old," Abby said, turning to the next keyboard over and typing. "It's probably just a surge. I'll check for . . . you . . ." She frowned, hitting the enter key about sixteen times.

"The hell?" Jordan said, hitting the side of her monitor, too. "No way that was a surge. It froze. Control-alt-delete, asshole. Wake up!"

He said those last two words just a little too loudly, and three different students whipped around in their seats to give him a death glare. Jordan sank down sheepishly.

Dan shifted to face his own computer, but he didn't really have a doubt what would happen. Warden Daniel Crawford. AND. Scarlets. He hit enter, his cursor stopped blinking, and next to him Jordan swore viciously, all exactly as he'd predicted.

"How hard would it be to make this happen?" Dan asked, frowning.

"Hard." Jordan glanced around the periphery of the AV room. "You would need to install an actual program on every single computer with whatever keywords and combinations you wanted to trigger the freeze. I'm not sure I could even program something like that."

"Well, it's a pain but maybe it will only slow us down." Abby spun around once completely in her desk chair and then said, "We can use our own laptops, right? They would be clean."

"Sure, but we won't have access to the college's digital archives from our own computers," Jordan said. "They would require a student ID for that kind of thing."

"I can use my phone for internet," Dan pointed out. "We all can."

"And as far as the archives go, we'll just have to do it the old-fashioned way." Abby slid out of her chair, going to collect her bag from the round table. "Jordan, show me where you found those newspapers. We can start there and try to find that article of Caroline's. That letter she wrote was October 1968. If she went ahead and published the article, it might have been soon after."

Dan nodded and followed Jordan up to the second level, which was even more deserted, quiet, and dark, with only every other row of lights turned on to conserve energy. The book stacks formed narrow aisles, broken up every dozen or so shelves with small areas to sit and study. Cubbies with computers ran along the stout wall overlooking the first floor.

At the top of the stairs, Jordan took a sharp left, bringing them through the maze of stacks. He and Abby chatted softly ahead, and Dan hung back, letting his eyes roam over the shelves and books, which all seemed to blur into one another. Shelf, aisle, shelf, aisle, over and over again, all of them abandoned. Shelf, aisle, shelf, boy, shelf, aisle . . . Dan stopped abruptly, then took two small steps back to look down the darkened lane formed by the two tall bookshelves.

The boy in the striped sweater and cutoff pants. Dan's mouth dried up, his tongue lying limp and numb in his mouth. He could feel a buzzing sensation starting in his lips, adrenaline hitting his system, making his whole body seize with sudden tremors. The boy in the shadows was drained of color, as if he were living in black and white, though his eyes seemed to glow faintly like coals. Blood dripped down through his hair and onto his forehead, into his eyes. . . .

Abby's and Jordan's quiet voices died away.

Dan blinked, expecting the boy to disappear, but he was still there, watching. Then he turned and walked down the aisle, away from Dan, only just visible in the darkness between the stacks. Without another thought, Dan followed.

Aisle after aisle, Dan chased the little apparition. He sped up, then decided to keep his distance, until the boy turned a sharp corner and Dan had to jog to make sure he didn't lose him. His heart pounded in his chest, that buzzy adrenaline numbness flooding through his veins faster now. Dan took the corner hard and fast and shouted, slamming chest first into Jordan. Dan stumbled back, the wind knocked clear out of his lungs.

"Dan! Where the hell did you come from?" Jordan spun, checking over his shoulder. "I thought you were right behind us."

"I was." He raced to think of an excuse other than *I followed a ghost child*. "I just took a shortcut."

"Scared me half to death."

"Are you okay? You guys hit each other pretty hard." Abby reached up to touch Dan's chest where he'd run into Jordan.

"I'm fine." *I'm not at all fine. I'm losing it.* "No, I'm not fine. . . . It's that little boy again. I just saw him." Dan glanced in every direction, but the boy was gone again. He turned to see where they had stopped, and a steep wall of shelves rose up to the ceiling. Binders upon binders were lined up in neat rows, the spines labeled with spans of years. *Winter 1961–Winter 1963*, *Spring 1963–Spring 1964*, and so on.

Right away, Dan noticed a gap, a clean, dust-free space where two binders obviously belonged.

And the boy led me right to this spot.

"You see things you shouldn't be able to see. You know things you shouldn't be able to know."

Damn it, Felix, stop being right about me.

"The years the warden ran Brookline," he murmured, fitting his hand into the empty space. "They're missing. The little kid led me right to it."

He heard Jordan whisper a barely audible "Creepy, Dan."

"But not everything is missing," Abby said excitedly. She pushed her arm into the gap left by the missing archive binders. He heard her fingernails scratch along the surface of the shelf, then she grunted softly, batting a slim, dusty binder toward them. The last swat was a little too rough, and the folder tumbled off the shelf. Dan managed to catch it before it could hit the carpet.

"They missed one. Fall 1968," Abby said, leaning over to read the spine. "It's something, at least. Let's hope Caroline published her article right after sending that letter."

"And this, too. . . ." Jordan palmed something out of the dusty shelf space and handed it to Dan. He could guess what it would be even before his hands closed over the musty card stock.

A photograph, but this one was less composed than the others. Dan recognized the birdcage from the last picture, the one their follower had left on the ground outside Lucy's house. But the cage wasn't empty anymore. In this photograph there was a bird inside, but it was broken and bleeding, its eyes staring, red and white feathers torn and littering the floor under its claws.

CHAPTER

16

an's phone chirped in his pocket, surprising him enough that he dropped his fork. It clattered noisily onto his tray, but that wasn't enough to interrupt Abby's host, who was in the middle of monologuing about her senior installation and the breakthrough she had made that afternoon.

"My brother finished his pre-med here," Lara was saying, "but even that wasn't good enough for my parents. They thought he would get into Berkeley, Princeton. . . . But the scholarship here was too good to pass up. Full ride."

He groped blindly for his fork, glancing down at his phone to find a new text message. It was from Jordan, who apparently felt it necessary to text him from about two feet away.

Does she ever shut up?

Dan smirked, glancing down the cafeteria bench at Jordan, who kept a cool outward facade.

Dan's smile didn't last long. He could feel the weight of the photographs in his pocket. Who would be morbid enough to take a picture of a dead bird? He could see the parrot's broken body whenever he lost focus and let his eyes close for a little too long.

"I think I might actually pass Psych 200 this semester," Micah said, interrupting Lara's story. He waited until Dan looked up to say, "Everything okay? I've hardly seen hide nor hair of you three today. Not sure you're getting the full prospie experience . . ."

"We saw the library," Dan deflected, picking at his mashed potatoes. The buzz of the dining hall rose around them, a constant blur of clanking silverware and laughter. "And the Commons . . . We got to wander quite a bit of the campus today, actually."

"And Lara took me to her installation this morning," Abby chimed in. "It's exciting work."

"You three coming to the carnival tonight?" Cal asked. He looked, in Dan's opinion, exhausted, with dark bags under his eyes and a sickly cast to his skin. Jordan glanced everywhere in the cafeteria except in Cal's direction, and Cal appeared to be doing the same, addressing every word specifically to Dan. "Probably going to be packed with drunk kids. Who knows what they'll get up to."

"Rowdy drunk kids aren't exactly a rousing endorsement, Cal," Micah said with another laugh. "But you're coming, right?"

"Wouldn't miss it," Jordan mumbled, swapping out his phone for his sudoku book and completely checking out of the conversation.

"Y'all are going to, uh, stick around this time, yeah?" Micah asked. Dan could hear the shift in tone, and shrank under the way he stared at each of them in turn.

"What are you talking about?" Lara reached across Micah for

the pepper, then doused her food in it.

"They just . . . had an adventure on top of the party, that's all."

"Can't blame 'em," Cal said, shrugging. "That party was too packed. The carnival will be, too, I guess, but at least it will be outside. Let me know if you guys need anything to help keep you warm." He stuck his thumb out and mimed drinking from it like a bottle.

Dan could see Micah's face turning darker shades of red by the minute.

"A lot of students worked hard on this, Cal," he said sternly. "The least you could do is show up sober. Anyway, there'll be plenty to do. Midway games, food, a maze . . . The dance and theater kids have cooked up some skits."

"The idiots in Student Affairs made me repaint the signs." Lara tossed Abby a sarcastic glance. "Apparently my design was too macabre. Philistines."

"Little kids come to this thing," Micah replied. "I can kind of see their point."

Dan's eyes landed on Jordan's sudoku puzzle, now half-hidden under his dinner tray, and he saw that he wasn't even solving the thing, but simply coloring in the empty squares.

When their plates were empty, they followed Micah and Lara to the garbage line. Cal had already left, muttering something about pregaming, whatever that was.

"Well, us volunteers have to get on over to the carnival," Micah said as they shuffled out of the cafeteria. "But you guys can wander by whenever you feel like it. Might want to get there early, before the lines get long."

"We'll be there," Dan assured him.

They stepped outside into the cold, each pulling on a different combination of hats and scarves and gloves.

"Catch you later," Lara said, waving to them, but primarily to Abby.

"Someone's been busy," Jordan observed, nodding to the path leading away from the cafeteria. The paved lanes crisscrossing the quad were lined with orange paper bags. A glowing votive sat in the bottom of each bag, throwing flickering, long shadows across the paths. Purple and black streamers decorated the dorms now, and plastic bats hung from the pillars and overhangs.

A few Halloween touches had been added to every building. Every building except Brookline. Dan stamped his feet, trying to coax warmth back into his legs. Behind him, he could feel Brookline there. He had to look, giving the asylum one quick glance over his shoulder. Just that was enough to send his legs wobbling.

"I'm wondering if we should ask Micah or Lara about the Scarlets thing. If it's like a local legend or rumor, they might know something about it." They ambled to the side of the stoop, avoiding the steady stream of students leaving the cafeteria. "Caroline's article was pretty vague. . . ."

Dan had taken the copy from the *Fall 1968* binder, but it was hardly worth reading again. Caroline Martin must have edited the article sometime after writing her letter—or someone else had. Anything seemed possible.

Abby stuck her hands deep into her coat pockets and gazed out at the flickering lights along the paths. "If the Scarlets went to the trouble of going through the town's mail, I'm sure their tracks are probably covered."

"We have to find out where those archive binders about the warden went," Dan said. He shivered, thinking of the boy leading him through the library. "Not just for what's in them, but for who took them." *And who left the dead bird behind.*

"Maybe it's our mystery computer programmer," Jordan suggested. "If searches about the warden are locked, then it figures that those records would go missing, too."

"I hate to point this out," Abby said softly, sniffling from the cold, "but Professor Reyes is running that seminar on Brookline. The archives might just be checked out. It's almost midterms, kids could be doing some extra studying, or the professor could be making copies for class handouts."

"I know," Dan replied. "It's not much to go on. None of this is. We should keep following Felix's map, otherwise we're still at square one."

A cold spike of anxiety lanced through Dan's chest as they crossed to the academic side. The green in front of Wilfurd Commons had been transformed into a black-and-purple carnival. More tents had sprung up, filling the empty spaces between buildings. Students in costumes, reeking of cheap alcohol, pushed by them, stumbling and shrieking with laughter. The townie families stuck together, herding their costumed children away from the loud college students.

"Wow, did Tim Burton binge on Laffy Taffy and vomit all over this place or what?" Jordan whispered.

"It certainly is . . . whimsical," Abby said. "I didn't realize there would be so many people here."

"Let's try to blend in," Dan suggested, which was harder than it first looked. The only other people not in ridiculous costumes were fellow prospies, who wandered through the Technicolor nightmare with their mouths open and chins tipped back, as they marveled at the tents, the wandering jugglers, the cotton candy vendors.

Midway games and popcorn stands lined the edges of the carnival, which seemed to be roughly in the shape of a circle. Lara's repainted signs pointed the way to the maze, to a haunted campus tour, and to the juggling stage. Dan glanced down the wide lane to his right, spotting a low, basic stage where a few students in leotards balanced on one another to make a pyramid.

A bullhorn cut through the air and all three of them turned to see a plump blond woman shouting from the back of a parked pickup truck. Red streamers hung from the taillights, a white banner dangling between them that read "KELLY LANG FOR STATE SENATE!"

"We could check out the maze," Abby said, trotting ahead. "It doesn't look too big, might just take us a minute."

"Do we need tickets or anything?" Jordan wondered, eagle eyeing a cotton candy seller.

"Looks like everything but food is free," Dan said. He recognized a few prospies hanging around a fenced-in area where a professor dunk tank had been set up. Luckily for the poor professor shivering on the bench, most of the students trying to dunk him were having a hard time aiming properly, which Dan guessed had something to do with whatever was in their plastic water bottles.

"All right, I'm up for the maze, but let's not get separated—these

things always make me dizzy," Jordan said, hooking arms with Dan and Abby.

They queued outside the biggest tent at the carnival. Masked students—no skulls, Dan noted—wandered up and down the line making halfhearted zombie noises.

"Are we scared yet?" Dan said, chuckling.

"At least it will be warmer inside," Abby said.

When they reached the head of the line, a girl in a convincing bearded-lady costume led them into the tent, where it was, sadly, just as cold. Hay bales marked out the maze, stacked high enough that even the tallest person wouldn't be able to see over and cheat.

"Good luck," the bearded lady said, closing off the tent flap behind them.

It was dark, darker than Dan expected. Abby took a few nervous steps forward, herding them along.

"I'm already dizzy," Jordan mumbled as they rounded the first corner. The only lighting came from above, a few fake lanterns anchored to the hay bale. A moist grassy smell drifted through the narrow lanes, dirt and strewn wood chips scattering as they ambled clumsily through the corridors.

Something zipped by to Dan's right, brushing his shoulder. It disappeared around the next corner before he could get a good look, but the only glimpse he *had* gotten made his jaw tighten.

A red cape.

"What was that?" Abby whispered.

"I'm going on ahead," Dan said, breaking off from the other two.

"Dan, no—don't!"

Jordan's voice faded behind him as he ran. Of course, the moment he went around the next turn he was met with a fork and had no idea which way the red cloak had gone. From the darkened passage to his right he heard a low laugh. His skin prickled, but he followed the sound, carefully tiptoeing around one sharp corner and then another. Very quickly, he was lost. Looking up, he hoped the shape of the tent above could help him orient, but a black swath of cloth hid the pattern in the ceiling.

"Lost?"

Gasping, Dan turned, coming face-to-face with the same red-and-black skull mask that had watched them before. He rocked back onto his heels, caught off balance by just how close the mask loomed to his face. In a moment of panic, Dan grabbed for the mask, but his balance tipped backward as the masked figure lunged forward, slamming into his shoulder and knocking him to the ground.

Dan scrambled to push back to his feet, dazed.

Another caped figure appeared next to him, and then another, and a fourth. They swarmed around him, laughing, close enough that he could feel the whisper of fabric as their cloaks brushed his face. Girls laughing, boys laughing . . . Dan couldn't make out one from the other. He curled onto his side, shivering, but not before seeing a flash of rubbery white, a flash of blue. He recognized the shoe just before it landed in his ribs.

Dan winced. He knew those shoes.

"Cal?" he whispered, finding the strength to climb to his knees. The moment he said it, the red cloaks vanished, rushing off down the maze and out of sight.

He felt a hand clutching his arm and looked down, strangely detached from the physical feeling of the fingers there. The hand belonged to Jordan. Dan looked up, puzzled, feeling everything swimming in slow motion. Then Jordan pulled, hard, and Dan slipped to the side, back to the ground. He felt the world spin once and then he couldn't feel Jordan's hand on his arm anymore.

The carnival darkened, not just the light but the colors. Everything looked dim. He wasn't staring up at a stilt walker anymore, he was staring up at everyone. The grown-ups made him feel so small.

Funnel cakes and popcorn. His stomach growled, but he had only a few dimes and he knew where he wanted to spend them.

He knew the way now and he ignored the taunting voices that called to him from the dark crevices between tents and trailers.

"Daniel, come out to play. . . . Come out to play. . . ."

Soon his brothers wouldn't taunt him like that. Soon they would be the ones who were afraid. They would cringe and hide under the covers, not him. He pushed his way through the crowd, through the forest of grown-up legs, of trousers and skirts. The tent was all the way at the end of the carnival, tucked away like a shameful thing, a secret.

The man was waiting outside the tent in his shabby top hat. He had a long, thick beard that made the boy's chin itch just looking at it. He smelled like a grandfather, like tobacco and leather. And when he smiled, his smile wasn't kind but it wasn't mean either.

"Well, look who we have here," the man said, standing up from a metal stool. "Did you bring your tickets, boy?"

"I did, sir."

"And more importantly, did you bring your bright young curiosity?"

"I did, sir, yes."

"Then I have this for you. . . ." The man swept aside his old tailed coat and pulled out a stone on a long silver chain. The stone was oblong and red and flashed like a star on fire. "Follow the star with your eyes, boy, follow it back and forth. Listen to the sound of my voice, the only sound in the world. . . ."

Dan could feel the cold seeping in. He was on the ground, his legs splayed out in front of him, and the damp grass was clinging to his jeans.

At least the Scarlets were gone. Nobody was kicking him now. Scarlets. *Plural.* This was even worse than he'd thought.

"He's back."

Dan blinked up at Jordan, who hovered over him. He reached up and both Abby and Jordan took his hands.

"The Scarlets," Dan muttered. "I just got . . . I saw them in the maze, and then the shoes . . . I saw Cal's shoes. It's not just one stalker, you guys, there are . . . There was a whole group of them! They *attacked* me." He rubbed at his forehead, still a little dizzy. "But that's not even the worst part. The nightmares? Yeah, they're not just when I'm asleep now. That one hit me out of nowhere. I don't know what triggered it this time."

"Is that happening a lot?" Abby asked, holding his arm tightly.

"Honestly, I don't know. I'm starting to wonder if that little ghost boy is like that—like a waking dream. Except this time, I was somewhere totally different. And I wasn't me."

"What did you mean you saw Cal's shoes? Did you see Cal wearing them? Was he in the maze?" Jordan helped him up from the grass. They were just outside the exit to the maze. Dan couldn't remember being carried out.

"Four Scarlets . . . They were all wearing the capes and the masks, but the cloaks weren't long enough. I saw those boat shoes you hate so much."

"Are you sure?" Abby pressed, steadying his other side. "More than one person could have shoes like that."

"No, they were his. I recognized them."

"Stay here, I'll grab you something to drink," Jordan said. "You look like you could use it."

Jordan cut through the lines of students queuing up for attractions and food, his dark, curly head disappearing behind a curtain of coats and winter hats. Abby tried to rub some warmth and comfort back into Dan's arm.

"I'm fine," he insisted, and smiled for her sake. "Really."

She jolted, scrambling to pull her phone out of her pocket. "It's Jordan. He didn't bring any money. Will you be okay? I'll just run over and give him a few dollars."

"Go," Dan assured her. "I'm all good now."

The quick grin Abby gave him didn't quite reach her eyes, and her lips tilted skeptically downward. He stood in a decreasingly empty spot, as more and more students, faculty, and towns-folk poured into the carnival. To his right he saw an entire row of food vendors, all of them from Camford and all of them proudly displaying signs saying their goods had been donated and proceeds would go to the mental health seminar Professor Reyes had mentioned. He tried to find Abby and Jordan among the different lines for cider and cocoa, but couldn't see them. He did, however, spy a strange tent off behind the food vendors. It sat alone, apart, huddled under the shadows of a giant, leaf-less tree.

Dan no longer went anywhere without the photos he had col-lected, and now he found himself reaching into his pocket for them, shuffling to the picture of the tent and the birdcage he had picked up outside Lucy's house.

They're the same.

Silly, he thought, but the tent seemed almost to shy away from the rest of the carnival, an outlier. An anomaly. His feet carried him past the lines of chatting carnival-goers, then past the food tables. He dodged between the hot dog line and the popcorn line, plunging into a sudden pool of silence.

A shadow loomed on his left, passing closer to him than he liked. Dan flinched, glancing up to see a cracked white face glaring down at him. A clown. His makeup had gone yellow and jaundiced around the eyes, his widened mouth like a slashed and bloody smile.

"Hey," Dan muttered, shouldering by the clown.

"You going to see the hypnotist freak, kid?" the clown rasped. He reeked of cigarettes. Before Dan could answer, a dirty white glove was shoved against his chest, leaving behind a crumpled-up strand of tickets. Dan took them numbly, feeling like he didn't really have a choice.

"Six for a nickel, can't beat the price." The clown threw back his head and laughed, then almost lost his bedraggled orange wig. "If you like that sort of thing anyway. Me? I don't like nobody messing around in this here skull."

The clown jabbed at his own head and then pushed out of Dan's way, coughing into his soiled glove.

Dan opened the hand that held the tickets, unspooling them as he walked across the damp grass as if he were leaving a trail of bread crumbs. The aged tickets looked like they might have been in that clown's sweaty hand for years. The paper cracked

at the edges, and huge block letters on the front advertised
"DR. MAUDIRE THE MAGNIFICENT—HYPNOTIST
EXTRAORDINAIRE." The doctor's list of accomplishments
filled the backs of the tickets. Apparently, he could cure insomnia, phobias, and even carnal appetites.

None of that much interested Dan. What interested him was
the matching sign outside the tent, along with the matching
birdcage, and the matching, well, *everything*. He checked the tent
against the photo again and frowned. It was identical, except
in reality the cage outside the tent stood empty. This had to be
some kind of joke.

Or someone wants you here.

They'd already decided the masked stalker hadn't dropped the
photo accidentally. And either way, Dan was going inside that
tent. He could feel the same inexplicable magnetism drawing
him toward it, the same pull he had felt leading him through
Brookline's old offices this summer, through the operating
theater and the patient rooms. . . .

Dan shoved the photo back in his jeans and took a deep breath,
watching the open flap of the hypnotist's tent flutter. Two dark
eyes peered out and then vanished. Someone was waiting.

Six for a nickel, an unbeatable price.

Dan glanced over his shoulder at the carnival, which seemed
miles away now, and then turned with his tickets and rushed
inside.

CHAPTER

17

*T*he inside of the tent smelled like spice and wood smoke. Another cage waited in the corner, this one also empty. Wide streamers of fabric hung from the center of the tent, pinned to ropes and poles to form narrow corridors and hiding places. Candles spewed purple wax as they burned away on waist-high sconces.

"Uh, hello?" Dan peered around a few of the fabric walls, swishing them out of the way. He moved a thick black curtain aside and jerked back, at once face-to-face with a gnarled old man with a bird on his shoulder. The bird was red and white, with just one eye.

I know that bird, how is it alive?

"I thought you might turn up here," the man said, adjusting his threadbare top hat. He grinned, his ancient teeth so worn they were almost translucent, chips of uneven agates dangling from loose sockets. The smell of spice was overwhelming, and Dan's nose itched furiously. He took a step back and then thrust his tickets toward the man as if in defense.

"Now what would you have me do with those?" The old man laughed, and the bird mimicked the sound. "Can't do over what's already been done, son."

"I don't know what you mean," Dan said, backing away farther.

"How did you know I would come here?"

The hypnotist's eyes gleamed in the candlelight. He laughed. "You ain't all that bright, son, but I see the resemblance. It's there if you squint real hard." And that he did, eyeing Dan up and down before tugging on his own suit lapels.

"Daniel Crawford, you mean." No point being coy. If the old man wanted to talk in riddles, then maybe some straightforward information would encourage him toward sense. "But that's not possible. You can't have seen Daniel Crawford and now me. You haven't aged since the dream. . . ."

The hypnotist bared his gums again and smiled wider, then reached into his coat and pulled out a weathered cigar case and a book of matches. He slipped the cigar between his lips and snapped his fingers, a match crackling to life. "You ever look at the sky? You know, clouds?"

"Sure," Dan said slowly.

"You might look at a cloud passing by and think, well, I'll be, that is the spitting image of a bunny rabbit. I might look at that same cloud and see a bat or a bear. Still others might look at that cloud and see nothing at all." Maudire, if that's who he was, puffed around the cigar and then urged the bird down off his shoulder and into its cage. The bird hopped along, screaming *Turk, turk!*

"You look at a raggedy old tent and some empty shadows and you see old Maudire. That makes you special, right? Ha! That makes you one of a kind," he said.

Dan fanned a plume of cigar smoke out of his face and frowned. "So what, you're saying I'm hallucinating this? But I can see you. I can smell you. . . ."

"You see what you see, son," the hypnotist said, shrugging. "Ain't for me to judge." He held up the string of tickets Dan had brought. Dan couldn't quite remember handing them over. "You paid good money for these, so you get something in return. But you can't do over what's already been done, so I'll give you something brand-new." He smirked around the glowing cigar and stared at his bird. "You can't do over what's already been done, but you sure can undo it. Not easy, but you can undo it."

"Undo what?" Dan heard his voice rise hotly. "What are you even talking about?"

"It'll all make sense when the time comes. . . . Every lock has a key, mmm? And every prison, too. The prison of the mind, now that's a tricky place to escape, but that's got a key, too. You're trapped in that little head of yours, son, but there's a way out. Some might call it a key, others a password, others a fail-safe. Doesn't matter what you call it, only that you *find* it."

"Were you like this with Daniel Crawford, too?" Dan muttered, thinking that he couldn't take a word this man said seriously. "Did you run him around in circles when he came to see you?"

"No, I certainly did not," Maudire said grimly. He tossed the cigar on the ground and stubbed it out with his boot. Then he sat on a low stool and perched his palms on his knees and sighed, long and hard. "No, I shot straight as an arrow with that little imp. Straight as an arrow. Biggest mistake of my life."

His eyes, hollow and haunted, rolled from the ground up to Dan, and for a second he was sure the hypnotist's eyes were filling with blood.

"That's all a nickel buys you, son," the hypnotist said. "Best nickel you ever spent."

"I didn't pay for the tickets," Dan said, backing slowly out of the tent.

The hypnotist chuckled, showing his yellow teeth again. "Oh, yes you did. You paid, didn't you? I know you did."

CHAPTER

18

*D*an stumbled out of the tent and into the cold, his nose still filled with the scent of spice and smoke.

Shit, Abby and Jordan are probably worried sick.

He dashed back toward the food vendors and found the carnival even more crowded than before. Through the constant mill and swirl of people, he spotted his friends standing in a small clearing near the popcorn stand.

"Hey!" he called, running up to them. "Sorry . . . I, uh, I saw an attraction I wanted to check out. I didn't mean to disappear on you guys like that." The clown who had given him the tickets ambled by, sneering at them. "Jeez, they could've toned down the makeup on these guys. . . . It's kinda sick."

"Dan, you have to stop wandering off like that, we were freaking out," Abby said, shaking her head. "I texted you like five times!"

He hadn't thought to check his phone and hadn't, he realized, even felt it buzz in his pocket. When he checked it now, he saw all five texts and sank down into his coat. "Seriously, I didn't mean to worry you guys. There was just this tent—the one over there—and it looks exactly like the one from that photo."

Abby was trying to hand him a bottle of water but she held on to it, watching as he produced the photo and held it up so his friends could make the comparison for themselves.

"Dan . . ." Jordan cleared his throat expectantly. "That's a tree."

Dan blinked hard, looking again at the picture and the tent. The . . . tent? The tree. Jordan was right. There was nothing there, just a blank patch of grass where Maudire's tent *ought* to be.

"That's not possible," Dan insisted. "I was there. I was inside the tent. I talked to the hypnotist, Dr. Maudire! I swear, you guys, I'm not making this up. He was telling me about some password or fail-safe or something. I didn't understand half of it."

"Drink this, Dan," Abby said, handing him the water. "You're disoriented, maybe dehydrated."

"He did say he was hallucinating before," Jordan pointed out. "It sounds like it's getting worse."

"I didn't say hallucinating. . . ." But there was no mistaking the absence of Maudire's tent. All the protesting in the world wouldn't change what he could now see plainly with his eyes. "I wouldn't make this up."

"And I don't think you are," Abby replied seriously. "I believe you, Dan, which makes it scarier in a way."

"Not to butt in," Jordan said quietly, elbowing them both, "but we've been spotted. Everyone look like you're having the time of your effing lives before your buddy Micah has a seizure."

Dan followed his friend's gaze, seeing Micah through the crowd waving his entire arm at them.

"Let's not get too wrapped up in conversation with him. We need to slip away and check out the addresses we have left."

"If you're not feeling well . . ."

"I'm okay now, Abby, I promise. Anyway, I want to ask him if he's seen Cal," Dan said. "For now just pretend we don't know anything. I want to see how he reacts."

Abby led the way to a volunteers' table where students handed out little maps of the carnival and answered questions. A few of them were leading walking haunted tours of the campus and surrounding streets. Micah gestured them over to his end of the table, a little command center set up not far from the food vendors. Cal waded through the mass of people toward them, no longer dressed in red robes and a mask, although that didn't prove anything. Lara was with him, and they had brought cups of cider.

It took Dan a moment to conjure up a fake smile. He avoided Cal's eyes, staring straight at the shoes he had spotted just minutes before.

"Thanks," Abby said, smiling brightly at Lara. "It's freezing out here."

"The last thing we need is some prospie dropping dead from frostbite," Cal muttered.

Dan hoped his anger wasn't showing too obviously on his face.

"Cal's grumpy because I convinced him to come along," Lara said. She was wearing one of the orange volunteer tees over a waffle-textured long-sleeve shirt. Her dark hair peeked out from under a chunky-knit pink hat with kitten ears perched on top.

"So what's up with this haunted tour?" Abby asked, making conversation with Lara. Cal turned away to chat with some upperclassmen who were also waiting for the tours, and bumped

Jordan with the big, overstuffed backpack he wore. It was so full the zipper was falling down of its own accord. Dan sipped his cider. It was watery, with a weird aftertaste.

"Oh, it's pretty cool stuff, actually. . . ."

But Dan wasn't listening.

"Come out and play, won't you come out to play, Daniel, Daniel. . . ."

He turned a full circle, slowly, but he couldn't find the source of the voice. It was the girl's soft whisper calling to him again.

"Daniel . . . Daniel . . ."

Now it was coming from the other direction. He spun back around, but too fast, knocking into Abby. The cider cup flew out of her hands, splattering across Cal's backpack.

"I'm so sorry!" she cried, darting forward. Lara jogged to the volunteer table and returned with a wad of napkins. Cal was already kneeling over his bag, though he didn't wipe any of the cider off with his expensive-looking leather gloves.

"Here," Abby said, grabbing the napkins and dabbing at the backpack. "It was an accident."

Her hand knocked the bursting zipper and the bag finally gave up, cracking open. The edge of a tall, white binder fell out from inside the bag. Dan spotted a 19 on the spine just before papers scattered in every direction, exploding out from the binder and littering the ground like fallen leaves. Abby squeaked in surprise and started to gather up the papers, some of which were being blown away by the wind. She and Cal collected them all, and then Dan watched as she sheepishly handed them over.

"I'm sorry, I didn't mean to make such a mess."

Cal snatched up the bag protectively, shielding it with his arms.

"Forget it," he muttered. "I'll clean it up."

As Cal stalked away, the stained backpack cradled in his arms like a baby, Dan tugged the others aside.

"You saw that, right? That binder . . . It was one of the missing ones. *He* has them."

"*And* he was chasing you around in that maze?" Jordan let out a dark laugh. "What do you think he's up to?"

"If he's possessed like Felix was, he could be doing it for anyone, with no motive of his own," Abby said despairingly.

"Either way, it does seem like all roads are leading straight to him," Dan admitted. "We have to get those binders and see what's inside."

"That might be easier than you think," she added with a sly grin. She pulled the edge of her coat open, revealing a dozen or so of the papers stashed inside.

"I am super into this kleptomaniac streak of yours," Jordan said, laughing.

"Did you really think I spilled all over him by accident?" she asked. "I was hoping to see a cloak in his backpack, but no luck."

"Hey! You guys want in on this next tour? There's room!" It was Lara, returning with a fresh cup of cider for Abby. "How about it?"

"Sounds perfect!" Abby shuffled forward, then swung back around to face them. She shoved the stolen papers in Jordan's direction. "Let's stick to the back of the group," she whispered. "The second we see an opening, we bolt."

CHAPTER

19

"*D*oes anyone else think it's weird that they're *not* talking about Brookline? Like at all?" Jordan asked.

The tour guide, following the lantern-lit paths of the campus, brought them to a stop outside a house one block from the chapel. Everyone, including Dan, huddled over their cups of cider for warmth.

"The tour just started," Abby pointed out in a whisper. "Give them a break."

"Still . . ."

"No negatives about the school, remember?" Dan asked. "They start talking about Brookline, kids will Google it or ask questions and then they're opening an industrial vat of worms. I bet they keep the whole thing PG."

"Stand in front of me," Jordan said. He had Abby's ill-gotten archive papers in one hand and his phone, which he was using for light, in the other. "I want to see what was so worth stealing from the library. Wake me up if the tour gets interesting."

Dan and Abby shifted to shield him from the group. Micah and Lara stood up next to the tour guide, but they were whispering back and forth, apparently arguing, judging by the looks on their faces.

"This house belonged to a former president of the college,"

the tour guide explained. She was short and stocky, with an athlete's build and long, curly blond hair. Behind her, a well-kept white Victorian house practically glowed from the amount of candles lit inside it. "President Amos Van der Holt. He was beloved by the students, but he died young under mysterious circumstances. It's said you can still see his shadow in the windows on November twenty-second, the day he died. The shadow always has a pipe, just like the one President Van der Holt smoked."

Abby snorted. Compared to the things they'd seen the past few months, a ghost smoking a pipe would almost be a welcome sight.

The tour moved on down the block, then turned right, traveled another block, and turned right again. The houses here were starting to look familiar. Every few steps or so Jordan's sneakers would collide with Dan's as he searched through the archive pages, head bent over his work.

"Guys, this is Ellis Street," Dan said. "The house from last night is right over there."

"Okay, *now* I'm creeped out," Jordan murmured, putting down the pages. "Good job, tour, you got me. What if they stop at that house?"

"Then we listen," Abby said, holding her cider right up under her chin. Dan could smell the cinnamon-spiked steam as it rose around her face. "And then we find a way to break off and get to the other houses. We're running out of time."

Sure enough, the group stopped just at the foot of the familiar paved driveway that led up to the house.

The tour guide jabbed her thumb over her shoulder in the

direction of the house and glanced down at a set of note cards in her other hand. "This house has been empty for going on twenty years now, but it was once home to the Cartwrights and their son Harry. Harry served as Camford's postmaster for six years, until 1971, when he was forced to resign. He became a suspect in the disappearance of several local women. . . ."

Dan squeezed his cup of cider a bit too hard; the Styrofoam creaked. He knew that name from his dreams—had, in fact, spoken to Harry Cartwright. *No, the warden spoke to Harry Cartwright, not me.*

"We found Caroline's letter in that house and she explicitly mentioned meeting a man named Harry," Abby whispered, pale even in the limited light washing over them. "Do you think she could have been one of the missing girls?"

"That's my bet," Jordan said. "If the secret society found out about her article and those letters she was sending, they would've wanted her to disappear. Here, look . . ." He discreetly held the papers from Cal's backpack at waist height, highlighting the top page with his phone light. He pointed to a faded, almost completely indecipherable photo of a farmhouse. "The school papers had articles about those disappearances."

"Well, on the bright side, maybe these papers were just in Cal's binder because he needed them for the tour, for research," Abby said. "I mean, he did help organize the carnival."

"I have a really hard time believing that," Dan muttered.

Several prospies crowded forward, huddling around the tour guide. "Did they ever find the missing people?" one asked.

"Can we go inside?" another shouted.

The tour guide tried to shrug off these questions with a smile, but she looked a little exasperated. Micah and Lara were still too lost in their discussion to be much help.

"Come on," Abby said, lingering toward the back of the group. "Now's our chance. . . . While they're busy."

With all eyes squarely on their tour guide and the Cartwright house, Dan followed close at Abby's heels. They slunk back and back until they broke away from the group, and Abby led them quickly to a copse of bushes in a neighbor's yard. Dan breathed a quick sigh of relief, certain they had made a clean getaway.

"Wandering off again?"

"Shit," Jordan muttered, wincing as Micah appeared around the tall, scraggly tops of the bushes. Jordan shoved the binder papers up under his jacket. "How do we ditch him?"

"We don't," Dan said. And then to Micah, "Hey! What's going on?"

"Not much. I guess Lara didn't like the way I was looking at Melissa—she was the tour guide—so we were having a little, uh, disagreement. I figured I'd give us both some breathing room, you know?"

"So you and Lara—are you guys a thing?" Dan asked.

"Used to be, way back in freshman year. But she's kind of the jealous type, if you know what I mean."

Jordan tugged urgently on Dan's sleeve, no doubt trying to signal that they should give Micah an excuse and be on their way. But Dan had a feeling they wouldn't be getting rid of Micah that easily. They had drawn his suspicion too many times and now they'd just have to deal.

"We were in the library today and found some creepy old news clippings about the town," Dan improvised. "The tour kind of took a nosedive—no offense—so we thought we'd check up on some *real* haunted houses."

Abby shot Dan an incredulous look. She clearly didn't agree with his plan, either.

"I suppose it is the season. . . . What house did you have in mind?"

"There's one not too far," Dan said, taking his phone out of his coat pocket and tapping the GPS app. "Let me just pull up the directions."

"And how do you know this house is haunted exactly?" Micah asked.

"We . . . found a news article talking about those missing women in the sixties, and one of them lived nearby." Now it was Abby's turn to improvise. Her voice shook, but Micah nodded, apparently buying it. "Spooky, right?"

"It might not be empty," Micah replied. "But we can take a look. Just don't scream, all right? If Lara realizes we snuck away, she'll chew my head off."

"Here," Dan said, handing him the Google map. "We're trying to get here. Do you know the street?"

"Virgil? Yeah. The Art House is over that way." Micah scratched his chin, squinting down at the paper. "I've been to a few parties around there. We can cut through the alley on Butler, shave off a minute or two of walking time."

"Perfect!" Dan said, just barely modulating his fake enthusiasm. "Lead on."

The wind picked up as they followed Micah across Ellis Street and toward a dark, narrow lane sandwiched between two houses.

A skeletal tree had managed to force its way to maturity in

the alley. Its branches scraped against the houses' eaves as the four of them scuttled down the lane. Dan glanced back to make sure no one from the group had seen them go and immediately wished he hadn't. The pale little boy in the striped sweater was there watching them, and even though Dan didn't let his eyes linger, he could swear the boy was smiling.

The alley dumped them out onto a weather-beaten strip of sidewalk. The trees were denser on this street, blocking out more of the already thin lamplight. Micah turned left, walking briskly toward an empty intersection. Most neighborhood trick-or-treaters had long since gone home, and the last groups out hardly paid them any attention, too fixated on their full bags of candy and grouchy parents. A few pumpkins remained on the stoops, glowing with sputtering candles.

"Almost there," Micah said as they crossed the intersection. He pulled up the neck of his coat, ducking down against the wind. "Still up for this?"

"It was my idea, wasn't it?" Dan caught up, striding next to him. He noticed a mint-green house across the street with a giant copper statue in the yard. "I take it that's the Art House?"

"How'd you guess?" Micah chuckled. "Looks like there aren't any cars in the driveway. Let's cross here."

Dan waited just a second or two before crossing, hanging back to check on Abby and Jordan. He wasn't exactly surprised by the scowl Abby had waiting for him.

"So what do you want to do if we find something?" she whispered, eyes locked on Micah.

"I don't know," Dan said. It was, sadly, the truth. "I hadn't considered that part."

"We don't know if Micah is one of them! He could have been right alongside Cal in that maze!"

"He's not like that. I think we might actually be able to trust him. He did warn us about Cal, remember?" And he had been the one to cover for Dan at the party, coming up with that smooth line for Abby. He wasn't an Ivy League wannabe like Cal—not at all the type to get caught up in a secret society. "Sometimes you have to adjust. This is adjusting."

"I'm stating for the record that this is a bad idea," Abby replied crisply.

"Noted . . ."

"And that you're being naive to trust anyone on this campus."

"He's already seen us," Dan mumbled. "We just won't clue him in on what we're looking for."

"You guys coming or what?" Micah gestured to them from the sidewalk. Behind him, a moldering two-story house waited in the shadows. Brown and dingy, it looked like a gingerbread house that had gotten damp. The roof sagged. The white house numbers near the front door were crooked. One had come unhinged except for the bottom screw and hung upside down.

"It certainly *looks* haunted," Jordan said, grimacing. "Are we really going inside that?"

"Yup," Dan replied.

"Too late to board the Nope Train to Screwthatsville?"

"Correct."

"So what now?" Micah asked, turning to them. "You bring a Ouija board or what?"

This was the moment of truth, Dan decided, in more ways than one. He took a deep breath, gathering his thoughts. If

Micah said no—if he returned to campus and reported them for trespassing or, worse, called the police—then their weekend would end badly and abruptly.

"Now we're going to break in and look around."

Micah's eyes narrowed dangerously and for a moment Dan was certain they were busted. He rubbed at the goatee on his chin and flicked his eyes to Jordan and then Abby. "I told you . . . I've gotten in trouble before. I don't want to get in trouble again, Dan."

"Does it look like anybody has lived there for years?" he replied. "No car in the drive. No lights. It's practically falling apart. We just want to look around inside."

"Yeah, and if anyone sees us go in, the cops get called and at the very least, I lose my job with the admissions office." Micah frowned, turning his gaze to the house. "Then again, I s'pose I didn't lead you all here thinking we were just gonna admire the view."

"That's the spirit," Jordan said drily. "Can we get off the sidewalk now? We're not exactly being subtle here."

Jordan didn't wait for consensus. He took off down the side of the driveway, sticking to the edge of the pavement where the overgrown grass encroached. This block in general looked more run-down than the last, with fewer cheerful houses and more old, dilapidated Victorian homes that didn't have pumpkins or lights. Nothing about these houses felt welcoming. Even with cider still warming his blood and the comforting scent of burning leaves in the air, he couldn't shake a sense that whatever was wrong with this house had spread, poisoning more than just its own crumbling clapboards.

They snaked along the drive to the garage and, next to it, a chain-link fence and a gate. It was one of those simple closures where you could just reach over and pull the latch, the kind that could only keep in small children and dogs. Jordan pulled the latch and the gate swung open with a piercing screech.

"That sliding door doesn't look secure," he whispered, holding the gate for them. "I'll try it—otherwise we'll have to use a window."

Micah hesitated at the gate, looking Jordan over with a snort. "You three do this kind of thing often?"

"My parents don't like me leaving the house unannounced," Jordan replied coolly. "I learned to circumvent their rules."

"Hey, man," Micah said with a laugh that was either defensive or amused, Dan couldn't tell. "Circumvent away. I just didn't know you were some kind of Houdini fan."

"Not much Houdini to this." With just a short tug on the handle, the sliding door jerked open. Jordan gestured inside, grinning. "Abracadabra?"

"Keep it down," Abby cautioned. "The neighbors could still be up."

Dan led them into the house, relieved to find his suspicions were correct; nobody was home, and nobody had been home in quite some time. About thirty years, judging by the brown shag carpeting and retro furniture. They crowded inside and Jordan closed the door behind them, leaving them standing in a dining area that transitioned into a kitchenette.

"All the pictures are missing," Abby said, going to a low, decorative table. She grabbed a dusty picture frame, the white backing showing through the glass. "And look . . ." She put down the frame and crept through an archway to the mudroom and then the living room beyond. "Everything is packed up. These look like moving boxes."

Dan followed. Dust flickered on the air. White sheets had been drawn over the couches and chairs. Even without the signs of abandonment, Dan *felt* the solitude of the place. Houses were meant to feel lived in, cozy. This one just felt . . .

"Cold," he whispered, watching his breath billow out. "It's freezing in here."

"I'm going to check out the bedrooms," Jordan said, passing by and disappearing down a dark hallway. Dan saw the bouncing light of his mobile as he went.

"I'll take the upstairs," Dan said, eager to make a quick round and then leave. He didn't know if he should trust his instincts, but if he did, those instincts were telling him to flee.

"What exactly are we looking for?" he heard Micah asking as he rounded the corner and found the stairs.

"Pictures, scrapbooks," Abby said, her voice fading as Dan left it behind. "You know, something spooky to commemorate the evening."

Their voices died away entirely, replaced by the sound of his own breathing and the soft tread of his shoes on the stairs. He could see the years of foot traffic worn into the wood. At the top, the landing was cramped, the ceiling low. There was a bathroom immediately in front of him, empty except for a heavily rusted claw-foot tub. He shined his mobile around, using the light app to illuminate the white and blue tiles and the porcelain sink with its ornate tap and handles. He moved on down the hall. The ceiling slanted and then cut away, a narrow hall opening up on his left. There he found a bedroom, or what remained of one, which was just a big bed frame and a collapsing mattress. Much like downstairs, a few picture frames still hung on the wall, clinging for dear life at skewed angles. There were no photos in them.

Dan retreated back down the hall, dodging left to check the last room. The floor creaked under his weight. The last door was small, hardly tall enough for an adult human to fit through. He had to stoop to get inside. His little light bounced like a glow bug around the room, showing him two sets of cramped bunk beds and a child-sized table hand painted with fire trucks and baseballs. Dan stood completely still in the center of the attic room. The ceiling sloped to a point like a barn's roof; the trunks and beds and leftover junk made the space feel utterly claustrophobic.

He went to the grimy window between the bunks and looked out at the house directly across the way. The houses were so close together there wasn't much of anything to see but wall. Sighing, he turned and made for the door. This house was a bust. Unless the others had found something downstairs, this was just an abandoned, empty time capsule, with no photos, no letters, no clues of any kind.

Swearing, Dan stopped, catching his breath as his shoe dragged across a loop-stitched rug. After regaining his balance, he realized he'd kicked the rug just enough to slide it over, and underneath where it had been, the scuffed boards had been decorated with paint. He knelt, his pulse coming quicker as he ran his fingers over the newer, shinier wood.

The rug had preserved the spot well, and the figure there, too. Some small, meticulous hand had painted the outline of a little boy. A boy Dan recognized from the stripes on his sweater. The pads of Dan's fingers touched something slightly cool, and he squinted into the low light, noticing a tiny catch.

Dan pulled on the hook, revealing a small rectangular hole. Dust came up from the darkness and choked him, and when he directed his phone inside, he found a tiny hiding space, just big enough for the cloth-wrapped metal box within. An old candy tin, perhaps, roughly the size of a shoe box, the stripes still bright and perfect. Dan cracked the lid carefully, revealing a child's journal, a satchel of marbles, a few playing cards, chewing gum wrappers. . . .

There was also a collection of old photographs, tied together with string. Judging by the photo on top, of a costumed little boy shoving a sword down his throat, Dan wasn't sure whether he wanted to see the rest. But his curiosity won out, and he untied the string with trembling fingers.

Whoever had collected these photos seemed to have been drawn to acts of the macabre. Pictures showed a woman who had thrown axes and daggers at a performing partner; a woman who stood balancing a series of torches on her body; and then, near the end, the creepiest combination of a fortune-teller and a clown that Dan had ever seen.

Shaking, Dan replaced the photos and set down the box, keeping the journal. It made perfect sense that he would be the one to find it, as if it had called to him, had known he would come for it.

Dan blew on the book softly, watching a veil of dust lift and shimmer in the air. The inside cover of the journal was worn but he could clearly read in huge red letters:

DANNY CRAWFORD'S! PRIVATE!!!

CHAPTER
20

Today the carnival is here. Patrick says it is a circus but he is dumb and even if he is older than me and says he knows more he is wrong. It is not a circus. A circus has animals like lions and giraffes and this year the only animals at the carnival are a few birds and the raccoons that get into the bins.

Patrick and Bernard go on the rides all day. Mom is too busy with the baby to notice that they steal coins from the saving jar under the sink to go again and again. They saw me when they took the coins and made me promise not to tell. I promised. They put a dirty sock in my mouth and held me under the bed anyway. I did not tell. I did not tell but I want to.

The rides are stupid. The only Good thing is the man in the hat. He did not make fun of my sweater even if it has holes and he said I was a very smart boy, smarter than my dumb brothers. He was Very Nice. There is a watch inside his coat and when he uses it he can make a woman flap like a chicken or a shy boy sing nursery songs. He said he would teach me how and show me his secrets.

I listened, I didn't forget a single word. I hope now I can make other people Do things too. Patrick and Bernard will have to shut up and listen to me now. They will have to do what I say.

There is a red rock on the back of his watch. It looks like a shooting star when he swings it. A bright burning star.

I hope the carnival never leaves.

But even if it leaves, I will still have the secrets. The secrets will never leave.

*D*an flipped to the next page, his heavy breathing ruffling the pages. Young Daniel Crawford had dated the entry not long after the first, and it began, *Today I took the swinging rock and tried to make Patrick cluck like a chicken. Tomorrow I will make him go up on the roof*. Patrick? Who was Patrick?

"Hey, find anything up here?"

Micah. His timing seriously couldn't be worse. Dan cringed, nudging the striped box back into the hiding place and slipping the journal inside his coat. He turned and smiled thinly up at Micah.

"Just some old junk. Must be where the kids slept," Dan said, standing and kicking the trapdoor shut. He couldn't do anything to hide the misplaced rug or the paintings on the floor, so he made no attempt to cover them up. "What'd you guys find downstairs?"

"Lots of packed boxes. Empty frames. I wouldn't wanna live here either, can't blame them for wanting to leave." He cast his eyes around the room and shivered. His eyes looked glassy, almost empty. Dan chalked it up to a trick of the dim light. "Kids lived in here? What the hell?"

"Creepy, right?" Dan nudged by him, ducking out under the door and into the hall. "Might as well have raised them in a broom closet."

"I didn't see any trace of that missing girl," Micah said, following him to the stairs. "Are you sure this is the right house?"

"They probably left town after she disappeared," Dan replied. "I can understand why they might want to move on."

"Really? I think they'd stay. I mean, what if she came back? If they were gone . . . Hell, that'd be so sad."

Dan didn't want to discuss it or quibble. He had his hands on the warden's childhood journal, a book that could give them all kinds of insight into the warden's mind. Whatever had turned that man into a monster could very well be hidden in those pages, and Dan felt jittery, almost hyper now that answers seemed so close at hand.

I should have listened to them. Bringing Micah along was a mistake.

But what could he do now? They went back downstairs, where Abby and Jordan were waiting, and not patiently. Jordan's eyes burned into his. He would show them the journal later, after he had a chance to look at it himself. Showing it around now, especially with Micah there, felt risky. He wanted badly to trust Micah, to think that they had another mind, another ally there on campus, but Dan wasn't even sure he wanted to show his *friends* the journal.

It was private.

"We found the address for one other house," Dan explained. "I doubt it's far."

"I need to lead the next round of tours," Micah replied. He pushed back the sleeve on his coat to check a watch. "That's in half an hour. I don't mind covering for y'all for a few minutes, but the other volunteers will be pissed if I don't come back."

"Well, we wouldn't want to get you in trouble with the other volunteers," Abby said, and though she was smiling, Dan thought it was pretty plain she wanted him to leave.

"Well," he said, smacking Dan lightly on the shoulder. "What's thirty minutes more? They won't mind. This is kinda fun and creepy. I'm hooked."

"Oh." It was Jordan, his eyes wide as he took out the Google map and handed it to Micah. "You . . . are?"

"Yeah! It's Halloween, man, this is a thrill." He leaned in close to them, closing his hand around the map and laughing, even adding a conspiratorial wink. "And I may have, you know, had a little something before the tour. Just to relax. Nothing too hard, just some recreational enhancement, eh?" He mimed puffing on a cigarette, though Dan assumed it was not plain old tobacco that had caused his easygoing mood.

Well *that* explained the glassy eyes.

"So . . . You're not going to snitch on us for leaving campus?" Jordan asked slowly.

"Hell no. That'd land me in hot water, too. Nah, I'm along for the ride tonight. Where to?"

Dan breathed a little easier, though he couldn't fully relax, not with the warden's old journal hidden in his coat.

"There," Abby said shortly, pointing out their next destination. She hopped from foot to foot. Dan felt the time crunch, too. "Do you know the way?"

"Piece of cake. Follow me." Micah spun on his heel, taking the map and leading them through the house and back to the busted sliding door.

But Abby slowed her steps, tugging on Jordan's and Dan's sleeves, pulling them in close to her sides. "Doesn't he seem just a little too eager?"

"He's stoned," Jordan whispered back. "He'd probably be excited to watch grass grow."

"Guys, I know you don't want him along but this is our out," Dan added, keeping a close eye on Micah to make sure he didn't overhear. "He can't get us in trouble. Not now. We have lever-age."

"And who do you think the school would believe? A bunch of prospies or the admissions office golden boy?" she hissed.

Dan shrugged and quickened his pace. "There's no time to second-guess. We'll just have to take our chances."

"Ticktock," Micah called from the door. "They'll do a head count back on campus in twenty-five minutes." He was grinning, and for a second, Dan wished he could experience this trip the way Micah was experiencing it—like something fun and dangerous to do with your friends. But Dan didn't have that luxury. With any luck, the journal pressed against his chest would help him close this chapter of his life—explain why he could see the things he saw, and maybe even help him stop seeing them for good.

And if Dan was *really* lucky, he might still have some friends on the other side of all this. If they could just forgive him for bringing Micah tonight.

"All right then," Dan said. "What are we waiting for?"

CHAPTER

21

A stiff wind chased them down Blake Street. Dan clutched his jacket and the journal closer to his body and shivered with the others outside a redbrick house with boarded windows and doors.

"Do you think it's condemned?" Abby asked, hesitating on the edge of the lawn. "It might not be safe to go inside."

"We have to," Dan said. Now more than ever he felt convinced they were on the right track. Felix's addresses had led them to Harry Cartwright's house and then Warden Crawford's childhood home. However Felix had come by those coordinates, they weren't coincidences—they were a constellation that just wasn't complete yet.

"Huh?" Micah turned around from where he was studying one of the boarded-up windows.

"Nothing . . . I said, um, we don't have to."

"How would we even get in?" Jordan led them around the lawn and driveway to a side door with a striped canvas overhang. They huddled around the door and Jordan kicked lamely at one of the boards holding it shut. "It's going to take more than a lockpick to get through that."

"Here," Micah said, grabbing one of the two-by-fours nailed to the frame. "This one looks loose. If we can get it free, I might

be able to pry the other boards off."

It was then that Dan realized how screwed they would have been without Micah. None of the three of them was strong enough to pull the board loose or use it to pop off the other well-secured boards. They would have been stuck trying to climb in a window.

Dan communicated as much to Jordan and Abby with one raised eyebrow.

"Whatever," Jordan muttered under his breath. "I'm not *that* impressed."

"I would've found another way in," Abby added.

"In those mittens?"

She didn't respond.

Meanwhile, a few steps away, Micah was using the loose board as a kind of giant crowbar, wedging it into the gap between the doorframe and the boards and pulling them loose. The boards groaned and then splintered, a little shower of dust falling to the ground like snow.

"There!" Micah grunted. "Just one more . . ."

The last board came free with a crisp popping sound. Dan, Abby, and Jordan ducked and swiveled in unison.

"Damn, that was loud." Micah stepped back from the door and dropped the two-by-four, scratching at the back of his neck sheepishly. "My bad."

"And now we wait for the police sirens," Jordan said.

Dan kicked the fallen wood closer to the house and nodded to the door. "Let's get inside. Someone *will* spot us if we keep skulking outside the door like this."

With a nervous glance around, Jordan slid up to the door.

"Let's just make this fast." Even with the boards removed the door wasn't going anywhere. Jordan knelt, fishing the lock-picking set out of his pocket and going to work. The knob turned suddenly a second later, rusted and loose. He stopped with his eyes closed, mouthing words Dan couldn't make out.

"What are you doing?"

"Praying that some kids are dumb enough to egg a house or smash some pumpkins *right now* and take the heat off. . . ."

"I don't even hear any dogs barking, and no lights came on," Dan pointed out. "Come on."

Jordan climbed quickly to his feet and shouldered open the door. By now, Dan was familiar with the smell of musty, deserted houses. The air hung heavy and sour from the mold and decaying wood.

"Do the lights still work?" Abby whispered from over his shoulder.

"It's been boarded up and left to rot," Jordan said. "I doubt anyone's paying the electricity. Lucky us."

Dan tried the nearest switch. Nothing happened. Why hadn't they thought to bring a flashlight? He pulled out his phone and turned the light app on. They seemed to be standing in a but-ler's pantry or mudroom, with shelves and cubbies built into the surrounding walls. A pair of grubby old white tennis shoes were mashed into one of the slots.

"Oh my God, yuck," Jordan groaned. "It smells like a wet dog exploded in here."

"Sh-hhhh." Dan didn't mean to hiss at him so loudly.

Jordan ignored him, sighing. "And to think I could be get-ting wasted on Goldschläger and introducing some adorable, uninitiated freshman to *Galaxy Quest* right now. . . ."

Farther in they found a living room, still furnished, with a low circular table and a few couches covered in awful psychedelic fabric. The carpet was worn and shaggy, with a myriad of alarming stains. Glass bottles were tipped against the base of the couches, and the walls were decorated with paddles, letters, pennants . . .

"This must have been a fraternity," Micah said, puffing out a thin laugh. "I wonder what they did to get shut down. I heard a few of the ones on campus had to be busted for meth labs back in the eighties."

"Ugh," Abby groaned, flipping the page on a vintage *Playboy* calendar pinned to the wall. "Classy."

"Split up," Dan said. "We have to be back on campus soon."

Jordan had picked up an empty bottle and given it a sniff. He let the bottle drop where he had found it. "I should not have done that. . . ."

Micah stopped roaming the living room and turned to give them each a long look, his mouth slightly open as if something major had just dawned on him. "You guys seem like you're looking for something in particular."

"I'm just . . . a serial killer buff, that's all. It's like a hobby of mine." Dan winced. Probably not the best lie to come up with when he had Micah out with them breaking and entering. "I've always wanted to solve a cold case, you know? Be the hero, maybe solve that missing-girls case or whatever . . ."

"And you think one of them lived here? In a *frat*?" He sounded understandably dubious.

"Not *live* lived here. The article said it was, um . . . uh . . . her last known whereabouts."

"Oh." With a shrug, Micah leaned down to inspect one of the retro coffee tables. "Hey, man, we've all got our hobbies. Just, uh, give me a heads-up if we're about to be axe-murdered or something."

"I think asbestos poisoning is a better bet," Jordan mumbled.

"On that note," Dan said wryly, "I'll check the basement."

This turned out to be easier said than done. Either the door was locked from the other side or the mechanism inside had jammed. Just his luck. Dan put his shoulder into it, slamming his weight against the door, once, twice . . . On the third hit the door gave, and a powerful stench of age and rot wafted up from below. He wanted to vomit and then run, but Felix had sent them there for a reason. There was no turning back now.

Dan covered his nose with his sleeve and carefully descended the stairs, illuminating and testing each one before going on to the next. The smell worsened the deeper he went, and for the first time that night he wondered if he was going to find something more than papers or photographs—something he wasn't prepared to handle.

At the bottom of the steps he shined his phone around, finding an old camping lantern sitting on an overturned crate. He twisted the knob on it, sighing with relief when a light jumped in the glass canister, filling the basement with a warm, spotty glow.

He turned, slowly, his fists clenched, his fingernails biting deep into his palms.

The first thing Dan saw was the chair, iron and rusted, with manacles attached to the arms and legs. An intense wave of

memory came over him and he froze.

It wasn't a body, but already he could tell that this was a terrible place. Lantern light bled across the room, flickering and fleeting, but finally steadying enough for him to see the table behind the chair, and beyond the table what looked like an old blackboard stand. Dan hadn't seen one of those since grade school—most classrooms had updated to plastic boards and markers after that.

His hands shook as he approached the table. It was littered with photographs, papers, and note cards. It looked as if someone had come here searching for something, scattering pages and stubs of pencils to the ground under the table.

Dan picked up one of the faded photographs. It was black-and-white, with two men seated in a formal setting, shaking hands. His skin felt suddenly icy as he noticed the man on the right had his face completely scratched out. It reminded him instantly of the picture that had started it all, the one he found waiting in his dorm room in Brookline.

He stuffed the photo in his pocket and started to pick over the pages on the table. Most of the notes he found were illegible, scribbled in a doctor's shorthand that looked more like random squiggles than actual sentences.

The pages fell out of his hands as he discarded them, the rustle of stiff paper on stiff paper sounding like a voice whispering, *Hurry, hurry.*

His eyes were drawn again to the blackboard. Just two words had been scrawled on it in grayish chalk.

TURN AROUND

"I wish," Dan muttered, ragged. "But I'm not done yet."

Turn around . . . He let the words ring in his head. The more they repeated, the more he felt certain there was something here he was missing. Manacled chair, a table of notes and photos that someone had frantically searched . . .

"Turn around," he said again, this time with a wry smile. "Not me," he said, leaning across the table and pushing at the blackboard. "You."

The hinges moaned, but the board spun slowly, gaining momentum as the weight fell toward the back. He had to push again, a little harder, to get it facing all the way around. Dan couldn't suppress a gasp of shock.

He fumbled for his phone, knowing this might be his only chance to record what he was seeing. Quickly, he snapped the clearest photo he could, hoping there would be enough light with his flash to capture everything.

It looked like a map of sorts, the kind of diagram a detective might use to keep track of the many leads in a case. Photographs, papers, and charts had been fixed to the board haphazardly, with strings leading between each piece, perhaps denoting connections. Some of the strings were red, others were white.

Dan pressed himself up close to the table, squinting, trying to read and absorb as quickly as he could—there was no way the photo had captured *every* detail. Overhead, he could hear the scraping of feet. His friends must be growing restless—they'd come looking for him any second. Although this, he decided, was something he would definitely need to share with Abby and Jordan.

He skimmed over patient charts, each accompanied by

photographs of young men seated in that manacled chair. The notes were endless.

Patient uncooperative . . .

As per Kentucky . . .

Patient shows promise . . .

They built it out of stone . . .

Dan had dabbled in speed reading, but this wasn't going to work.

Without thinking, he started to snatch up whatever he could reach, ripping down the charts and photos and cards. He could reconstruct the connections later with the help of the picture he took.

This is it. This is it. You're so close now. . . .

At the bottom of the board, he noticed a packet of yellowed pages that were clipped together. Some kind of pamphlet, maybe, or a journal. Dan finished shoveling what he could into his coat and zipped it up, then made one final reach, taking the clipped-together pages.

Thunk . . . Thunk . . .

His pulse leaped. *Damn it.* Footsteps on the stairs. His time was up. Whatever this place was, he would have to make sense of it later.

"Well, I've seen enough dirty old jock straps to last a lifetime," Jordan was saying, appearing next to the lantern. "How about yoooowhoa. What is this place?"

"Not a frat I'd recommend joining," Dan replied. "Someone was running experiments down here. A lot of them."

Jordan visibly shivered, then whispered, "Tell me you took photos."

"Better. We should get somewhere private—without Micah. I need to show you guys what I found."

The footsteps on the stairs, this time, were not slow. Abby thundered down the steps, colliding headfirst into Jordan, who turned at the last second and managed to sling an arm around her.

"We . . . need . . . to go!" she blurted in between gasps for air. She pointed to the top of the stairs. "I was . . . on the second floor, looked out the window. There are people. I don't know . . . They're everywhere. They circled the house!" Her eyes were huge in the lantern light. She clutched Jordan's jacket, trying to tug him up the stairs.

Dan bent to snuff out the lantern and then followed them, each taking the steps two at a time. Micah waited for them on the first floor, his face pale as a ghost's.

"I think I can figure a way out," he said softly. "It's . . . a plan at least."

Glancing out the window, Dan could see the dark silhouettes of people perfectly stamped against the streetlights. One figure stood apart from the rest, in the center of a yellow pool of lamplight. Masked. Cloaked. The gaping, hollow eyes of the mask seemed to swallow him whole. As more and more of the figures stepped out of the shadows, Dan saw that they were all cloaked and masked. The Scarlets had found them. If this was some prank of Cal's, Dan didn't want to stick around to find out the punch line.

"Caroline was right," Dan whispered, his throat tense, closing up and making it almost impossible to breathe. "They're real."

Micah crouched and led them to the side door that went back outside. They lined up under one of the windows. Through the rotted door slats, Dan heard a low hum that built and built, growing into a chant.

"What are they saying?" Jordan hissed, eyes darting behind his glasses.

Dan tightened his grip on the papers tucked against his chest. He felt sick.

"My name," Dan said. "They're chanting my name."

CHAPTER

22

"Don't listen to them." Micah's hand was on his shoulder, grasping and shaking. It was probably a good thing, too, because Dan was feeling so nauseated he could hardly keep his eyes open. "Just get ready to run, yeah? Can you run?"

"Sure, of course," Dan said, nodding. Another hand was on him then, Abby's, and that was far more welcome. She touched his wrist, saying gently, "We'll all hold hands. We can get out of here together."

"She's right. Stick together and get back to campus," Micah said. "Ready?"

Dan nodded, holding tight to the many treasures he had found that night.

"Here goes nothin', then," Micah said, nudging open the broken door.

"Where are you going?" Jordan demanded.

"Out there. I'll draw their attention, you just get the hell out of dodge." He inched toward the opening door.

"*That's* your big plan? How high *are* you?"

"Just run, would ya?" And then he was gone, off like a shot across the overgrown lawn. Dan forced himself up from the ground. He didn't trust his legs just then, but he didn't have a choice—Micah was already sprinting toward the street, and the cloaked Scarlets surrounding the house broke, chasing after him, swarming like a horde of zombies.

Dan watched them converge, gaining ground with each second, their red cloaks fanning out behind them as they gave chase.

"That's our cue," Abby said. She was the first to go, holding Dan by the elbow and Jordan by his wrist. She yanked them out the door, pelting toward the sidewalk as fast as her little Ugg boots would carry her.

"Slow down!" Dan said, struggling to match her pace.

"Keep up!" she countered.

Dan glanced to his left, over his shoulder, watching as Micah led what looked like a dozen red ghosts down the street. He shouldn't have looked. He was never that coordinated to begin with, and now he was tripping, thudding to the ground so hard his teeth rattled. The papers he had been clutching to his chest flew up and away in a spectacular arc. Dan watched them go, flopping like a fish out of water as he tried to regain his feet.

"Leave it!" Abby screamed.

They had made too much noise, drawn too much attention. Some of Micah's pursuers stopped and turned, watching for a moment that felt like years. Then they came for him, swift red shapes racing across the lawn, those horrible masked faces homing in on him.

"I can't leave it," Dan said, crawling on elbows and knees through the damp grass. He groped in the darkness, fingers growing slick and then muddy as he tried to find the lost pages. He could feel the nearing footsteps shuddering through the earth and into his chest.

A pair of Chuck Taylors zipped by, and Jordan with them.

"I've got them!" he shouted. "Now get your ass up!"

Both Jordan and Abby scooped him off the ground, lifting him by his elbows. Dan's feet were already churning in mid-air. There was no time to gain his balance; Abby and Jordan whisked him away, avoiding the streetlamp at the corner. Dan didn't dare chance another look—he knew they were still being followed.

His lungs burned; his eyes stung with tears from the cold air whipping past his face. One block flew by and then another. Dan knew they were headed in the right direction from the campus chapel steeple rising above the trees. In the distance, he heard the sounds of the carnival, twinkling music and laughter.

"They're gone. . . ." Jordan slowed to a stop, bending to rest his hands on his knees and catch his breath. His dark hair was limp, his cheeks sweaty and bright red. "I think we lost them."

"Where can we go?" Dan asked. They regrouped under a tree across from the chapel. The carnival continued to their left, the academic buildings of the campus clustered behind the church. "We need somewhere private. Safe."

"We can try one of the library study rooms," Abby suggested. She leaned heavily against the tree, gasping.

"If someone comes for us there, we'll be cornered," Jordan replied. "We need somewhere open."

Dan was only half listening. He watched the shadows closely, ready for those chanting Scarlets to show up any second. What would they do to him if they caught him? He didn't want to think about it, not if there was a chance they could avoid that same fate. Jordan and Abby were probably thinking the same thing, judging by how they hung their heads, as if exhausted by the weight of what they had seen.

"What about the computer lab under our dorm?" Abby asked. "There's one right before the tunnels. I remember seeing it in the orientation map."

"It's worth looking at. . . . Dan? Dan, are you listening?"

"Hm? Right. The computer lab. Sure." He turned to look at Jordan, noticing the rumpled notes clutched to his stomach. "Could I have those back?"

"What, like right now?" Jordan snorted. "Yeah, here. Take them. They give me the creeps."

Abby was already heading in the direction of the residential side of campus. The two boys scrambled to keep up. "You don't even know what's in them yet," she pointed out.

"Yeah, because manacle chair and creepazoid basement probably means those notes are filled with rainbows and bunny rabbits. Come on . . . Nothing good could come from that place."

"Jordan's right. I found all kinds of photographs and charts. . . ." Dan peeled open his coat, his sweater damp underneath.

"Jesus, look at you. Do you have watches and handbags in there, too?"

"No, I just . . . I just . . . took whatever I saw. I didn't know what was important. Here, look at these." Dan handed out a few pictures to them but kept the young warden's diary close to his side.

Abby held one up, squinting. It wasn't until they passed under a streetlamp that she gasped. "You guys need to look at this."

"What is it?" Dan crowded next to her. She held up the picture he had already seen, the one with a scratched-out face beside a hook-nosed man in a trim black suit. "Whoa, look at the carpet."

"That's the CIA seal," Jordan said with an incredulous laugh.

"Who do you think is there with him?" Abby asked softly.

"I'll give you three guesses and the first two don't count," Jordan said.

Dan found himself nodding. The coat, the pocket watch . . . He had seen enough old photos of the warden to spot the man's stance, his style. "Warden Crawford."

Laughing, Jordan pulled away, putting both gloved palms on his head. "This is crazy-pants. What the hell would that guy be doing meeting with the CIA?"

"I don't know," Dan admitted. He held up the pamphlet. "But whatever it is, I bet we'll find it in here."

CHAPTER

23

*T*he computer lab was spare and sterile, a long, low room snuggled up under Erickson Dormitory. Dan found himself relieved to see there were two doors, one on each end of the room, so that it felt more like a bunker than a computer lab. It being Halloween night, nobody was there to study or do homework, and the heat seemed to have been turned off. It was freezing.

One of the pale blue lights overhead flickered, buzzing irregularly, just irritating enough to make Dan's eye twitch.

Abby was on the floor next to Jordan's computer, using Dan's phone and the image on it to try to roughly reconstruct the layout of the blackboard. The young warden's journal still sat heavy against his side. Dan wanted badly to start reading it, but only when he had time to himself.

"Jordan? Do me a favor," Abby said, pulling off her mittens and hat and piling them haphazardly next to her project. "Take this list of names and see if you get any hits on the college website. Alums will come back to work for the school a lot of times, so maybe we'll get lucky and find someone who was there for all of this."

"Brilliant idea," Jordan said with real admiration in his voice. He took the list from her and started typing furiously. "I think it's a safe bet that the warden and the Scarlets are connected. That name-chanting . . . Ugh. I don't even want to think about it."

Neither did Dan.

He turned his attention to the pamphlet of notes. Sitting on the edge of a table a few feet behind Jordan's chair, he swung his legs nervously back and forth. While coming inside had brought an initial blast of warmth, the cold seemed to have found its way back into his bones.

The topmost pieces of paper felt brittle, stained with dark, broken rings, as if from coffee cups. Some of the pencil notes in the margins had worn away to obscurity from age. Dan propped the pages on his knees, afraid that handling the pamphlet would only damage the pages more. A note card had been clipped to the front of the stack.

"Kentucky, 1953,'" he read quietly. "He would have been in his prime then."

"So you're sure he wrote that?" Jordan asked.

"Yes," Dan replied, flipping to the first page. "I know his handwriting by now."

It rained all day yesterday and this morning. I wrongly assumed it would be warm here in the spring, but the days are chill and cloudy, and the rain seems never to stop. Dr. Forester believes that might disrupt the subjects' concentration and expressed his relief that milder weather persists. I attempted to share my theories regarding a three-pronged approach—physically, sensory, spiritually—but Forester insists on exploring only the physical. This shortsightedness will be his downfall. I'm sure of it.

Perhaps I should not begrudge Forester his purely scientific approach. This is not a privately-funded experiment. Every I must be dotted, every

It rained all day yesterday and this morning. I wrongly assumed it would be warm here in the spring, but the days are chill and cloudy, and the rain seems never to stop. Dr. Forester believes that night disrupt the subject's concentration and expressed his belief that milder weather persists. I attempted to share my theories regarding a three-pronged approach—physically, sensory, spiritually—but Forester insists on exploring only the physical. This short sightedness will be his downfall. I'm sure of it. Perhaps I should not begrudge Forester his purely scientific approach. This is not a privately-funded experiment. Every I must be dotted, every I crossed. Still, all avenues should be investigated, we seek to unlock the core secrets of the mind and that may not be possible using chemicals and suggestion alone.

T crossed. *Still, all avenues should be investigated, we seek to unlock the core secrets of the mind and that may not be possible using chemicals and suggestions alone.*

Dan flipped to the next page. Half of what he was looking at was incomprehensible, blocked-off charts with shorthand scribbles only a doctor could decipher. No patient names were listed, just numbers, presumably to maintain some kind of anonymity. He wondered if there was a corresponding list somewhere that contained the patients' identities.

The warden's writing picked up again on the page after that.

As I expected, when administered the drug, subjects hallucinate and babble, but we are no closer to producing a clean slate. One prostitute—I have forgotten her name—chased her own shadow for four hours. Not the breakthrough any of us were hoping for. Patient 67 has been given lysergic acid diethylamide for eight consecutive days. Forester plans to continue this persistent dosage. For how long he would not say.

Yet all of this remains irrelevant. When I wrested that jewel from Dr. Maudire's clenched hands, I did so believing I would one day put it to use for the greater good. I might not consider myself a patriot, but the thought of having utter control over a person's mind in the long term . . . If I must suffer Forester's fool antics to get closer to the answer, then I can play the docile assistant.

He remains convinced that we will find a way to manufacture the ultimate truth serum, and reprogram the mind. A simpleton could be made a genius, a genius a fool. The implications for espionage, for warfare, are immense. But that is not where my interest lies. To control the now is a simple thing, but to control the future? That is worth striving for.

For a long moment, Dan stared down at the page in his lap. This went way beyond what he had expected to find. If the date on the note card was correct, it meant the warden had been laying the groundwork for his experiments at Brookline for years before he became the warden there. Whatever research he had begun in Kentucky he had continued in even more gruesome ways at the asylum.

Abby spoke up suddenly, craning her neck to look up at Jordan from her place on the floor. "What's lysergic acid die . . . thyla . . . mide?" She stumbled over the word, then picked up a note card and held it up for Jordan. "This. What is that?"

"It's in mine, too," Dan said.

Jordan took the card and opened a new browser window, typing with quick, loud keystrokes. "Huh. That's weird. It's LSD."

"You mean like acid?" Abby asked, snorting. "That can't be right."

"Click on that top entry," Dan said. Over Jordan's shoulder he could see the Wikipedia entry for the drug. "Skim it."

"Hey . . . ," Jordan said softly, reading, then louder. "Whoa. Whoa, hey." He pointed frantically at the screen, twisting around to give Dan a wide-eyed grimace. "The CIA experimented with this stuff. They thought they could use it for mind control and like drop bombs of it on Russia. Chemical warfare, messed-up stuff. My history teacher used to rant about this. I guess I just assumed he was full of it." Glancing at the screen, he sat up straighter. "MKUltra. That's it. That's what he used to rant about in fifth period."

"It sounds like the warden wasn't happy with how the experiments were going," Dan said. He did some quick mental math.

"Nineteen fifty-three . . . Eisenhower was president then."

"That explains the picture." Abby took it from where she had placed it on the floor.

"So the warden gets picked to be part of CIA experiments and goes to Kentucky, but he's unsatisfied with the methods and, what? Leaves to come here and start up his own experiments on mental patients?" It was more information than they'd had before, but Dan couldn't help feeling they were still missing something. There was the mention of Dr. Maudire and the jewel. And in the young warden's journal, he called his special rock "the bright burning star." Could it be the same jewel that was on Lucy's necklace? What did it have to do with Felix?

His fingers itched to grab that other journal, the one still hidden in his coat. Instead, he looked at the next page of the pamphlet. The entry was short, just a few lines. He hadn't considered that handwriting could actually look angry, but this did.

> *Forester is a myopic old fool. He continues to thwart me, and even went so far as to chide me for circumventing the parameters of the experiment. Me! Chide me! When he is the weak link in the chain. Maybe if he were my patient, I could unlock his true potential and then he would not be so limiting or so dull.*

The entries became shorter and shorter.

> *Forester dismissed me permanently today. That is well enough. I've had a breakthrough, and as I suspected, it was only possible through the three-pronged approach. The drug, the operation, the stone. It is not yet perfect, but I have found the secret to creating my own true agents. Control. I have it at last.*

A few pages later and there was hardly anything written at all.

Sanctum, a holy or sacred place—what could be more sacred than possessing the power of your own true thoughts? Sanctum. It is both lock and key.

When Dan turned to the next set of notes, the paper looked much newer, not nearly as stained or crinkled. Again, they were clipped with a note card, and the date caught his attention—1960. Seven years later. That was quite a gap. He shivered to think what the warden might have gotten up to in those missing years.

I have found him at last. My perfect subject. There will be more perfect ones, I'm sure, but he was the first. An alcoholic, homeless, nobody would miss him. One hundred and seventy-four days with the drugs in his system. A marvel it didn't permanently damage his mind. It was a simple thing to arrange the surgery and see that his lobotomy was completed without incident.

Now all that remains is the third and final step, reprogramming his mind with hypnosis, and thereby exposing him to Dr. Maudire's jewel. I have never believed in the power of trinkets. Reasoning, logic, knowledge, science—in these things I believe. But objects? It's silly even to entertain the thought . . . but my hypnosis is never more potent than when I use the trickster's stone. There is something unique about this stone, I'm convinced of this. Even a man of science must amend his beliefs when the same result occurs again and again.

Maudire claimed he stole it from a mad spinster's grave, and the act of robbing a dead woman gave the gem its terrible power. A wild fantasy, I'm certain, meant to capture the imagination of a lonely little boy.

It worked, though perhaps not in the old fool's favor. Did its power increase, I wonder, when I strangled its owner?

It does not matter. What matters is that I have tracked my perfect subject, my dear Harry Cartwright, and soon he will be my thrall.

So Maudire really was dead. Dan had never met the man himself, just his apparition. How did that work exactly? Did the old magician leave behind some kind of imprint? It was one thing to *see* another person's memories, it was another thing entirely to have a conversation with them. Shuddering, Dan skimmed back up the page. "Listen to this. . . ."

He read that last entry to them, feeling the chill in the room deepen as he went. When he finished, he let the pamphlet fall onto his legs. He considered his next words very carefully, then reached into his coat and fished out the young warden's journal. It wouldn't be right to hide it; it frightened him, really, that he'd had the inclination to do so in the first place.

"What's that?" Abby asked, her mouth hanging open a little in surprise.

"I found it tonight. In that first house . . . I didn't want to say anything in front of Micah."

"I think that dude is on the level," Jordan said wryly. "I know I gave him a hard time earlier, but he didn't have to run off like that so we could get away."

"Do you think he's okay?" Abby glanced swiftly between them. "I almost feel like we should have called the police."

"I don't know," Dan said. "The guy is tough, though. I bet he got away. Right now I just want to focus on piecing this all together." He handed the journal to Abby, who took it with just two fingers, as if it were a smelly dead thing. "I think the warden grew up in that house. I found a hidden trapdoor under a rug with an old tin and that journal. He wrote it when he was a kid. It's . . . kind of sad, actually."

"'Today Patrick went up to the roof. Wake up, Patrick, I said, wake up now and fly!'" Abby read, having opened to a random entry. "'When he came back down again he was all broken and his head had gone lumpy.'"

"I think Patrick was one of his brothers," Dan explained. "He talks about wanting to control them. He was being bullied. It's weird because I'd thought Daniel was the oldest of three. That's what Pastor Bittle told me this summer. But apparently he had a fourth brother."

"Wait, let me get this straight," Jordan cut in. "He was pissed at his brother so he pushed him off the *roof*?"

Dan shook his head. "Not pushed. Hypnotized."

From the floor, Abby gasped, but it came out half-choked. "Oh my God, he drew a picture of it."

She held up the book for them to see, and she was right. There, under the short description of Patrick's fall, was a crude crayon drawing of a boy on his back, his limbs twisted at unnatural angles. The mangled boy wore a striped sweater and too-short pants. Dan's eyes widened—he hadn't been seeing young Daniel in his hallucinations. There was one line of writing under the picture.

Patrick will stay quiet now.

CHAPTER

24

"So the warden was an evil creeper even as a child," Jordan said, taking off his glasses to clean them on his sweater. "Good to know."

"It goes deeper than that," Dan replied, a little impatient with Jordan for making light of it. "We knew he was obsessed with preserving his legacy, but it's about more than that. He couldn't control his brothers, he couldn't control Forester, he couldn't control that Maudire guy he strangled. . . ."

"But he figured out a way to do it," Abby said. She put the child's journal on the carpet and pushed it away as if she couldn't stand to touch it. "He got close with Harry Cartwright during those experiments, and then tracked him down when it was over. Do you think that's how he ended up returning to Camford?"

"Hmm . . ." Jordan leaned back in the desk chair, bouncing a little. He tented his hands and squinted up at the ceiling. "He gets chosen to participate in covert CIA experiments, he thinks they're crap—which they were, by the way; they never figured out how to do jack shit with the LSD, if Mr. Chandahar is right—"

"Who on earth is Mr. Chandahar?" Abby interjected.

"My history teacher . . . the conspiracy nut? Anyway, Crazy-Pants Crawford—no offense—"

Dan snorted. "None taken."

"—manages to subdue Harry Cartwright with drugs and surgery, then the experiments end and Cartwright goes on his merry way to buddy up to Caroline and maybe those other girls, too. Warden Looney Tunes—no offense—"

"Still none taken."

"—finds out good ole Harry went to Camford to start life as a postmaster, but then the warden shows up and women start going missing and, hey! Do you think that's where Harry took the girls? To the warden? Maybe he wasn't at Brookline yet. Maybe he needed test subjects or something."

Dan shivered, remembering his vision of the warden at Harry Cartwright's house, so clearly manipulating him. No wonder the man was so docile; Crawford had partially lobotomized him.

"Okay, screw this, I need a snack." Jordan pushed up from the desk, stretching and yawning. "Ouch. It's almost one in the morning. I'm going to hit a vending machine. Do you guys want anything?"

"Be careful, Jordan, those weirdos could still be out there," Abby said. She got to her feet, following Jordan's example and stretching.

"I'll be quick," he reassured them.

"I'll take a water," Abby added. "Dan?"

"Water's good. Watch your back, Jordan, seriously."

"I'll be fine," Jordan insisted, shuffling to the door. "And no, those are not famous last words. My last words would be way more epic. Anyway, if I'm not back in ten minutes, send Wentworth Miller and a cheese pizza."

Dan put down the notes, rubbing his eyes. He felt vaguely tired—that is, his body was tired, but his mind was still sharp and awake. Something nagged. For all the information they had gathered, the puzzle wasn't quite complete. Why had Felix wanted them to find all this?

He looked at Abby, who had shifted into Jordan's vacated chair. She smiled across the aisle at Dan, leaning her chin on one hand.

"We've hardly had five minutes to breathe since we got here," she said. "How are you holding up?"

"This is . . . a lot. I mean, I knew we were dealing with an evil guy but this just goes deeper than I could have imagined." Dan could feel a headache starting. That's what happened when he went this long without taking his meds.

"It does seem a bit over our heads," Abby agreed. "But how are *you*? Outside of all this."

"I want it to be over. I want to be able to relax again and enjoy my time with you guys. With you." His cheeks burned and he glanced down at his shoes. "I mean . . . I like spending time with you. I'd like to do it more often. I was really hoping you would get to take me to Lara's installation."

"Me too, Dan. I'd like to think that one day when this is over, you and I can see . . . Well . . ." She laughed, shaking her head. "Jeez, talking about LSD and the CIA is easier, go figure. Anyway, what I'm trying to say is: I don't know what we are right now, but I'd like to find out."

Dan nodded, grateful that she could articulate what he couldn't. All he knew for certain was that looking at her made his fears and doubts feel less insurmountable. If that wasn't the start of love, it was at least something to hold on to. "I'd like that, too. I just . . . The past few weeks it feels like you and Jordan have been distant. Was I just imagining it?"

It was her turn to blush. "I can't speak for Jordan, but I've been scared, you know? I mean, we went through a pretty rough summer together, and it wasn't totally your fault, but . . . I guess I started to feel like if I wanted to move on from that, I needed to move on from you. Not to mention, I didn't want to get attached and then watch you go off to UCLA or something. I guess I was just holding back to protect myself, but maybe that wasn't fair."

"No." Dan shook his head quickly. "It makes perfect sense. And I think you're right to worry and watch out for yourself. Who knows where we'll end up? Better to wait and see once everything's back to normal."

"Normal? You're hallucinating, I'm hearing voices—maybe normal isn't in the cards for us right now."

She laughed, but Dan was distracted, his mind latching on to something she had said. . . .

"What is it? Dan? What happened?"

"My hallucinations," he murmured, wishing his clumsy mouth would catch up to his thoughts. "They didn't start until I got here, did they?"

It is not yet perfect, but I have found the secret to creating my own true agents. Control. I have it at last.

"The warden," Dan blurted, grabbing the pamphlet and flipping pages furiously. "He said he figured it out . . . or got close. He said he could make agents, hypnotize them—that the drug was *part* of it. What if that's why I'm hallucinating? Listen . . ." He started to read over the journal entry. "'I have found the secret to creating my own true agents.' Those agents . . . they could be trying to drug us. They could be doing it already."

"Who's they?" Abby asked. Dan was sure this was significant, but Abby didn't look convinced in the slightest. "Drugging us? You don't think that's awfully far-fetched, even after everything?"

"It wouldn't be hard, would it? We eat food prepared by other people. The drinks are all out of their dispensers. Maybe it's far-fetched but it's *possible*."

"Are you sure you're not just . . . hoping that's the case? I mean, wouldn't you feel better knowing the hallucinations weren't from you but something else?"

She had a point, but Dan didn't really stop to consider it. He was already racing ahead, piecing together more and more of what felt like a plausible scenario. "This whole time we've assumed the warden's influence was confined to Brookline, but what if that's wrong? What if the whole college was in on the experiments? The whole *community*? It makes sense, Abby. How could he keep what was going on covered up unless he had help? Someone had to be running interference for him while he did his experiments at the asylum."

"Dan, slow down," Abby said, "slow down. . . ."

"He wanted control. That was always the goal. That was it all along, I wanted to control people, unlock their true potential as interpreted by me."

"Dan!" She was almost shouting now. Abby leaped up out of the chair and crossed to him, grabbing his forearm and shaking. "Dan! Stop!"

"What?" Dan was out of breath. They stared at each other

in tense silence, and then Abby shook his arm, this time more gently.

"You're talking in first person. Can't you hear yourself? *I* did this. . . . *I* wanted that. . . ."

That was irrelevant. She was interrupting his line of thinking, and he had to keep the thread. He had to write it all down before he forgot.

"That's not the point," Dan muttered, avoiding her gaze.

"Yes, it is, Dan. Yes, it is the point. I'll be honest, I don't really give a crap what 'Warden Crawford' did forty years ago. I care about *us*, Dan. I care about my aunt Lucy. I care about the people who are still alive, and I came back here to this miserable place so we could all get better and move on with our lives. But you're not getting better. You're turning into someone else." Trembling, she took a step back, as if frightened of who was looking back at her.

"I'm me," he said, exasperated. "Daniel. Daniel Crawford. I'm . . . *me*!"

"*Dan* Crawford," she said. It was almost a whisper, and hoarse.

"What?"

"Dan. You never call yourself Daniel."

Dan felt the wind go out of his sail. He'd become so obsessed with uncovering all the lives the warden had ruined with his influence, he'd lost sight of how *he* was affecting the lives of the two people who mattered most to him in the world. If he kept this up, they wouldn't have a friendship, they'd have a shared trauma—one that held them together like a lock that had rusted over.

"Damn it," he said, dropping his head into his hands. "You're right. I have to keep us separate."

"From now on we should take some precautions," she said, still keeping her distance. "Jordan's coming back with bottled water. Maybe we should only eat and drink things from the vending machines. We're not here much longer, it shouldn't be too difficult."

"That's a good idea," Dan said. "We can stock up tonight."

"Dan . . . Even if there is 'something in the water,' or whatever, I have to say that for all the nightmares and the voices and stuff, Jordan and I have never experienced anything close to what's happening to you." Abby tucked a piece of hair behind her ear with a sigh. "I'm not trying to poke holes in your theory. . . ."

"I know. And you . . . you're right about that. It's not a perfect explanation."

Jordan appeared at the door, his arms laden with bottled waters, Diet Mountain Dew, three bags of chips, and an enormous box of Twizzlers.

"What?" he said at the combined force of their staring. "I'm a growing boy. Here." He tossed them each a water. "Yikes. You could cut the tension in here with a knife. What's going on?"

"Dan thinks someone might be trying to drug us," Abby explained, smoothing down the front of her sweater. Dan silently thanked her for glossing over his outburst. "So from now on, we're only going to eat and drink things that are prepackaged."

"Wow." Jordan slid back into his desk chair and ripped open a bag of Doritos. "That's . . . that's a lot to swallow. But better safe than sorry, I suppose."

"I think maybe this whole thing is bigger than the asylum," Dan added. "Maybe even bigger than the college."

Jordan positioned the open bag of chips above his face and shook until a little avalanche of nuclear orange triangles fell into his open mouth. He reached for his Diet Mountain Dew and went back to reading the MKUltra Wikipedia entry.

On the floor, Dan's phone buzzed, shimmying across the carpet. He scooped it up and squinted down at the glowing screen.

He had a text message. From Micah.

They know ur in Erickson. Get out now.

The phone buzzed in Dan's hand. Another message arrived, this time from an unregistered number.

We see you

Before he could tell the others, Jordan let out a whining "Heeey. What gives? This thing just shut off. . . ." He smacked his palm against the monitor. Dan froze, watching as every monitor in the lab switched off, one by one, the screens going blank.

"We need to go," Dan whispered. "Now."

"Go where?" Abby cried, kneeling to pick up the pictures and cards.

"Grab whatever you can carry," he said, shoving his phone away. "I have an idea."

CHAPTER

25

"This had better work," Jordan whispered, fidgeting in the hedge next to Dan. "This goddamn stupid fern is getting to second base. . . ."

"Shhhh." Abby was hidden somewhere to his left, invisible behind a thick row of overgrown juniper bushes.

The temperature had dropped steadily, and now, wedged behind a shrub with damp leaves brushing his face, Dan struggled to keep his teeth from chattering. He hugged the journal and notes to his chest. If he shivered, if he *breathed*, it might be enough to give away their hiding spot.

The minutes stretched on. Maybe he was wrong. Maybe the warning message was just that, a warning, and nobody would come. Dan decided he would give it another five minutes. If nobody came, then they would have to come up with another plan.

Trembling, miserable, Dan was about to call it off when he heard the squeak of sneakers shuffling across the wet grass. One cloaked figure, then two, followed by two more . . . All told, six people showed, hidden under heavy red capes and skull masks. Dan shrank back as one of the leering masks turned toward him. It was impossible to tell if the guy saw him hidden there in the bushes.

Finally, the Scarlets went into the dorm. Dan didn't dare exhale until the door shut behind the last one.

"It's really them," Abby whispered. "The Scarlets. I wonder how many there are."

"If you start counting alums, there could be hundreds. Maybe thousands."

"You're starting to sound like my history teacher," Jordan said. "And I'm freaked out that it's beginning to sound like sense."

"They'll be back soon," Dan reminded him. "Let's stay quiet."

Not ten seconds later, the door of the dormitory burst open with a bang. Dan huddled closer to the ground, watching as three of the six red-robed students emerged. The person in front was tall, probably male, and he stalled right under the lamp, looking in every direction. Jordan tapped Dan on the shoulder and then pointed. Dan followed Jordan's finger through the branches and leaves to the pavement and a pair of boat shoes.

"Come on!" Cal's voice boomed across the lawn and the paths. "They'll be done checking the other exits. You idiots. How did you let those morons get away? You!" He strode forward and shoved one of the other Scarlets. "You warned him, didn't you?"

"Back off, I didn't do anything."

Dan's heart sank—it was Micah's muffled voice behind one of the ugly masks.

"Yeah, we'll see about that." Cal shoved him again, harder. "If you're lying, you know what she'll do to you, and this time your weird magic grandpa won't be enough to save you."

"Don't you think I know that?" Micah pushed back, his fists thumping on Cal's chest.

Cal ignored the push, standing his ground. "She's been putting this together for years, you idiot. Mess this up now, and she'll ruin your life. Doubt the college will want to keep you around when they know what *really* got you sent to juvie."

"You don't know the first thing about it," he shot back, getting in Cal's face.

"Theft, right? That's what you tell everyone? What a joke. *You're* a joke."

"You need to shut up right now," Micah growled, shoving Cal again. "Right. Now."

"No wonder you work so hard to be everyone's best bud." Snorting, Cal turned his back on Micah and took a few steps toward the bush concealing Jordan. "Think everyone would still kiss your ass if they knew you got drunk and plowed into a tree? What was the poor girl's name? Julie? Jessie?"

Micah swung, hard, and Cal just managed to dodge out of the way.

"Careful," Cal warned, clucking his tongue softly. "You're in enough trouble as it is."

Grunting and gasping for air, Micah backed away, hands in the air. His shoulders slumped as the fight leaked out of him. "I didn't do anything, Cal. Back off."

"We'll see. Tell your dumbass ex she better stay in line, too, or she'll have to *wake up*, got it?"

"Leave Lara out of this," Micah rumbled.

The three missing Scarlets returned, and then all six of them left down the path, walking and then running. Dan held up his hand, signaling for his friends to wait. If they left the shelter of the bushes too early they'd be spotted, and he didn't want to find out what the Scarlets would do to them if they were discovered.

The Scarlets were almost across the quad and out of sight when Dan crawled out from his hiding place. Abby tumbled out of the juniper bush across the path from them and brushed the stray leaves from her coat.

"I hate saying this, but we have to follow them," Dan said.

Jordan glanced between him and Abby quickly. "We'll be completely outnumbered!"

"We can lag behind so they don't notice us. Jordan, we have to hurry!" Abby said, breaking into a run. "They're almost gone."

Together, they ran up the path leading from the dorm, following the direction the robed figures had gone. Dan could just make out a flutter of red disappearing around a corner ahead and to the left. He didn't want to make too much noise, but he hazarded a few breathless words.

"I bet I know where Felix's last coordinate goes," he huffed. "They're going to lead us right to it."

✗ ✗ ✗ ✗ ✗

Clinging to the shadows and whatever trees they found along the way, they followed the six robed figures north and then west of the campus. Dan had never gone this far on foot from the school, and when he glanced over his shoulder the steeple of the campus chapel was no longer visible. The modest houses clustered around the school gave way to larger, more expensive houses in a well-manicured neighborhood.

They had less cover to hide behind now, with each row of shrubs trimmed down to uniform cubes. House after house, Dan tried to time their dashes between cover, watching to make sure no cars were passing and none of their targets lagged behind.

Part of him didn't want to believe what Cal had said about Micah, but why else would someone like him fall in with a cult? Even Dan could see the temptation—join the Scarlets and have a stain on your past wiped clean. Hadn't Micah even said he was here on scholarship?

At last Cal and his cohorts turned up the lane to a three-story mansion. The house looked like it had been cut from one enormous block of gray stone. Unlike the other houses in the neighborhood, which had all gone dark except for the occasional porch light, this house was completely lit up. Every window glowed with a red candle in the sill. Even from a distance Dan could make out the shape of the candles. Skulls.

He had seen a candle just like those in Micah's room, and one at the house party.

"Is this like a meeting hall or something?" Abby mused aloud, crouching close to Dan. They hid behind a cluster of perfectly round bushes. A few of the berries from the bush had overripened and fallen, staining the grass red at their feet.

"I don't see any cars," Dan said. "And this is pretty far from campus. . . ."

"Since whatever we're about to do will probably get us killed, I want to go on record now saying I was right about the boat shoes," Jordan whispered.

"Fine. Okay. You were right about the shoes," Dan said. "We're all very proud."

"What *is* the plan?" Abby asked urgently. "We can't just go strolling up to the front door."

"There isn't a plan. We just need to get close enough to take a look inside. When we do, we might be able to see who else is one of them."

"And if they don't take off their masks?" Abby peered around the edge of one of the bushes, chewing her lower lip.

"Then we'll have to think of something else," Jordan said. "At least we'll get an idea of how many weirdos we're dealing with."

"Let's try the back," Dan murmured, inching forward. "We can take the driveway wide and stay away from the windows."

"I don't know about this. . . ." Abby fiddled with her mittens, rocking back and forth on her heels. "We're going to be totally outnumbered. Maybe we should wait until morning. They'll be gone for the most part and then we can see if the house has any doors Jordan can unlock."

They didn't have time to argue, not now, not when they were this close.

"I have to see this through, Abby," Dan said finally. "Felix said to follow, and that's what I'm going to do."

"But there are other ways we could—"

"No, Abby, this is it. You can stay behind if you want, but I'm going to get a closer look. I want to know who's after us. I want to know exactly who we're up against." He was freezing and frightened, and rapidly losing his patience. Why didn't she understand? He didn't like the idea of this any more than she did, but *liking* didn't enter into it.

The warden and his legacy and whoever was a part of it would never leave them alone until they dismantled the twisted system he had put in place.

"But Dan, if we wait—"

"I just want it to end, Abby. That's all I want, to know how to fix this once and for all." Dan wasn't waiting any longer. They could follow him or they could stay put, but he wasn't hesitating another second.

He darted out from behind the bushes, skirting the driveway, jogging past it, and then turning to run up parallel to the pavement. The house loomed closer, taller than he had originally thought. It was cold, featureless, just a stone rectangle with evenly spaced windows and a sober slate roof.

When he reached the end of the drive, he was standing opposite the front door, with an empty three-car garage to his right. There was a gap between the house and the garage and he sprinted for it. When he rounded the corner of the house he pushed himself up against the wall, waiting there to catch his breath.

The moment Abby and Jordan appeared, crowding his side, Dan felt a wave of guilt wash over him. The stress and fear were making him hot-tempered and impatient, and his friends didn't deserve that. It had been his idea to come back to this place. He was the one the Scarlets were after. But still, his friends followed him.

"I'm sorry," he whispered as they regrouped against the house. "I just . . ."

"I get it. It's not like we could walk away from this," Abby replied. "Not really."

"Well, whatever we're doing, can we hurry it up? My toes are going numb and this place is giving me the creeps."

Jordan was right. They were already wasting too much time. Dan led them toward the window a few feet ahead. It was low enough that if he didn't duck, the top of his head would be visible from inside. All three of them crept below the bottom edge of the window, and then Dan turned, his hands freezing and stiff, and carefully rose up until he could just see in.

Luck was on his side, but he held his breath, signaling to the others that they could look.

On the other side of the window was a long, tall room with a gleaming wooden floor. A chandelier with red candles hung in the very center, and the hot wax running into the silvery catches looked like thick rivers of blood. Red-caped figures, at least a dozen, formed a semicircle around a high-backed chair. Dan's grip on the windowsill tightened. He recognized the chair. It looked almost exactly like the one in the frat house basement.

"What are they saying?" Abby breathed in his ear.

She was right, they were chanting something in a low hum that built, louder and louder until Dan could finally make out the words.

"They built it out of stone. . . . They built it out of stone. . . ."

Why did that seem so familiar?

On the right half of the semicircle he spotted Cal's boat shoes, but nobody was removing their hoods. When the chant grew loud enough to actually shake the pane of glass in front of his eyes, the words cut out abruptly. An open doorway on the right side of the room flickered with shadow, and then another red-robed figure entered, followed by three others.

"Isn't that . . . ?" Jordan murmured.

She hadn't bothered wearing a mask or hood.

"Yes." Dan recognized her instantly—the short dark hair, the gap-toothed smile. "Professor Reyes. And I've seen that tall guy on campus. I think he's another professor. The blond woman was at the carnival. Kelly something. God, she was campaigning for state senate."

"I can't believe this. . . ." Abby shook her head, glancing away.

Dan smiled, grim. "I can."

She walked solemnly to the chair and stood behind it. Around her neck, a shard of red stone flickered, dancing in the candlelight.

"That's it," Dan whispered. "That's the gem he kept writing about. It's the warden's."

"How did she get it?" Abby asked.

"I don't know. Maybe she was his protégé."

"Or his victim," Jordan suggested softly.

Professor Reyes propped her hands on the back of the chair, taking a long moment to look around at those assembled. They were in danger of being spotted now, with the window facing her directly. Dan hoped the bright lights inside would make it more difficult to see into the darkness outside, but just in case, he lowered his head a fraction.

Even through the glass, Dan could hear Professor Reyes perfectly as she lifted her head and said, "Where is he?"

"We . . . We lost him, and the two others." It was Cal, who shuffled his boat shoes back and forth nervously.

"Not *him*, the other one. The traitor."

If Dan had felt guilty before for convincing Jordan and Abby to return to the college, he felt even guiltier now watching as three more robed strangers hauled Micah into the room. A mittened hand closed over his and squeezed. Dan shared a look with Abby, feeling his gut twist sickeningly.

Micah looked drugged and beaten, fresh bruises darkening his jaw and right cheek. Surely he would be fighting them? He wasn't a small guy by any means, and Dan had seen those martial arts trophies in his room. But he slumped against the shoulders of the people carrying him, one lens of his glasses shattered and the other missing altogether.

"We have to do something," Dan whispered.

"Like what?" At Jordan's words, Abby's hand tightened even more on Dan's fingers.

"I don't know. . . . But he helped us escape. We have to help him."

"Yeah, and then we get caught and the whole thing was for nothing."

He felt even sicker when Abby whispered, "Jordan's right."

The Scarlets wrestled Micah into the high-backed chair in front of the professor and slammed the manacles around his wrists. There were iron fasteners for his ankles, too. Dan watched, his throat closing with helpless panic as one of them pulled a belt from inside the folds of his robe and secured it around Micah's forehead, keeping his head locked back against the chair.

"My tools?" Professor Reyes asked drily, as if she were asking someone to pass the salt.

A robed figure bowed and scuttled out of the room, returning only a moment later with a shiny silver tray laden with only three objects—a piece of gauze, a snub-nosed mallet, and a spike.

"Oh, no. No, no, no," Jordan gasped.

Micah began to stir, becoming aware suddenly of his bindings and fighting them.

"Be still," Professor Reyes barked. Her dark eyes glittered, beetle black. "You would not like it if I slipped. There's hardly time for this, but not even your family line protects you from more *permanent* solutions."

On his knuckles, Abby's mitten grew damp with sweat.

"Let this be a reminder to all of you what happens when you disobey. When you *meddle*. You could have frightened him off, scared him away, when I am *this close* to the answer. . . ." She stepped to the side of the chair, took the spike and then the hammer, and leaned over, carefully pulling back Micah's right eyelid and setting the spike in place. "Hold him still. It's time he woke up. . . ."

Two figures did just that.

Micah's eyes darted frantically, then locked on Dan's through the window. Dan inhaled, hard, biting down on his tongue to keep from shouting. The mallet swung back, gaining momentum to strike. Next to him, Dan could feel Abby recoil, hiding her eyes. He refused to look away.

And in the last second, when he heard the mallet hit the spike, he was certain he saw Micah mouth the word "run."

CHAPTER

26

*T*he sound went straight through him, a hollow *thunk* like a piece of meat being dropped on a tile floor. Dan wished he hadn't looked. He wished harder that he had done something to stop it.

"You don't belong here."

Dan spun, tearing his eyes away from the aftermath of Micah's lobotomy to find a Scarlet standing directly behind them. None of them spoke. Dan felt icy fear squeeze the words and air right out of him.

The figure reached up and pulled back her mask, revealing a pretty if disheveled face. It took a second for Dan to recognize her.

"Lara!" Abby practically swooned with relief. "Wait! You're one of these monsters?"

"I was. Not anymore. Not that I can leave, but . . . I never thought they would do that to one of us. To *Micah*." Her lip trembled, her eyes glossy with tears. Then she blinked, hard, and her face was no longer scared but determined. "You can't be here. If they find you . . . Better not to think about it. Follow me, okay? This side of the house is practically empty. Nobody will spot us."

"What is this place?" Dan asked, no longer so intent on

getting inside. He had seen enough.

"Professor Reyes lives here. She inherited it from Warden Crawford. She calls him *father*, but I don't think they're actually related. He left it to her in his will." Lara led them along the back of the house, ducking whenever they neared a window. "Now leave, understand me? You can't be seen."

"Where are we supposed to go?" Jordan whispered. "You're here, Cal is a psycho, and Micah is . . . We don't have anywhere *to* go."

"Find somewhere to hide. The student union never locks up. . . . Pick a hallway somewhere and try to avoid everyone you can. Keep your phones on. If they catch wind of where you are, I'll text."

"Lara . . ." Abby ran up next to her, grabbing her wrist. "Why are you doing this? If they find out, you'll be hurt, too."

"I can't care about that right now. This isn't what I . . . This isn't who I want to be. . . ." Lara didn't slow her pace, charging on through the darkness until they reached the narrow row of trees separating the mansion from the next property over. "I thought this was for academics, for connections! They said they could get my art into any New York gallery I wanted. Or they could get me into med school if I ever *changed my mind*. Ha." She stopped, checking in every direction to make sure they hadn't been followed. "Stay safe. I'll check in with you when I can. Find a way off campus. Get a bus, get a plane . . . Just get away."

"Hang on," Dan said sternly. "I have more questions. . . ."

"Not now. They'll be looking for me." She sighed and pulled the hood of her robe back up. "Call me tomorrow. I'll answer all your questions then."

"Dan, let her go. I don't want her to get in trouble." Abby tugged on his arm until she succeeded in yanking him into the trees. "Be careful, Lara."

"You too." With that, she rushed across the yard, a blur of scarlet.

They picked their way across the streets and campus, pausing in the shadows near buildings and trees until they could dash out into the open without being seen. That was fairly easy, given how late it was.

Exhausted, they finally reached Wilfurd Commons and snaked through the dimly lit halls until they found a back corridor where delivery trucks dropped off food and soda. They collapsed against the wall, each of them silent for a long moment.

A half-dead halogen light flickered overhead, buzzing intermittently. The vending machines down the hall let off a similar but more consistent hum.

"I want to go over everything again," Dan mumbled, pulling the journals and notes out of his coat.

"Can we just sit quietly for ten minutes?" Jordan grumbled. "I just need to . . . I don't know. Process? We just saw . . . And all those people in there. What the hell is wrong with this place?"

"Dan was right," Abby said, pulling off her mittens and then letting her arms drop like lead weights onto her thighs. "This goes way, way deeper than we thought."

"I mean, why the hell would people join a group like that?" Jordan asked. He tipped his head back against the wall and closed his eyes.

"You heard Lara—connections, prestige. Micah said his uncle

went here, and I'll bet he was a Scarlet, too. And not that it's a worse fate at this point, but Micah might still be in juvie if they hadn't fixed his record." Dan rubbed his eyes. He couldn't fall asleep. Not yet. "Cal's dad was the dean. It's probably a family thing."

"Lara's brother is an alum," Abby said. "He was probably a member."

"My guess is it was a secret society just like any other until the warden got his hooks in it. I bet members don't even know all the things they did that were really for his benefit. And whatever he was trying to do, it looks like Professor Reyes is still doing it now. I just wish I knew what she meant about being 'this close to an answer.' An answer to what?"

"What *I* want to know is, does this secret society have somebody in the Camford police force?" Jordan muttered.

Dan didn't even want to think about that yet. "Did you have any luck cross-referencing the names from the blackboard with alums before the computers crapped out?"

"Nope."

"I still have these," Abby said, showing him a few squares of folded newspaper. "Remember? Cal had them in his backpack at the carnival."

A spark of hope lit in Dan's chest, the first in a while, and it was enough to jolt him back awake. "Let's take a look."

"Knock yourselves out," Jordan murmured. "I'm gonna grab a nap."

"We can take turns." Abby smoothed out the photocopied newspapers from the archives between her legs and Dan's. "Here, I'll set a phone alarm. . . ."

"What is it?" Dan asked. She sounded worried, and Dan glanced over to see her checking her phone.

"My battery is low. Really low. Yours?"

Dan slipped the phone out of his coat pocket and grimaced. "Same. Damn it. My charger is in Micah's room, and there's no way I can go back there. Although . . . Jordan could pick the lock."

That jerked Jordan abruptly out of his nap. "No. No freaking way, Dan, you are kidding me with that shit. I am not going back to that dorm. I do that and I'm one breath away from being inspiration for the next 'totally fictional' *Law and Order* episode."

"Then how do we get Lara's call? Is your battery any good?"

Jordan glanced down at the iPhone resting on his stomach. "Half charge. If I turn it off until morning, I can conserve it."

"I'll text Lara his number," Abby said. "At least that way she can find us."

"Okeydoke. Wake me when it's my turn to keep watch," Jordan said, already half-asleep.

Dan leaned over the flattened paper, skimming his fingers across the various titles of news stories and editorials. Most of it was total fluff, news about sports teams and upcoming dances or plays. His eyes blurred and he couldn't read, sadness surprising him, overtaking him to the point where he couldn't keep his hand from trembling. Then Abby's hand was there, resting on his, reassuring and comforting with its steady warmth.

As he dozed, Jordan softly repeated sequences of numbers under his breath, the words slurring together.

"I'm so sorry, Dan. I know you liked him."

"He'll probably be a vegetable now," he said bitterly. "Just . . , blank. And that's *if* he survived it. He was a good guy . . . I think. I mean, whatever he used to be, he still tried to help us."

"Maybe he was trying to do better, you know? Atone? He might have come around and realized the Scarlets weren't in the right," Abby suggested. "And if we had stuck with him?" She rubbed his hand lightly. "They would have caught us, too, and then what? We would be just like him now. I know it's hard, but you have to think logically about this."

"Ha. That's funny."

"What?"

"An artist telling me to think logically. But you're right. . . . I know you are. It's not that. It's that we didn't do anything to stop it." Dan sighed, forcing his eyes to focus on the newsprint. "I feel like that's been the case ever since we got to Brookline this summer—stuff keeps happening *to* us, but we can't do a damn thing about it."

"We can and we will," Abby assured him. "This isn't over yet."

Dan nodded, swallowing past the tight knot of loss tangled in his throat. He hated that feeling, like he was either going to throw up or cry or both. He flipped the newspaper page over, finding an article about a sorority organizing a charity event for a professor's medical expenses. Dan was about to move to the next page when Abby's hand shot out, smacking the paper back down to the floor.

"That girl," she said, pointing to the picture of the sorority girls lined up and smiling. "Who does she remind you of?"

Squinting, Dan looked at the folded arms and crossed legs of a girl who didn't look very happy to have her picture taken. Standing on the far left side of the row of girls, she was practically

scowling. She was slimmer then and had a different haircut, but her features were the same.

"Professor Reyes," he said. Dan shrugged, not finding any real significance in the picture. "So she was in a sorority, so what?"

Abby chewed her lip, brows furrowed as she stared down at the paper, deep in thought.

"What?" Dan pressed. "What is it?"

"Just a hunch, I guess. I mean . . . We know the warden was controlling Harry Cartwright, and we know he was implicated in the disappearances of those women in town. Remember that letter we found in his house? Caroline's? She was in the Scarlets, she hated it, wanted to leave . . ."

"*Caroline.*" Dan's eyes grew wide with sudden curiosity. "You think Caroline Martin is the professor?" He skimmed the tiny print under the newspaper photo. There it was, in black-and-white—the first name on the left: *C. Martin*.

"Reyes must be her married name," Abby suggested. "Or maybe she just chose it herself after the warden brainwashed her. Maybe *he* chose it. It makes sense, right? If she figured out what the warden was up to with the Scarlets and wanted to leave, he would do whatever he could to keep her from spreading it around."

"So he silenced Caroline by making her one of his experiments, and now she does it to her own followers," Dan said, nodding. "And the other women, the other disappearances . . . They might have been the same. They were going to expose him."

"Just like Micah . . ." Abby said sadly. "And Lara, too, if they find out she's helping us."

"It's a cycle. Professor Reyes is just doing what the warden programmed her to do."

"That's so depressing." She touched the professor's name under the sorority photo. "Do you really think he hypnotized her? Can something like that even last this long? I wonder how you, you know, break her out of it. The warden would have done this to her thirty years ago."

"Which means maybe the Scarlets are really her thralls or whatever and they don't even know it," Dan said, and now that he saw the scope of the warden's work laid before him, more and more pieces began to slide, terribly, into place. "Maybe Cal has been totally brainwashed. Or maybe your aunt Lucy. I mean, she did seem totally different this time. And Felix . . . Maybe this is what happened to him, too!"

At that, Abby sat up straighter. "Felix? But he gave you the addresses to figure all this out. . . ."

"Which proves he really is fighting back. This summer, it seemed like there were moments when he was himself, and moments when he was the Sculptor. So maybe the brainwashing didn't completely take. Maybe Professor Reyes doesn't have the warden's skill. She has the stone and probably his drug cocktail, but his notes were still in the frat. Maybe she never saw them. . . ." That little spark of hope flared again, but only weakly.

"So maybe it can be reversed," Abby said brightly.

He thought of his meeting with Maudire, or his ghost, or Warden Crawford's vision, or whatever the heck it was.

You can't do over what's already been done, but you sure can undo it. Not easy, but you can undo it.

If the warden's brainwashing really could be undone, then maybe the fail-safe Maudire had talked about was hidden somewhere in the journals. Dan nodded, closing the newspaper, grimly determined. "I hope it can be reversed. Because as soon as we help the others, we're going to do whatever it takes to reverse it on me."

"Wait, you think—"

"I do think. And I'm ready to have my mind back to myself."

CHAPTER

27

The old hypnotist had teeth like daggers nestled in the wiry tangle of his beard. He looked clean from far away, but up close you could see dirt in the deep crags of his face.

Old meant frail. Old meant even a little boy could beat him.

Inside the tent it smelled like weird berries, berries that had been soaked in a fancy woman's perfume. He knew the smell would stay in his clothes for days, and Mother would yell at him about it. Where have you been? Why do you smell like that? You'll upset the baby! He would make up a lie later when he walked back home with Patrick and Bernard.

But right now he needed the stone on the chain. If he ever wanted Patrick to go up to the roof, he would need the stone. Inside the tent there were all kinds of strange things—a bird with red feathers and one eye that hopped back and forth on its perch shrieking, "Turk! Turk!" and big heavy candlesticks bubbling with purple wax.

He was the old man's favorite and that meant his guard would be down.

"Do you know where I acquired this particular gem?" The hypnotist laughed all the time. He laughed after every sentence, sometimes every word. "Old Maudire pulled it from a grave, my boy, what do you think of that? Ha ha!"

"Turk! Turk!"

Daniel glared at the bird. He wondered if the bird would tell on him, since it could talk. It didn't matter. He needed the gem if he ever wanted Patrick to shut up.

"She was a cold old widow, never wanted her children to do anything but what they were told, boy, drove them crazy, ha ha! Proud. Puffed up. Some call me

puffed up, but they're wrong. I took the stone from the widow's grave, from her plantation, Arnaud Plantation, a white house, pretty, with trees and a little river. One of her boys drowned in that river. Her girl cracked her skull on the tree. Ha ha! I whispered sweet to her when I dug her up, whispered, 'Wake up, chérie, wake up!' They buried that cursed widow in secret, boy, and nobody would have the guts to take her jewels but me! See? Me, Old Maudire . . ."

"Turk!"

"Can I see it again?" Daniel asked. He wasn't listening to the story. He didn't care. Maybe the stone was magic or maybe it was ordinary. Either way he knew it hypnotized people in a special way. It had worked on him, hadn't it? And tricks never worked on him.

"One more time, boy, one more time, and then you must be off home!" The hypnotist pulled the red gleaming slice of agate from his vest pocket and dangled it in front of Daniel's eyes. It looked like earth's blood, like something cruel and primal that had come up from the bottom of the world.

It was warm in his palm, though it looked like it should have been cold.

"Turk! Turk!"

Daniel looked at the stone for a long time, and waited until the hypnotist turned around to pour a cup of tea from the little smoking stove in the corner. Then he put the stone in his pocket, took up one of the heavy candlesticks in both hands, and swung it as hard as he could. Purple wax scalded his palm, but he hardly felt it. There was more blood than he expected, and it came out of his smashed melon head so fast, so thick . . .

The candlestick was too heavy for his little hands. He dropped it and climbed on Maudire's back and wrapped his hands around the old hypnotist's neck. It was good he was so old and frail; his neck was just a warm, pulsing pipe under Daniel's hands, no bigger around than one of Mother's milk bottles.

The purple wax on his wrist cooled and cracked off, and under his hands Maudire stopped moving.

"Turk!"

Daniel hated that bird. He took another candlestick and tipped it over, pouring hot wax all over the bird. His wings were clipped, and he couldn't fly, but he could shriek as the wax scalded and burned. Then he hit the bird, too, because he hated it, because he didn't want to hear that stupid word anymore.

What was a Turk anyway?

Daniel wiped his hands on the tattered, striped carpet and left the tent.

He smiled as he walked through the carnival; he had the stone now and tomorrow Patrick would shut up for good.

CHAPTER

28

*D*an never seemed to slide gracefully out of sleep these days. He shot up, feeling a hand clutch at his arm. For a second he was sure it was the Scarlets coming for him, or that bearded old man from his dreams, but instead it was Abby.

She shook him lightly, her phone vibrating its alarm in her palm.

"What time is it?" he asked, groggy.

"Eight," Abby mumbled, "in the morning. I . . . uh, might have fallen asleep, too. But it looks like nobody found us. So . . . hooray?"

Jordan was missing, but he soon arrived from around the corner, a bounty of junk food heaped high in his arms. Dan's stomach rumbled in anticipation.

"Soup's up," Jordan said, smiling despite the dark smudges under his eyes. He tossed Dan a bottle of orange juice and a frosted cinnamon bun in a plastic wrapper. "You look rough. Bad dreams?"

"Aren't they always?" Dan replied, cracking open the orange juice and guzzling.

"Mine were bad, too," Abby said softly. She leaned forward from the wall and started to gather her hair into a ponytail. "Lucy and Lara were chasing me, but they didn't have faces. I only knew it was them because they kept laughing." She shivered. "It was awful."

"So what do we do now?" Jordan leaned against the wall opposite from them and turned on his phone. He stared at it glumly while he chewed a disintegrating powdered doughnut. "Just wait for Lara to call? What happens if she doesn't?"

"She will. She has to."

Dan wasn't so sure. He *hoped* Abby was right, but after seeing Micah's fate, he refused to underestimate Professor Reyes and what she would do to keep control of her followers—what she would do to find him.

He sighed and choked down a bite of cinnamon roll. It wasn't smart to take his meds on an empty stomach. He was just glad he carried them everywhere, or going back to pick the lock on Micah's room would have been a necessity. How was he ever going to get his stuff back? What if they never saw Micah again? "Maybe Lara can tell us who we can actually trust around here. She's a Scarlet, so she must know who *isn't* one. There might still be a chance that the police aren't mixed up in all of this."

"What I wanna know is why they didn't just leave when the weird shit started happening," Jordan said, flipping his phone around in his palm idly. "You'd think after the first ice pick lobotomy someone would've spoken up."

"Right, just like we left the second things got hairy this summer?" Abby snorted drily.

"Touché."

Abby scooted closer, picking up Dan's notes and glancing over them while Jordan took a seat and browsed the newspaper from the archive.

"It's strange to look at her like this," Jordan said. He opened to the picture of the sorority girls lined up. "She looks . . . normal. You think she was already mixed up with the warden?"

"I think so, yeah," Dan replied. His teeth felt furry. He hadn't been able to wash his face or brush his teeth since the morning before. "The timelines match up."

"So even then, she was . . ." And here Jordan stopped himself, twinkling his fingertips in front of his eyes. "Bedazzled or whatever."

"What's this?" A fast reader, Abby was already done skimming through most of the packet. "'Sanctum, a holy or sacred place,'" she read. "'What could be more sacred than possessing the power of your own true thoughts? Sanctum. It is both lock and key.'" With a puzzled *hmm* sound she lowered the pages. "Do you think the house we found was this sanctum? If that was his house, it would make sense."

"Probably," Dan said, "or it could be Brookline. Hell, it could be that stupid rock of his."

He thought of his dream and the young Daniel Crawford bludgeoning the hypnotist like it was nothing at all. Instructing his older brother to leap to his death because he was a bully. Of course the only sacred thing to such a person would be his own thoughts.

"It's such an odd way to phrase it," Abby continued. "And he seems so obsessed with logic and science and knowledge. All this junk about holiness and it being sacred seems out of place."

"At this point I wouldn't write anything off," Jordan said, then paused, starting a little as his phone buzzed its way across the carpet. "Do I answer?"

"Let me," Abby said, snatching up the phone. She tucked a piece of dark hair behind her ear three times even though it stayed put the first time.

The cinnamon roll in Dan's stomach turned sour. He half expected Professor Reyes to be on the other end when Abby picked up.

"Hello? Lara? Oh, thank God you're safe. Sure . . . Is everything . . . Yeah, yeah we can meet you there. Oh . . . Just me? I . . . I don't know. I mean, yeah, sure, I'll come alone." Dan shook his head urgently at her but Abby ignored him. "No problem. I'll be there as soon as I can." Abby hung up, breathing heavily. Her knuckles were bluish white around the phone. "She sounded frightened."

"Wouldn't you?" Jordan muttered.

"She wants just me to go. . . . You two will have to hang behind. Maybe I can talk her down."

"You should've asked if she was alone," Dan said. *Especially if she sounded afraid.* "Where are you meeting her?"

"At her studio in the art building," Abby replied, gathering up her coat and mittens and standing. "Where I went to see her installation. It's out of the way, and I don't think anyone will be there this early on a Sunday. . . . Maybe just a janitor or two."

"You know this is a trap, right?" Jordan asked, helping Abby straighten the hood on her coat, which had gotten tangled.

"Of course it is," she said with a tired laugh. "But what are our options at this point?"

"We won't let you go in there alone," Dan assured her, pulling on his cold-weather gear and packing up their notes.

"I'm going to hide these," he said. "If we're walking into a trap, the last thing I want is Professor Reyes getting her hands on our notes. Here." He shifted the files and journals into an orderly pile and handed them to Abby. "Stick these in the girls' bathroom, a vent maybe."

She disappeared down the hall momentarily, and returned with her coat zipped and her hat pulled down snugly over her ears. "Trap or not," Abby said, "I think I have an idea."

CHAPTER

29

As they stood outside the art building shivering in the milky sunlight, Dan found himself wondering if he would ever be warm again. He hadn't expected to miss the uncomfortably cramped hallway where they had spent the night, but anything was better than listening to his teeth rattle around in his skull while his feet started to go numb.

The art building was low and wide, with two warped columns protecting the entrance. The stout profile and oddly shaped columns reminded him of a bulldog's bowlegged stance.

"When you said 'idea,' I thought you meant like a *plan* plan, not charging in, conspicuously absent guns blazing," Jordan said, stamping his feet and blowing on his fingers.

Abby hushed him. He and Dan were standing to either side of the door, not visible to whoever might be lurking inside the art building.

"It is a plan, which you would see if you just shut up for one minute." She took out Jordan's phone and inched off her mitten to dial. Before tapping the number she said, "I'm going to call Lara and tell her the door's locked, that I can't get in. It will force her to come out here. When she opens the door we can grab her and go. That way if there's anyone waiting inside to ambush us they won't get the drop."

"That's . . . not a bad plan actually," Jordan admitted with a shrug.

"Shhh, it's ringing. Get ready, we won't have much time to get away."

Silence. Dan rubbed his arms furiously, trying to coax feeling back into them. He felt like they were waiting for the executioner to show up; even if Lara could help them, first she would have to actually cooperate and evade the Scarlets. For a moment he closed his eyes and imagined himself back home, warm, hands wrapped around a steamy cup of cocoa with a blanket over his lap.

"It went to voice mail," Abby said. She tried the number again. "She's not picking up. . . . Crap. One more try."

"Hang on." Jordan shifted closer to her, as close as he could get without being visible through the glass windows surrounding the door. "Do you hear that?"

Abby put her ear to the door.

Dan couldn't hear anything but a few birds calling to one another on top of the building next door.

"Is that the 'Monster Mash'?"

"It's her ringtone," Abby said, holding up the phone. "Maybe we should go in."

"Dial again, let's make sure," Dan suggested.

He strained to listen for the ringtone, and almost as soon as Abby hit redial he heard a faint twinkling that gradually transformed into a melody. The fact that her phone had rung through three times now worried him. It didn't make sense. If there was an ambush waiting for them inside, then she would have put her phone on silent or interrupted the calls, or, hell, *answered*.

"We should go in," Abby said, handing Jordan back his phone. "She would've picked up by now."

"I'm with you on this one," Dan agreed. "Something's not right." Then he reached out and put his hand over the door-knob, blocking them from going in. "And if there really is an ambush waiting for us inside, run and split up. They'll have a harder time catching us that way. If you get away, turn your phones back on and we'll find somewhere to meet up."

"Got it," Jordan said.

"Try to be quiet," Abby added, pushing Dan's hand away and turning the doorknob. "We might be able to get a quick peek and then hightail it."

Dan soon realized a "quick peek" wasn't going to be in the cards. Something smooth and white was lying on the floor just inside the foyer. He paused, but Abby had already rushed ahead, bending to pick it up.

"Okay, what is *that*?" Jordan whispered, pointing frantically.

"It's a hand," Abby replied quietly. "A mannequin hand." She frowned, looking up slowly from the plastic fingers to Dan's face. "This is part of her project."

Dan took a careful step out of the foyer and into the corridor that bisected it. To the left the hall was empty, with several doors leading off into what he presumed were practice studios. To the right . . .

"There's another one," Abby said, trotting off to retrieve it. This piece was a foot. "Guys . . . I really don't like this. Lara would never take her own work apart. This project meant the world to her."

"Where's her studio?" Dan asked, although he hardly needed

to. He could already see another cast-off piece of mannequin behind her. The discarded body parts made a trail down the hall. Abby turned and led them the right way, pausing to look over each crumb left on the trail. A thigh . . . a forearm . . . a head.

When they reached the torso, Dan realized they were standing outside a half-open door. Abby was quick to reach for it, but Dan delayed her. Her hand was shaking uncontrollably when he took hold of it.

"Whatever we find in there," he murmured, looking at them both in turn, "don't scream."

Abby put her palm flat on the door and pushed. The hinges creaked mournfully, the door swinging open slowly, revealing yet more of the trail of mannequin parts. Broken riggings hung from the ceiling, the ropes and wires still dangling as if recently ripped apart. A few nails and screws hung from the ends of the wires. The mannequins had probably been suspended, he thought, wishing he could've seen what the piece was supposed to look like.

At his side, Abby gasped softly, sprinting past the morbid trail of plastic body parts to the flesh-and-blood body lying in the center of the studio.

He almost broke his own rule, feeling the urge to scream rise fast and painful in his throat.

It was Lara, lying sprawled on the ground with her head cocked to one side. She was almost smiling, like someone who had thought of a joke and couldn't wait to share it. Her hands were curled under her body. The blood was still pooling out from her, and Abby had to take a quick step back to avoid it

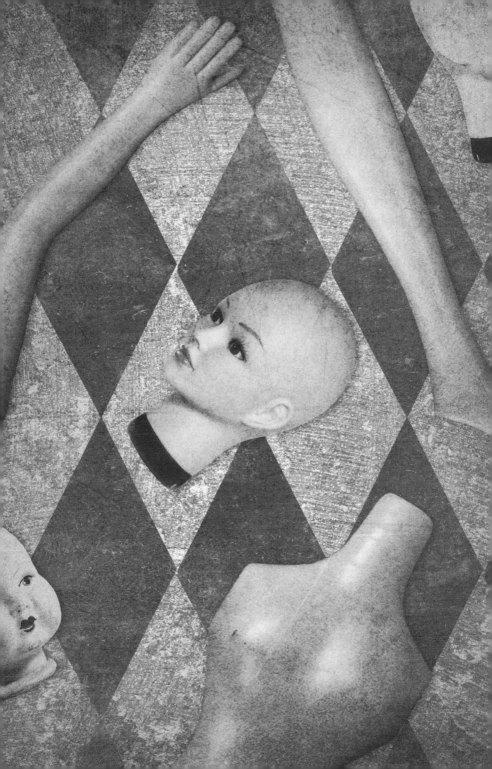

touching her sneakers.

"Oh my God," Abby said, holding one trembling hand over her mouth.

Carefully, Dan and Jordan picked their way across the studio to her. Abby followed a few shaky steps behind. Cal or the professor, Dan wondered, but he didn't say anything, putting an arm around Abby and squeezing her while she wiped at the tears on her face.

"I know it's awful, Abby, but we have to leave her," Dan whispered.

"We can't . . . Not like this . . ."

He started to pull her back, away from the body. The mannequin parts slipped out of Abby's grasp, clattering to the floor.

"We can't be seen here," Dan added. He watched Jordan kneel down and wipe the end of his jacket over the mannequin pieces Abby had touched. "If we don't go now, someone will find us. That's exactly what Professor Reyes would want, to have us detained. To find me."

Abby wrenched herself out of his grasp, spinning and planting her feet. "Can you just shut up about all this warden crap for once? That's a person! A real person! We can't leave her here. We have to call 911, we have to *do* something."

"Abs, she's dead," Jordan said gently. "There's nothing we can do." He turned to Dan and made a futile half gesture to the door. "Maybe we could call 911 and hang up. At least then we know someone would come."

"We have to get out of here," Dan replied, going to the door. He wasn't about to stand around and get caught and then blamed for a death he had nothing to do with. Maybe if she was still alive they could dawdle, but she wasn't. "If this is a setup, the police could already be on their way, don't you get it?"

Dan glanced up at the ceiling, looking for cameras. They should never have come.

"I'm not leaving her," Abby said finally, crossing her arms.

"Then stay," Dan grumbled. "But I'm not sticking around here another minute."

Jordan hesitated, then followed Dan to the door. Only a few seconds later and he heard Abby running to catch up with them in the hall. "Dan . . ."

"Follow me," he said brusquely. "I know what we can do."

"Dan, wait—" Abby pulled on his arm, but he didn't slow down until they reached the end of the corridor and a side door marked "EXIT." Right next to it was a little red box with a handle.

"Wait," she said again, pleading.

"I can't, Abby, and neither can you." He pointed to the fire alarm. "When you're ready, pull it. Look, I know you're upset. I am too. But I'm also *scared*, okay? Are you forgetting? You were supposed to come alone. Alone. The whole thing was a trap."

"All the more reason she deserves our pity!" Abby fired back. "Not . . . whatever this is! Someone *murdered* her!"

"We can't stay and wait for the police. It's not one of our options right now, so pull the fire alarm or don't. I'm leaving."

CHAPTER

30

The outside cold hit him like a slap in the face. He jogged, hands deep in his pockets, his feet pounding the ground harder than necessary. At least this way he got a little warmer. Not much, but anything was better than letting the image of Lara's lifeless face creep back into focus.

This wasn't Professor Reyes. This was the warden. But he couldn't lash out at the warden, so the professor would have to do. She had attacked Micah and now she had attacked Lara. It didn't take much extrapolating to see that they were next. Swearing, he blinked, hard, forcing back the panic threatening to rob his nerve altogether.

Behind him, the shrill fire alarm sounded and then Abby and Jordan were next to him, and it only made the guilt worse.

He knew it was the right thing to do, leaving like that, otherwise they would be caught either by the police or the Scarlets, and neither option would get them safely out of Camford.

Abby marched right by him. She stopped about ten feet beyond where he'd come to a rest; then she turned right around and came back toward him.

"I don't like what we just did," Abby said resolutely. "And I don't care if it's dangerous, I'm going to the police."

"What? Abby, you know that's not a good idea."

"We have information," she half yelled. Jordan appeared at her side, taking her by the arm and leading her away from the building.

"We can't have this conversation right here," he warned them.

Jordan brought Abby down the path, away from the art building and toward a paved circular park area. A few academic buildings now lay between them and the scene of the crime.

"You don't agree with me, I get that, Dan, but we know who killed Lara! And I know you think the whole town is wrapped up in this conspiracy, but it just . . . It's just ridiculous!" She caught her breath, clasping her hands together and wringing them. "We don't have any evidence that this goes further than the college."

"What about Harry Cartwright? And the senator? What about the entire town throwing that insane carnival?" Dan replied hotly. "He was with the post office. The warden didn't seem to have any trouble getting him to steal mail. That senator didn't even flinch when they . . . when they hurt Micah."

"But when we were searching around those houses, even Micah was worried about getting caught by the police, and he's a Scarlet!"

Dan tapped his foot, anxious, hearing the sound of a distant fire engine grow closer and louder. "He was probably putting on an act for our benefit. . . ."

"But you were so sure we could trust him," Jordan said slowly, watching Dan from under a severely arched brow. "It feels like we only have half the facts here, and . . . And as much as I think you might be right, Dan, it feels wrong to just disappear when we could at least try the police."

"Because they did such a bang-up job over the summer!" Dan forced his voice back down from a shout. The Scarlets could be watching them right now. They probably were. Whoever killed Lara might be lurking around, watching them argue and enjoying every minute of it.

"Incompetence is not the same thing as corruption," Abby pointed out. "I don't know what else we can do. Lara was our way out."

She pulled out her phone, and Dan could see the map application brighten her screen. "I'll go alone, that's fine. You two can stay here and try to figure out a miracle cure."

Dan had to physically stop himself from swatting the phone out of her hands. She was already searching for directions to the police station.

"I'm going with you, Abs. I really don't want you going there alone," Jordan said, placing a light hand on her shoulder.

"I know this can work," Dan stated, pleading now. "We're so close to figuring it out. What Felix wanted us to see, what he wanted us to follow. And my vision! Maudire, he said there was a way to undo everything! *He* would know, right? We're close."

"Maybe we are." Abby turned away, following the little trail marked out on her phone. "And we still will be after we do the right thing. We can both be right, Dan, and I'd rather base my decisions on reality rather than some *vision*."

"Please, don't go," he said softly, but they were already walking down the path leading to town.

Abby glanced back at him, smiling sadly. Even when he tried, Dan couldn't persuade his feet to follow.

CHAPTER

31

steady thrumming pain grew at the base of Dan's neck. It was concern, he knew, concern that was turning into a physical ache.

"I'm not too proud," he insisted. "I'm trusting my gut this time."

Even if it was pride, he had to believe that this was the right choice. He watched Abby and Jordan disappear down the hill and stood there waiting, and waiting.

They'd turn around. They'd come to their senses. Any minute now they would race back up the hill. He could follow, maybe, at a distance, and make sure they weren't ambushed by Scarlets.

Strangely, Dan felt most safe here, out in the open. At least here he would have a chance to run and get away. The skin on his face started to burn from the cold, so he walked, aimlessly at first but then with more purpose, an idea forming in his mind. He followed in the direction his friends had gone, taking the path that bisected campus and then plunged down the hill and through the town sprawled below. When he reached the hill he stopped and went left, eventually coming to the little graveyard where they had paused the first day back on campus.

The abandoned liquor bottle that had served as a frat boy's pillow was still there, ice forming on the glass.

Dan sidestepped the low gate that closed off the cemetery and listened to the frosty grass crunch under his shoes. Even when he stopped and stood still his heart pounded. He couldn't tear his thoughts away from Abby and Jordan. He was letting them get caught. He was letting them down.

But he stood by what he said to them: there had to be a way to reverse the hypnotism. If not, they had come back to the college and risked their lives all over again for nothing.

Dan had to smile, albeit ironically, at the gravestone near his feet. Just as he expected, the heavy roses of the Scarlet's skull were laid on the grave of Roger L. Erickson. Erickson Dorm. He looked at the dates. This Mr. Erickson had died eighteen months ago. What had Micah said? Cal's father was the dean? How much had the Scarlets gotten away with on campus because the dean had helped turn heads the other way? *Beloved father, son, mentor . . .*

"Bastard."

He didn't need to turn to know who was behind him.

"He really was. Nobody liked the guy, least of all me."

A pair of familiar boat shoes sidled up next to Dan's feet. Cal wasn't wearing his red cape this time, just a thick sweater, corduroy trousers, and his expensive leather gloves. He sighed, longingly maybe, and then clucked his tongue.

Dan's already drumming pulse raced harder. His chest throbbed as he considered his options. He was no athlete, and Cal looked strong and lean enough to run him down.

"I'm getting a call," Cal said, drawing a phone out of his pocket. "Hello, officers? Yeah, you're going to have two little morons showing up at the station soon. Be a peach and have them brought up the hill for us. You too. Bye-bye."

"You're the bastard," Dan muttered.

"Probably," Cal said casually.

"Call the police back, tell them to leave my friends alone."

"Or what?" He laughed, tossing his reddish hair out of his eyes. "Your friends are going to end up docile as can be or dead, just like your buddy Micah."

Dan flinched. Dead?

"How much of this is you being you, Cal, and how much of this is you 'being docile'?"

That seemed to give Cal pause. He pushed both hands through his hair and sighed. His eyes grew cool and distant. "You know, that's the least boring thing you've ever said to me. I almost wish I had an answer for you. I got an early start. Dad was in so deep. When you drink the Kool-Aid for as long as I have you can't tell where your thoughts start and someone else's begin."

With his hand already in his pocket, Dan could easily reach his phone. He tried to punch in Abby's speed dial number, hoping there would be enough juice left to get the call through. And then what? It would be too late. . . . Maybe if she got the call and heard them talking she would know to turn and run.

Dan heard the grass and gravel shift on the path behind them. More Scarlets, he assumed, but it was worse.

"You've done so well, Cal, just like our Felix. . . ." It was Professor Reyes. Dan turned to look at her, chilled by her serene smile.

He took off, trying to run and leap the cemetery fence, but Cal was too fast.

Once Cal had his iron grip on Dan's arms, Dan stopped

struggling and stared coolly at Professor Reyes. He had been headed for this moment, but now, facing her, he didn't feel ready. She was dressed in a black cardigan and trousers, everything black except the gleaming red slice of agate on a chain around her neck. "Haven't they all done so well, Daniel?"

"Dan," he said sharply. "Felix . . . You put him up to it?"

"Of course I did." She laughed, and it raked down his spine like sharp fingernails. "That boy doesn't breathe unless he's given permission."

"Why are you doing this?" Dan whispered. His hands felt frozen, and Cal's arms squeezed the breath out of his lungs. "Why don't you just stop and leave us all alone?"

"You of all people should know I can't do that." She laughed again, tossing her head. "Now you'll come with me and we'll have a little talk. Felix has done his part, and so has Cal." Grinning, Professor Reyes took one menacing step toward him. The stone around her neck flashed.

"Yes, my puppets have played their parts well," she said, touching the stone around her throat lovingly, "and now they're done. But your part to play, Daniel Crawford, is just beginning."

He tried to throw his weight back against Cal; he bucked and jabbed his head back, but Cal anticipated his every move. Professor Reyes smiled, drawing a long syringe from her pants pocket. He smelled her heavy perfume, saw the greedy glint in her eye. The prick of the needle stung Dan's arm before he could even scream.

CHAPTER

32

*H*e thought it would go better. The method was refined. . . . How could he have blundered now, when he felt so secure in his techniques? But what was done was done. There was no reason to dwell on failure.

Beside him, the young woman was frail still, recovering. A thick blanket was wrapped around her shoulders. He wanted no secrets where his methods were concerned. This was the price they—he—paid for perfection. For control.

"Look at them, Caroline," he said. She was staring at her feet, not at the long wooden boxes laid out on the grass. Behind them, the manse lay silent, the stones darker and colder under the heavy-bottomed clouds. Mist swirled around the foundation, trickling down the garden toward them.

The women would go into the ground in the backyard. The cemetery was too risky, his influence not yet secure at the college or with the town administrators.

"Look at them," he repeated, more sternly this time.

Caroline lifted her head. The very top of it was shaved bald, the beginnings of dark stubble peeking through like a newly seeded patch of earth. Wispy black hair clung to the back of her neck. The stitches over her skull were still pink and raw. Her surgery had gone flawlessly. The others . . . It was too bad. He should have performed the surgeries first instead of wasting time with their drug regimen.

Ah well, he thought, lesson learned. Nothing ventured, nothing gained.

"We will simply have to practice," he said with a sigh. "The spike technique is far subtler, but demands a defter hand than I have developed."

Caroline gazed up at him, still unwilling to look at the boxes going into the ground.

"There was so much blood," she whispered. Her hands were balled up in the blanket, and there they began to tremble. "So much blood."

She was right, of course. Head wounds always were so confoundedly messy.

"Now, now, Caroline, don't be vulgar. If you would like to discuss the procedures we can, but we will do so scientifically and with none of these theatrics."

He rested a fatherly hand on her shoulder.

"I will teach you. We will practice together! Won't that be fun? I'm sure you'll prove a worthy student."

CHAPTER

33

*D*an woke with his head swirling. It took him a moment to remember the graveyard, the professor, the syringe. . . .

He tried to sit up, but his head pounded so hard he almost vomited. His tongue felt swollen and dry, his throat parched. Slowly, he peeled his eyes open. Even half-drugged and groggy, Dan recognized the dusty shelves and the smell of a moldering foundation. File cabinets . . . A sprawling wooden desk . . . He was back in the warden's office.

Brookline.

He expected to be bound, but there was nothing holding him down this time. Someone had shoved him into the warden's old office chair. When he stood, his muscles ached as if he had been beaten to a pulp. Skull-shaped candles flickered on every surface, red wax bubbling over dishes, running down the file cabinets, and cooling there. Brookline had been closed down to students, but Professor Reyes still used it for the senior psychology majors in her seminar.

"Good, you're awake again." She stepped through the warden's glass-paned office door and left it open. Her sober black clothing was gone, replaced with a Scarlet's robe.

"Again?" Dan croaked, touching his burning throat.

"Mmhm. We roused you just long enough to make sure the

hypnotism took." She smiled at him, showing the wide gap between her two front teeth. "And good news! It did."

Adrenaline shot through his body in a panicked jolt. He touched his nose, his forehead. "You didn't . . ."

"Oh, no. Not yet." She nodded to a tray of medical instruments on the desk in front of him. He recognized the spike from the night before. "That comes later."

"Why later?" Dan had to stall her. Maybe he could distract her long enough to go for the spike. She wasn't very big; he might be able to overpower her. "Why wait?"

"Because the process can be . . . unpredictable, and you have information I need now, before your brain might get turned to a puddle of goo." She smirked and pointed to the chair he had just risen from. "Have a seat, Daniel, so we can talk like civilized adults."

"I don't think so," he said, summoning every last ounce of strength to grab the spike and lunge for her.

He had almost closed his hand around it when she said, "You will not touch that, Daniel."

It was as if he had put the spike through his own head, pain lancing through his skull and down his spine until he did exactly as she said. He couldn't move, couldn't make his body obey his thoughts and commands.

"Now would you like to sit?" she asked calmly. Professor Reyes dropped into a chair across the desk with an impatient little sigh.

"What did you do to me?"

"What I do to everyone who can't be civilized and controlled. Now sit." She reached up and pushed back the hood on her robe, then calmly pulled off her own hair. It was a wig, Dan realized, and underneath he could see that her hair had never quite grown around the scars from her lobotomy.

Not knowing what else to do, Dan sat down, eyes lingering on the tray of tools.

"You won't be able to hurt me, you know," she said lightly. "You're under my control now."

Dan's mind raced. There had to be a way out of this. There had to be a way to gain control of his mind again. "You don't have to do this. You can let me go." She hardly seemed to be listening. Dan hurried on. "You can't blame yourself, Caroline. He took over everything—he took over a fraternity, he took over the Scarlets, then you and the college. You never had a chance. He kidnapped you and turned you into one of his puppets. You're a victim here, not a villain."

Caroline hesitated, her lower lip quivering. Then she laughed, hard, so hard a little spray of spit landed on her robe. "Nice try. *Very* stirring speech. But I'm afraid you're wrong, Daniel. I am not a victim, I most certainly am the villain. I haven't gotten to choose much in my life but this much I choose: I *am* the villain." She turned slightly in her chair and called through the open office door, "You can bring them in now."

It was a sadly familiar sight. Abby and Jordan were brought in, strapped again to gurneys. Cal was the one to wheel them in, one at a time. When they were all inside the office, Cal stood to one side, sneering arrogantly at Dan.

"Your friends are much better when they're tied up, yes? So much more *docile*."

Abby and Jordan were awake, both of them struggling against

the fasteners holding them down. Dan watched, miserable, as Cal collapsed the legs and wheels on the gurneys and propped them up vertically against the wall. His friends cried out, now facing him directly, both of them as tightly bound as mummies.

"Why don't you just hypnotize them, too?" Dan muttered.

"What makes you think I haven't?" Professor Reyes stood and walked over to Jordan, looking up him and down with plain disinterest. "Actually, *I* haven't, but our friend the Sculptor did. Or is he Felix? Or is he the Sculptor?" She laughed—cackled— and Dan shot up out of the chair, only to feel that same horrible burning sear through his head.

"The nightmares . . . the voices . . . You really had no idea?" Professor Reyes *tsk-tsk*ed him playfully. "He had you down there in that operating theater all to himself. Armed with my knowledge, it was only natural for him to have a little fun. He isn't very skilled, though. He couldn't control you. But I can."

"Leave them out of this," Dan said, clutching the edge of the warden's desk. The heat of the candles in the room was overbearing. Sweaty, faint, he dropped back down into the chair. "You said you wanted information, fine. I'll give it to you."

Professor Reyes nodded to Cal, who went obediently to the desk and picked up the spike and mallet. Then he retreated to Jordan's side and Dan felt his skin prickle with fear.

"I bet you want the notes," Dan said, trying to keep her attention away from Jordan. "I don't know where they are."

"But you read them," she said, showing her teeth. It couldn't be called a smile.

"Yes, I read them."

"I so hoped you would. I bet you thought you were so clever, figuring out the coordinates, finding all the crumbs I laid out for you. The notes were there for you, and you being of his blood . . . I knew you would understand them better than I ever could. One piece was always missing. You see him, don't you? In dreams, in real life . . . You see the warden. You can see what others cannot, Daniel. That was why it had to be *you*. I couldn't very well dig up Maudire and question him myself, could I?" Her mouth twisted viciously as she said it. Caroline pulled on the necklace around her neck and it came free in her hand, then she leaned onto the desk and dangled it in front of Dan, letting it swing gently back and forth. He couldn't help but look at it and feel a strange urge to never take his eyes away.

"Felix led you right to it. I led you right to it. The carnival, the photos . . . If I could just trigger the right memories, I knew you would give me the answer. Maudire was the one who told you about the password. So simple. So unbelievably simple. Why hadn't I thought of that? You found it, didn't you? You know the word that undoes all his programming, all his work. . . ." She picked up one hand from the desk and slammed it back down. Dan shot back in his seat, shaking.

"I don't know what you mean. . . ." And it was true. She was right about Maudire suggesting there might be a fail-safe, but he never said what exactly that was. . . .

"Do it," she growled, and Dan watched, paralyzed, as Cal lifted the spike and positioned it above Jordan's eye.

"Hey!" Jordan flinched, then went perfectly still. "Don't . . . Don't do it. Dan will tell you the word! Of course he will! Won't you, Dan? You will, won't you?" Sweat poured down Jordan's forehead. His voice had gone high, panicked.

Dan shook his head slowly; he didn't know it. Why didn't he know it?

Think . . . Think . . .

"Stop! I'll tell you," Dan said, but it was just to stall. He couldn't focus, couldn't think. He didn't know what she wanted to hear. He tried to visualize the pamphlet and the notes but the harder he tried the more the words blurred together.

"Tell me what it is," Caroline screamed, shrill, the red stone moving faster and faster in front of his eyes. It looked like a star, red, burning, cracking his skull right open until her words sounded like they were coming from inside his head. "Tell me the password, Daniel Crawford, tell me and I will have control over myself once more. I will be freed. The rest of you can rot, but *I* will be free. *Tell me.*"

Out of the corner of his eye he could see Cal pull back the mallet. He was going to strike.

"I know it!" Dan shouted. "Don't-hurt-him-I-know-it!"

Abby was shrieking, flailing against her bonds.

Why didn't he know? Why couldn't he help them?

"Do you?" Professor Reyes grinned at him from behind the swinging stone. "Maybe this is the wrong kind of encouragement. Maybe you're more like *him* than I thought." Her eyes drifted down to the table and the tray of instruments. "Pick up the scalpel, Daniel, and hold it to your neck."

It was like his mind and his body were two separate entities. He couldn't control his arm or the hand that reached out and closed around the knife.

"There's a good boy."

Dan watched the blade come closer and closer until the cool tip of it touched his neck. His mouth opened in a silent, help-less scream of dread.

"You don't care about your friends—threatening them does nothing. You only care about yourself. . . . Just like he did." She lowered her voice to a steady, emotionless whisper. "Now say the word that will set me free or you'll have to start cutting."

His eyes flew to Abby, then to Jordan. They watched him, unblinking, Abby whispering a stream of words he couldn't make out. Tears gushed down her cheeks. Dan pictured the pamphlet again, but it was no use. There was nothing there.

"He didn't write it down," Dan babbled, tripping over his words. "He didn't. . . . I know he didn't. I would remember. He didn't write it down, I swear! I swear he didn't. Oh God, don't make me do this. . . ."

It was just one word, one syllable that he heard and had to obey. The professor's conditioning was too strong and Dan was powerless against it.

"Wake up, Daniel, and *cut*."

He hardly felt it at first, the knife biting into his skin as he began to slowly, slowly drag it across his throat. Then he felt warm wetness against his fingertips and the room began to dip. He couldn't blame Micah now, or Lara, or even Cal—he would have done anything Caroline said under that combination of drugs and hypnosis. He tried to fight it, but his mind was a blank, his limbs seemingly belonging to someone else.

"A little fear to jog your memory," Caroline whispered sav-agely. "And if you can't remember . . . Oh well."

The blood was coming faster now but he couldn't stop it, and he didn't know how to answer her so he knew it would just pour out and out.

Then he heard something pierce through the blank canvas of his mind. It was a splash of color, of inspiration, and the instant he heard it he could think again. He was free.

"Sanctum!" Abby screamed it, and then screamed it again, louder and with more conviction. "Sanctum! The password is sanctum!"

Caroline reeled, blinking fast before settling her gaze on Dan. From the blankness of her expression came a sneer, her lips twisting as she advanced toward him. "That's it! The password! And so simple, too! I almost feel like a fool. But that's all I needed from you," she said. "I don't need you anymore. Now I can stamp out the last of that monster's bloodline!"

He saw and heard the spike hit the floor. Cal had dropped it. The professor lunged across the desk, grabbing Dan around the throat and squeezing. Spots danced on Dan's vision. He spun the scalpel in his hand and raised it high, using the last of his air and strength to plunge the scalpel down into the professor's back.

She clawed at him, spinning and falling down onto the desk as she tried to reach the knife. The red stone fell out of her grasp, bouncing on the papers littering the warden's desk. Dan snatched it up and vaulted over the table, ignoring the tremor in his hands and the blood covering them to rip at the bonds holding Abby down. Cal had already started undoing Jordan's.

Breathing hard, Dan stole a glance at Cal, who was bent double, shaking his head as if he'd been punched in the jaw and couldn't get his bearings.

"I'll kill you!" Caroline was screaming, still scrabbling on the desk trying to pull the scalpel out of her back. Candles spilled onto the floor, rolling away, some going out and others spreading their flames to the files and books scattered on the floor. "I'll kill you all!"

The flames spread to her robe and took, and it looked as if she couldn't decide whether to deal with the knife or the fire licking up her sides.

Dan yanked at the last buckle, the one fastening Abby's head to the gurney. She tumbled out of her bindings and into his grasp.

"We have to get out of here," Jordan shouted, grabbing Dan by the sleeve of his coat and pulling. "Now!"

Jordan led them to the door, Dan and Abby fast on his heels, but it was blocked. Cal stood in the way, his handsome face drawn and weary. Whatever spark had been in his eyes when Dan first met him was gone now. Dan didn't want to fight him, but he wasn't going to stop now, not when the flames were already spreading, eating up the office and turning the room into a furnace.

"Go," Cal said, shoving Jordan through the door. "Get out of here, go!"

The others filed through, but Dan skidded to a halt just outside. "You can come with us," he said breathlessly, turning to Cal. Behind him, the fire roared, the dusty old books and papers acting like kindling, igniting instantly. It wouldn't be long before the flames reached the door.

"No," Cal said with a sad smile. "She can't get out. She has to go down with his place. Take your friends and get out of here. Let me do one damn decent thing." He turned away then, and over his shoulder murmured, "And tell your girlfriend thanks for me."

"Dan! Let's go!" Abby jerked him backward by his collar, forcing him to follow her and the others down the corridor.

He remembered the way so well, like he had just been down in the depths of Brookline yesterday. The smell of char and smoke filled the air, and he could still feel the heat of the fire as they rushed down the hall and away from the office. When they were almost to the lobby of the old asylum, Dan looked back to see the flames pouring out of the warden's office and down the corridor.

They reached the outer door and found it locked. Jordan didn't bother with the handle, ramming his shoulder against the metal and wood until it gave, spilling them out into the cooler air of the abandoned dormitory.

"Out the back," Jordan said, already running. Dan could hear the faint crackle of fire spreading across the asylum behind them. "We don't want to be seen coming out of here."

As they rounded the corner and ran for the back entrance to Brookline, Dan spotted the red latch handle of a fire alarm. Cold evening air rushed in around him as Abby and Jordan broke through the outer doors and Dan pulled the fire alarm. The bells sounded at once, deafening as they filled the echoing hall.

Outside it was twilight, purple-and-orange dusk sitting just above the tops of the trees. Dan took a few steps out the door and turned, trying to catch his breath as he heard a distant, guttural rumbling.

There was an earsplitting crack and the whole of Brookline sagged. The foundation was disintegrating. Brookline was going to fall.

CHAPTER

34

*T*he flames spread faster than Dan expected, and by the time he, Abby, and Jordan rounded the side of the building and approached the front, a crowd had already gathered.

"The cops took our phones," Jordan muttered bleakly. "I hope someone calls 911 and gets Cal out of there."

Dan and Abby stood looking at him in stunned silence.

"What?" he mumbled. "Cal was probably an okay guy before the brainwashing. Who knows, maybe the boat shoes weren't even his idea."

Abby clapped him lightly on the shoulder. "I hope they can get him out."

A fire engine screeched onto the lawn, sending the onlookers running in every direction. Dan tried to fix his rumpled coat and clothing, nervous that they looked like they had just escaped Brookline's destruction. The last thing he wanted was to explain what had happened inside.

"Dan! Your neck!" Abby appeared in front of him, pulling a handful of wet wipes from her pocket. She tore one open with her teeth and pressed it firmly to the cut on his throat. It hurt more then than it ever had before. "Luckily I don't think it's very deep."

"Yeah," he said with a dark laugh. "Luckily."

Firefighters poured out of the truck, swiftly organizing and finding the nearest hydrant along the quad path. Dan recognized a few of the prospective students in the group milling on the lawn.

He felt Abby's fingers entwine comfortably with his, and he turned to her, exhausted but still managing a tiny smile. She helped him put a fresh wet wipe on his cut and he pressed it hard to stop the bleeding.

"How did you figure it out?" he asked softly. "The password . . . I mean, I know we both read that thing in his notes, but that was pretty amazing what you did back there."

"It just stuck out to me," she said with a modest shrug. "It didn't fit with the rest of his mumbo jumbo so I thought it had to be important. To be honest it was mostly a guess. I would've just started screaming random words if that one didn't work."

"I'm glad we hid those stupid notes," he muttered.

"Should we go get them?" she asked.

"Later. Cal wanted me to thank you," Dan added. He watched the firefighters shouting to one another, though the fire was visible on the first floor now, the windows glowing like a jack-o'-lantern's eyes. "Maybe he'll get to thank you in person."

"God, I hope so. He shouldn't have stayed in there." Abby gave his hand one last press. "I'm going to check on Jordan. You going to be okay?"

He nodded. "Yeah, I'm just . . . eager to get out of here and go home."

As Abby turned and wandered toward Jordan, Dan wondered what he would tell Paul and Sandy about his neck. *Or maybe it's time to tell them the truth about everything.*

A few firefighters emerged from Brookline's front door with a stretcher. Even from where they stood, Dan could tell it was Cal being pulled out alive. A few yards ahead of him, silhouetted against the blaze, he could see Abby and Jordan standing side by side. Jordan's shoulders slumped with relief. Dan shuffled up to his friends, feeling exhaustion overtake him at last.

"So what now?" Dan asked, though he didn't direct it to anyone in particular. It was as much a question put to himself. He slipped his hand into his pocket and closed his fingers around the smooth face of the red stone. "We just . . . go around shouting 'sanctum' at people hoping it does something?"

"I don't know," Abby replied with a shrug. "But I'm glad we get to go home."

Dan took Abby's hand and hardened his jaw, watching Brookline burn. Dancing flecks of fire shot out from the windows, blown about on the breeze. He didn't say it, but Dan hoped no more stretchers came out of Brookline, that the monster Caroline Reyes had become—had been made into—would be gone forever, buried in the most appropriate place Dan could imagine.

CHAPTER

35

*T*wo hours later, he and Jordan waited for their rides out of town with a light rain just beginning to fall. Abby faced them on the sidewalk, huddled under her hood with her mittens deep in her pockets.

"I'm only staying one extra day," she said, "just to see Aunt Lucy and make sure she's okay. You don't need to worry, I'll text like every five minutes."

"Cold comfort, Abs. I hate the idea of you staying here one more minute," Jordan replied sourly.

Dan found himself nodding, but his mind was elsewhere. He couldn't seem to stop holding the stone in his pocket. He rubbed his thumb over the smooth, glassy surface, his eyes fixed on a point in the road over Abby's shoulder.

Rain gathered in the potholes and he felt each droplet hit the top of his head, drip, drip, his thumb moving back and forth across the stone in the same rhythm.

"Dan?" Abby was smiling at him, then went on tiptoes and kissed his cheek. "Everything okay? You seem distracted."

"Just . . . thinking. I mean, in a way, we 'solved the mystery' or whatever, but is that really going to help us? What if we get back home and realize it wasn't any kind of hypnosis or brainwashing or anything, and we were all just traumatized by the summer?"

"Then we'll just have to move on," Abby said. "Like every-body else." She motioned behind her, to where other prospies were no doubt reassuring their very concerned parents that the building that had caught fire was empty.

"Besides, we *weren't* hypnotized. It was all the drugs, remem-ber?" Jordan said, nudging him.

"Very funny, Jordan," Dan mumbled.

"Anyway you have all those notes and junk now so you can see if there's anything in there about your family," Jordan added. "But in the meantime, just cheer up, yeah? We're going home."

"You're right," Dan said. He glanced at Abby and smiled. "Putting this behind us—that's the way to go."

Soon he would be back with Paul and Sandy, safe and dis-tracted by school, college applications, all the things he was supposed to care about.

"That's your bus, Jordan," Abby said, pointing down the road. Through the steady rain and mist, a pair of glaring orange lights appeared. "I'll be in touch. You two take care of yourselves, all right?"

She gave Dan another quick kiss on the cheek and hugged Jordan, then she crossed the street before the bus pulled up. Dan watched her disappear up the path, the same one they had taken up to campus just two short days ago. The bus stopped directly in front of the curb, obstructing Dan's view of the path. Jordan's bus pulled up and Dan's taxi waited just behind it.

"Safe travels, Dan. It was good to hang out with you again even if you are a huge pain in the ass." Jordan hugged him close and Dan chuckled, watching as his friend saluted and hopped onto the bus.

When it was Dan's turn, he hauled his bag, now stuffed with the recovered journals and research, into the trunk of the taxi. The driver hardly looked at him when Dan got in.

Dan took the small red stone out of his pocket and stared down at it. The taxi idled, waiting for traffic to pass before pulling out from the curb. It was strange to think that Brookline was probably completely gone at this point, burned out, just a smoking remnant waiting to be demolished.

Most of its sordid history was with him now, stuffed in his bag and cradled in his palm.

Dan looked out the window, feeling his heart spasm in his chest. Numbness settled in his fingers, and he couldn't feel the weight of the stone anymore.

There across the street, standing on the path where Abby had been just seconds before, was a familiar face, not the ghost of Patrick, but almost definitely a ghost. He was tall and broad, with wire-rimmed glasses and a goatee, and he waved at the taxi as it drove away. His eyes were both black, and thickly clotting blood dripped out of one nostril.

Micah.

"Sanctum," Dan whispered, fogging the glass. "Sanctum."

It didn't matter how many times he said it, Micah, pale as a specter, was there, watching him go.

Dan squinted, pressing his nose to the cold glass, not believing his eyes. Micah waved and waved, now with both hands, and when a car cruised by Dan flinched and blinked. When he opened his eyes, Micah was gone, as if he had never been there at all.

ACKNOWLEDGMENTS

Without fail, my family and friends are always instrumental in the making of any novel; their patience, support, and love see me through it all. I also want to acknowledge the hefty contribution of Andrew Harwell, and thank him for his guidance and expertise. As always, I would never have gotten to write this project without Kate McKean, my superstar agent. Lastly, a big thanks to Olivia DeLeon, Kim VandeWater, and the fantastic team at HarperCollins.

The images in this book are custom photo illustrations created
by Faceout Studio and feature photographs from real vintage carnivals.

Turn the page for a spine-tingling sneak peek at the
third book in Madeleine Roux's bestselling Asylum series

CATACOMB

When Dan and his friends take a senior road trip to
America's most haunted city, some long-buried secrets
threaten more than just the summer. Now Dan can only
hope to make it out of New Orleans alive. . . .

*T*hese were the rules as they were first put down:

First, that the Artist should choose an Object dear to the deceased.

Second, that the Artist feel neither guilt nor remorse in the taking.

Third, and most important, that the Object would not hold power until blooded. And that the more innocent the blood for the blooding, the more powerful the result.

Chapter 1

At first the idea of a cross-country road trip had been hard to stomach. If sleeping in a tent wasn't horrible enough, Dan had felt anxious, almost sick, at the prospect of being away from his computer, his books, his *alone time* for two whole weeks. But that was the deal Jordan offered when he wrote to them with the big news: he was moving to New Orleans to live with his uncle.

Perfect chance, his email had said, *to have some time together. You two nerds can help me move down there, and we'll get a last hurrah before we all traipse off to college.*

Dan couldn't argue with that, or with any reason to spend more time with Abby. She'd visited him in Pittsburgh once a few months ago, and they'd been talking online more or less every week. But two weeks away from parents and chaperones . . . He didn't want to get ahead of himself, but maybe their relationship could finally flourish, or at least survive, with some much-needed quality time together.

The Great Senior Exodus, Jordan had called it. And now, a day after leaving Jordan's miserable parents behind in Virginia, the trip was finally starting to live up to that name.

"These are incredible," Jordan was saying, flicking through the pictures Abby had taken and then uploaded onto his laptop

for safekeeping. "Dan, you should really check these out."

"I know it's kind of cliché, photographing Americana in black and white, but lately I've been obsessing over Diane Arbus and Ansel Adams. They were the focus of my senior project, and Mr. Blaise really loved it."

Dan leaned forward between the seats to look at the photographs with Jordan. "They're definitely worth the stops," he said. They really were something. Open landscapes and deserted buildings—through Abby's eyes, they were desolate, but also beautiful. "So Blaise finally gave you an A, then?"

"Yup. No more stupid A minuses for me." She beamed. Jordan offered up a high five, which Abby managed without taking her eyes off the road. "He actually grew up in Alabama. He's the one who gave me ideas for sites to photograph."

They had already stopped a few—well, *many*—times to allow Abby to take photos, but Dan didn't mind the extra time on the road. He could ride forever in this car with his friends, even if his turns driving got a little tedious.

"I know it's lame to take us so far out of the way, but you're not in too much of a hurry to get there, are you, Jordan?"

"You've already apologized about a million times. Don't worry about it. I'd say something if it was annoying."

"Yes," she said with a laugh. "I'm sure you would."

If he was honest, Dan wasn't in too much of a hurry to get there, either.

It had been nine months since they'd watched the Brookline asylum burn to the ground. The three of them had barely escaped with their lives, and they'd managed that much only with the help of a boy named Micah, who had died trying to buy them time to escape their pursuers. Micah had had a rough, short life, and he'd grown up in Louisiana—a fact Dan had never told Abby or Jordan. Now, just when it seemed like the ghosts of the past were finally content to leave Dan and his friends alone, Dan and his friends were headed to the most haunted city in America. It felt like they were tempting fate, to say the least.

"You okay back there?" Abby asked, cruising smoothly down Highway 59.

"Yeah, I'm good, Abs," Dan said. He wasn't sure if that was a lie. But before Abby could call him on it, Jordan's phone dinged—or rather, a clip of Beyoncé fired off loud enough to make all three of them jump.

Dan knew what that meant. "You're still talking to Cal?"

"On and off," Jordan said, quickly reading the text message. "The on part is why Mom won't pay for school. Not sure what I'd do without Uncle Steve."

"You could stop talking to Cal," Dan suggested.

"And let my parents *win*? Not likely." He peered around the center console at Dan, his bare feet propped up on the dashboard. Late afternoon sunlight glinted off the shiny new black lip piercing Jordan had insisted on getting in Louisville. "He says physical therapy is a real shit show sometimes, but his life feels like paradise after New Hampshire College. Hey! I just realized that at Uncle Steve's, I'll be able to Skype with him without my mother the drama queen bursting into tears."

Dan shifted again, even antsier now at the mention of New Hampshire College. If he let his mind wander or dwell, he would feel the heat of the flames that had engulfed Brookline and everything in it. He wanted to believe that Brookline's effect on him had ended that day—that the evil had died with Warden Crawford and Professor Reyes—but his last moments at the college had given him cause to doubt.

He'd had another vision. He'd seen Micah's ghost, waving good-bye.

He hadn't had any visions since then, and for that, Dan was grateful. It felt like a signal: it was time to let it all go and move on. Even the files and journals he had saved from the ordeal held no interest anymore.

Well, except for one small thing.

Before the trip, Abby and Jordan had threatened to subject Dan to a search of his things for any junk he might have brought from Brookline. They'd said it like a joke—like, no way Dan would really do that to them, right?

But in the end, they hadn't dumped out his bag, which meant they hadn't found the file he had brought along. The one that had been folded in half at the bottom of the stack they'd rescued from Professor Reyes's things. The one labeled *POSSIBLE FAMILY / CONNECTIONS?*, inside which he'd found a paper-clipped pile of papers, connected by a name that had made his heart shoot into his mouth.

MARCUS DANIEL CRAWFORD.

Nine months ago, that pile of papers had seemed like a gift, the reward at the end of a long, hard search for answers about his mysterious past. A sparse family tree had confirmed what he'd already suspected: Marcus was his father, and he was also the nephew of the warden through the warden's youngest brother, Bill. But a single line had also been drawn from Marcus to someone named Evelyn. Was that his mother? It seemed so incomplete. He'd tried to find any Evelyn Crawford online who seemed like a match, but with no promising results and no maiden name, he hadn't had much else to go on.

There was more in the stack—an old postcard, a map, even a police report detailing a time his father had been arrested for breaking and entering—but maddeningly, nothing that would help him pick out his father from the numerous Marcus Daniel Crawfords he found online, and nothing else about his potential mother.

Still. Even after the pile of papers had come to feel less like a gift than a curse, he'd kept the folder hidden. And when he'd packed his bags for this trip, the thought of Paul and Sandy going through his room and finding the folder had been enough to make him bring it—to keep it in sight.

As if on cue, Dan's phone buzzed, not with Beyoncé but with the more subdued jingle indicating Sandy was texting. He checked the message, smiling down into the faint glow of the screen.

How are the intrepid roadtrippers doing? Please tell me you are eating more than beef jerky and Skittles! Call at the next good stopping place.

Dan texted back to reassure her that they were doing their best to eat actual, normal food.

"How's Sandy?" Jordan asked, craning around to look at him again.

"She's good. Just making sure we aren't stuffing ourselves with junk the whole way to Louisiana," Dan replied. He flicked his eyes up to see Jordan swallowing with some difficulty—the insides of his lips were a guilty shade of Skittles orange.

"It's a road trip. What does she think we're going to do?" Jordan asked. "Boil quinoa on the radiator?"

"That's not a half-bad idea," Abby teased. "We are *not* stopping at McDonald's tonight."

"But—"

"No. I checked to see if there was anything to eat other than fast food on the route. Turns out we can avoid the Montgomery traffic and stop at a cute little family-owned diner off 271."

"Diners have hamburgers," Jordan pointed out sagely. "So really, that doesn't change much."

"Hey, I'm just providing a few more options. What you stuff down your gullet is none of my business," she said.

"And thank God for that," Jordan muttered. "Quinoa is for goats."

"I'm with Abby," Dan said. "I could use a salad, or just, you know, a vegetable of any kind. I'm starting to shrivel up from all the beef jerky."

He heard the satisfied smile in Abby's voice as she sat up straighter in the driver's seat and said, "That's settled then. The place I found is called the Mutton Chop, and the same family has owned it for generations. We can get a little local history for my photography project *and* a decent meal."

"I'm still getting a burger," Jordan muttered. He twisted to face the windshield, sighing as he slid down into his seat and began to text at lightning speed. "Soon I'll be on the all-gumbo, all-jambalaya diet. Gotta get my burgers in while I still can."

The images in this book are custom photo illustrations created
by Faceout Studio and feature real found photographs from New Orleans.